"He's dead. My Aaron is dead."

"Mistress Esther, please," said Isaac, reaching out a hand to comfort the sobbing woman. "Let us examine him first. Sometimes—"

"It's too late, Master Isaac," she wailed. "I know. I've seen the dead before."

"If you will come with me," said a quiet voice from the foot of the stairs. "I will take you to him, Master Isaac."

"It's Daniel, isn't it?" said Isaac, quietly. "If you will lead the way, we will follow." The procession trailed up the stairs to a small sleeping chamber over the bakery. Isaac stood in the doorway, listening, and sniffing the air. "When did he die?" he asked.

"Just moments before your arrival, sir. Even before there was time to arrange his body decently, Mama heard you and rushed down the stairs."

"Take me to him," said Isaac. Raquel took her father's hand and led him to the head of the sadly disarranged bed. Isaac ran his fingers over the body where it lay, contorted and twisted, exactly as it had fallen in his death throes. "His death was not peaceful," he remarked.

CURE
──*for a*──
CHARLATAN

Caroline Roe

BERKLEY PRIME CRIME, NEW YORK

This is a work of fiction. Names, characters, places, and incidents are either the product of the author's imagination or are used fictitiously, and any resemblance to actual persons, living or dead, business establishments, events, or locales is entirely coincidental.

CURE FOR A CHARLATAN

A Berkley Prime Crime Book / published by arrangement with the author

PRINTING HISTORY
Berkley Prime Crime edition / February 1999

The Penguin Putnam Inc. World Wide Web site address is
http://www.penguinputnam.com

ISBN: 0-425-16734-8

Berkley Prime Crime Books are published
by The Berkley Publishing Group,
a member of Penguin Putnam Inc.,
375 Hudson Street, New York, New York 10014.
The name BERKLEY PRIME CRIME and the BERKLEY PRIME CRIME
design are trademarks belonging to Penguin Putnam Inc.

PRINTED IN THE UNITED STATES OF AMERICA

10   9   8   7   6   5   4   3   2

This book is most affectionately
dedicated to
Bella Pomer
whose faith, energy,
and critical eye have never failed me

I would like to thank the many generous people who have helped: Sìlvia Planas of the Institut d'Estudis Nàhmanides and the staff at the Centre Bonastruc ça Porta in Girona; Margaret Charlton and Charles Sale for invaluable advice on flowers, herbs, and alpine plants; and Negin Zanpour for essential insights into the Muslim community of the time. My never-failing research collaborator, Deborah Schlow, and my daughter, Anne Roe, have been unstinting in their help. And most particularly, the book could not have been written without Harry Roe, who has traced along with me every step of the road that Isaac walked.

CAST OF CHARACTERS

The Jewish Quarter:
  Isaac, the physician
  Judith, his wife
  Nathan and Miriam, their youngest children, twins
  Rebecca Mallol, their estranged daughter
  Raquel, their second daughter, Isaac's assistant
  Naomi, Leah, and Ibrahim, their servants
  Yusuf, Isaac's apprentice, a Muslim orphan from
    Granada
  Mossé, a baker
  Esther, his wife
  Daniel, their eldest son, heir to his uncle Ephraim
  Aaron, their younger son
  Sara, ten, their daughter
  Mordecai, a wealthy man of business
  Blanca and Dalia, his daughters
  Ephraim, a glover
  Dolsa, his wife
  Salomó des Mestre, the banker's son, Yusuf's
    youthful tutor
  Abraham Ravaya, Astruch Caravida, Astruch des
    Mestre, Bonastruch Bonafet, Mahir Ravaya, Vidal
    Bellshom, members of the council

The Cathedral:
  Berenguer de Cruilles, Bishop of Girona
  Francesc Monterranes, his confidant and chief assistant
  Bernat sa Frigola, his secretary
  Nicholau Mallol, cathedral scribe and Rebecca's
    husband
  Carles Mallol, their son age two
  Lorens, a seminarian
  Bertran, a seminarian, cousin of the Bishop

The Brothel:
  Marieta, keeper of the establishment
  Guillem de Montpellier, scholar, magus, and boarder
    at Marieta's
  Lup, his servant
  Hasan, known as Ali, Guillem's slave
  Zeynab, known as Romea, musician and dancer,
    Marieta's slave

The City:
  Ramon, a weaver
  Marc, his son
  Pons Manet, a wealthy wool merchant
  Joana, his wife
  Jaume, their elder son
  Francesca, their daughter-in-law

The Court:
  Francesc Adrober, a judge, head of the court
  Guillema, a prostitute, and Venguda de Costa, a wife,
    the victims
  Tomas de Costa, Marc de Puig, Pere Vives, and
    Bernat, the accused

ONE

"How much money?" murmured the thin, ascetic-looking man vaguely, like one whose thoughts were on higher things. He wore the sober black tunic of a scholar or priest, and looked out of place in the tawdry surroundings of the cheap tavern. "We've done well enough. It's time we moved south."

Outside, Girona lay still and somnolent, waiting patiently for the cool of evening. The room was dark and close, its atmosphere thick with the remembrance of spilled wine and long-departed drinkers. Not a whisper of air penetrated the open shutters; flies buzzed lazily, as if their hearts weren't in the task. Rodrigue, the tavern keeper, sweated and dozed in a corner, ignoring his only customers.

"You call this doing well?" said the other contemptuously, jangling a purse filled with coins in his companion's face. "Listen, Guillem, my cheap little friend. On a good day, you bring in enough for a room and a plate of soup."

"It's not been that bad," protested Guillem.

"I'm talking about gold, you fool. Gold. Enough to live like a lord."

"You're mad," said Guillem. "Girona may be filled with well-fed merchants and their silk-clad wives, but they do not waste their gold on trifles."

"That is true. Consequently there will be more for us."

He shook his head doubtfully. "How do we lay our hands on it?"

"That's not your concern. I know who has it, and how to get it."

Guillem leaned forward. "You speak in earnest," he said, in amazement. And before his companion could reply, "How much danger lies in it?"

The other gave him a curious, sidelong glance. "It is no crime to steal that which was stolen," he said.

The scholar bit down on his upper lip, in a nervous gesture that irritated his companion. "How do we do it?" he asked finally.

"Mama?" said Miriam.

"What do you want?" snapped Judith, wife to Isaac the physician. She was not a long-suffering woman by nature, and what she had of patience had already been sorely tried that morning. Summer had ground on relentlessly far into September, and she was hot under her dark veil. The shady thoroughfares and vaulted streets of the *Call*, Girona's thriving Jewish Quarter, felt like a giant bath, heated by the fierce sun working on damp mists rising from the rivers. She panted and sweated as she climbed the hilly street.

Her maid, Leah, had felt dizzy and faint with headache that morning, and had taken to her bed. Naomi, the cook, was locked in the kitchen, crashing pots and dishes about in a fury, and Miriam had been trailing after her mother, demanding to be amused. Judith's well-organized household was collapsing in every direction.

It was her husband's fault. Isaac, normally the most gracious of men, had been up most of the night with an ailing child, and his own patience was stretched thin. He had come down to breakfast hungry and thirsty. Judith had picked out a fine ripe pear for him, and set it on his plate with a tempting small roll. "Is there nothing else?" he had said. "Am I required to fast because of a little heat?"

Naomi entered the courtyard as he was speaking, and his shaft ricocheted off the bosom of its target, his wife, to go straight into the vulnerable heart of the cook.

"Papa," whispered Raquel, "Naomi is right here beside us."

Isaac, furious at himself for the blunder his sightlessness had led him into, had left the table abruptly, upsetting a jug of water, and retreated to his study. Naomi, bristling with hurt pride, had barricaded herself in the kitchen, turning the solidly built stone house into an inferno with her preparations. With Leah in her bed, and the kitchen boy needed to keep the fires going, the cook commandeered Ibrahim, the houseman, as errand boy. But when he received a summons to make a third visit to the market, his usual phlegmatic indifference vanished. He planted himself in front of his mistress, seething with righteous rage. The courtyard wasn't swept, any more than the house, or the master's study, and when did she suppose he was to do his own work? Judith rejected the impulse to dismiss the whole houseful of them, with the possible exception of the kitchen boy, who already had to bear the brunt of the cook's rage, and began to sort out the chaos. She placated Ibrahim by promising to finish the marketing herself, set her daughter, Raquel, to straighten the beds, then caught a sulky Miriam by the hand, and fled the house.

"Well? What's wrong?" she asked her youngest daughter.

"Why can't I go to school with Nathan, Mama? Papa says that girls ought to go to school as well as boys. And I'm seven, too. There's nothing to do, and no one to play with, and everyone is cross with me."

"You can't, and that's that," said Judith. "I don't want to talk about it. If you stopped complaining and made yourself useful, no one would be cross. Now hurry up." She dragged her grimly up the main street of the Quarter and marched her through the gate at the north end. They emerged at the foot of the hill going up to the cathedral, where Judith paused in the shade in a fruitless attempt to cool down.

"Where are we going, Mama?"

"You'll find out when we get there."

A feeble breeze from the west tumbled over the high city wall, and brought with it the smell of yeast, hot bread, and spices to mother and daughter. Judith pulled her veil close and, gripping Miriam firmly, turned down the street to the bakery. They walked past the baskets of bread at the door, toward a red-faced woman standing behind the worktable considering a sizable mound of fresh dough. A sturdy girl of ten or eleven was transferring loaves from the oven onto wooden racks at the back of the shop.

"Morning, Mistress Judith," said the baker's wife, looking up in surprise.

"Good morning, Mistress Esther," said Judith, frowning as she looked around for the particular round loaf that Naomi seemed to feel was an essential part of today's dinner.

"A fine day. What can I offer you that Ibrahim didn't fetch this morning?" said Esther, diplomatically reminding the physician's wife that she had all the bread she needed, in case absence of mind had brought her into the shop. "A spice bun for a hungry little girl?"

But Miriam had disappeared into the cavernous back of the shop, and was enthralled at the spectacle of young Sara stacking up cooled loaves in baskets to be transferred to the front.

"Ibrahim!" said Judith, in a voice heavy with meaning, and launched into the sad tale of her morning: the cook's ill temper, her husband's thoughtlessness, and the general rebelliousness and sulkiness of everyone in the house, children and servants alike. "Here I am, with a houseful of servants who eat their heads off and collect wages you wouldn't believe, and have less to do at home than anyone could believe, and I'm doing my own marketing. I don't know what's got into everyone," she said. "People used to be content to work hard and lead honest lives, but now . . ." Her voice trailed away ominously. "And what are you doing here by yourselves, you and Sara, baking as well as minding the shop? Where is everyone?"

The baker's wife shrugged. "Mossé is off at the mill. And Aaron is—well—you know how he's been lately. The new apprentice is sick again and gone home to be looked after by his mother, he says, and the boy is fast asleep somewhere, I expect. Not that he's any use. Our maid left to get married, and the new girl is making a mess of things in the kitchen right now." As she talked, she sprinkled the dough with flour, smoothing it out and turning it with practiced hands.

Judith had heard most of the litany of complaints before, but it was clear that she had missed some important piece of news concerning the state of mind or health of the baker's second son. Forgetting her own domestic crises for the moment, she turned her entire attention to Mistress Esther.

"But times have changed, Mistress Judith," said that worthy and hardworking woman, beginning to knead the mound. "Take our boys." With every phrase, she turned, folded, and thumped the dough as if it were her husband's thick skull under her hands. "I told Mossé again and again that sending Daniel out to apprentice—even if it was to my brother—was flying in the face of the Lord, who granted us a clever firstborn son to carry on after us. But he never listens," she said, with a particularly heavy thump. "No matter how often he's wrong, he still never listens."

"But isn't Aaron—"

"Oh, Aaron tries," said Esther. "But he'll never be the man his brother is."

"I know that Isaac came to visit him," said Judith, probing delicately. Her husband's discretion when talking about his patients was a constant source of irritation to her. Without exception, she learned of her neighbors' maladies and complaints from others, who snickered, and pretended to be surprised at her ignorance. "Is he better?"

"I don't know," said Esther, with a sigh. "Thank you, sir," she said automatically as a customer dropped a farthing for a small loaf into her jar. "Sometimes I think he's getting worse. I don't know what to do about him. And that's not my only worry, mistress." She lowered her voice, and leaned toward the physician's wife. "There's a thief about. I counted the money today, because Mossé is off to the mill, and I'm almost certain that we're short. And it's not the first time. I keep very close track."

Judith agreed that keeping close track was important. "Maybe Mossé—"

"He always tells me when he does. He took the coin to pay for the grain, but there's more missing than that. There's only our key to the strongbox, and I keep it by me all the time. So unless he took the key while I was sleeping, I don't know how that money disappeared." She paused and glanced over at the two children, who were giggling together over something or other. "Unless he's giving it to some woman. And if he is, Mistress Judith, he'll be a sorry man when I find out who she is. And she'll be even sorrier."

Judith glanced at Esther's square jaw and muscular arms, and silently agreed. Mossé would no doubt be very sorry. For Mossé's sake, and her own, she hoped it was a thief. Mossé was a good baker, with a lighter touch than old Ruca. She'd hate to lose him.

"No one else could—"

"Certainly not, mistress. Who else would have the key? And the box is very strong. It's a woman, or it's sorcery, that's what I say."

"There are your sons," suggested Judith.

"Not even Mossé would be foolish enough to give the key to the strongbox to a couple of boys," said his wife with scorn.

"Daniel must be close to twenty, Mistress Esther. He's a man now."

"Even so. Think of the temptation. And the trouble they

could get into with all that extra money. Women. Drink.''
She lowered her voice again. ''Unspeakable vices and
wickedness.'' Her eyes shone with excitement. ''Not that
we're rich, mistress,'' she added hastily, ''but that's our
money to pay tax, and rent for the shop, and to save for
bad times. No—the boys don't even know where we keep
it.''

Judith doubted that, and reached for the round loaf she
had come for.

''Not that Aaron would ever steal from us,'' added his
mother.

''Of course not,'' said Judith, who privately thought Esther and Mossé knew nothing about their own children.

''He was always the quiet, good one. If it were Daniel,
now, who was living here—'' She nodded energetically.
''I could believe that. He might take some money to show
how easy it was. As a jest. But then he would tell me, and
give it back, and we'd laugh about it together. He's like
that.''

''Did he ever do that?''

''Well—'' Esther seemed uncertain. ''Not since he was
a boy of eight and took some sweetmeats from a locked
cupboard.''

''What's the matter with Aaron?'' asked Judith, the
thought of the chaos that was building at home prodding
her on.

''In my opinion, it's old Mordecai's daughter,'' said Esther.

''Dalia?'' asked Judith. At sixteen, shy, awkward Aaron
was an unlikely suitor for the rich merchant's lively daughter.

''Dalia. He's wasting away because of her. I know it.
Only he's so shy, he turns red in the face and leaves when
she comes in.'' The rhythm of turn, fold, and thump in-
tensified. ''She's a little vixen, you know—tormenting and
teasing him whenever she sees him. But Mordecai's a rich
man, he is. His cellar is filled with the money he made in
boots before he turned to other things. And no wonder at

those prices. Not like us, who can only ask so much for a loaf, and have to pay the cost of grain, and wood for the fires, and tax. Always the tax. How can a family get ahead? Except by making a good marriage. And whenever I suggest arranging a match for him, he gets furious at me. I don't know what to do, mistress. The other day,'' she added, lowering her voice, "he said he didn't want to be a baker. He wanted to be a scholar—a clerk. Mossé is upset.''

"A teacher? Or a rabbi?" said Judith in amazement. "Aaron?''

"No," said his mother. Her busy hands stopped. "Not even that. Something else. He's restless, and not sleeping, and wanders about at all hours of the night. It has to be love," she said uneasily. "What else can it be? He's so tired all the time he can scarcely lift a sack of flour, but instead of resting when he can, he disappears in the evening—the Lord only knows where. Do you think Master Isaac can cure him?''

"Of love?" said Judith. "I don't think even my husband could do that.''

That evening, fifteen or twenty people were gathered in the meadow on the other side of the Onyar River, listening to the scholarly looking man from the tavern. He had been speaking for more than a quarter of an hour, and most of his audience stared at him apathetically, without comprehending, like cows in a field watching a passerby; it passed the time until something more entertaining happened along. A few, however, regarded him with lively curiosity, and a group of three young men in front listened with avid interest. On the edge of the crowd, a little boy, bored and restless, picked up a stone, raised his arm, and prepared to throw it. The speaker's companion, poorly dressed in a patched and threadbare tunic, with unkempt gray hair and a scarred face, caught the boy's wrist and squeezed.

"Ow!" the boy squeaked. "You're hurting me.''

"Good," said the man. "Remember that. The next time

it won't be just your wrist. Now disappear!"

The lad turned and ran into a clump of tall grasses by the edge of the meadow, where he vanished into the dry stalks and feathery ears, each one as high as the tallest man there.

"Friends," said the orator, ignoring this petty interruption, "those few things that I, Master Guillem of Montpellier, have imparted to you are but a small portion of the knowledge of the ancients, the hidden wisdom of the Magi, which I have learned at the University at Montpellier, and from various astrologers, seers, and mystics I have sought out in my travels throughout the world. By saying the words that I will teach you, all holy words, none of them tainted with sorcery or heresy, and by using the herbs I will tell you of, you may restore health and vigor to the body, strengthen the mind, and gain wisdom to understand those things that are now hidden from you. These will bring you health, wisdom, and prosperity."

"What about grace?" said one of the three young men, who was also dressed as a clerk.

"For that you must go to the church," said the speaker quickly. "She will teach you how to seek grace. Now, I ask you most humbly, if you wish to learn these things, that when my friend and helper, Lup, comes around, you give him what you can, to help us buy our bread and assist the poor."

"I can guess what kind of poor they'll be assisting," said a prosperous-looking gentleman at the back to the man standing beside him.

"Poor tavern keepers and streetwalkers?" observed his companion.

"I've met their kind before. But they'll be gone soon. Those two have the smell of officers about them." He nodded at two horsemen moving at a rapid canter toward the meadow.

As they strolled along the road back to Girona, in the light of the setting sun, they heard shouts and jeers from the little crowd, and the penetrating voice of Master Guillem. "We will meet tomorrow," he was calling. "You are foolish to try and silence me, when I can bring prosperity and health to the citizens of the city." The two comfortable-looking gentlemen grinned at each other and went their separate ways.

The officers looked and sounded bored. "We don't want to silence you, Master Guillem," said one. "We want you to seek a license to speak."

"But we're well outside the city gates," objected the speaker.

"Nonetheless, you must have a document of permission."

"So you can have a fat fee," muttered Lup, thrusting the money bag into his tunic for safekeeping. He looked at Master Guillem, nodded in the direction of the three young men, gangly youths of sixteen or seventeen years, and turned to the rest of the crowd. "You heard the gentlemen," he called out. "Back to your houses."

As the crowd began to drift away, their meager entertainment for the evening snatched away from them by the authorities, Master Guillem moved swiftly in on the three boys.

"Good evening, gentlemen," he said in sober tones. "I regret that our meeting was broken up. The good men who run the city suffer from a certain, shall we say, narrow-mindedness."

"They're not from the city," observed one the boys.

Master Guillem ignored the interruption. "Are you interested in acquiring wisdom?"

"We are," said the young man who seemed to be leader of the three. He, too, wore the black tunic of a scholar. "But we don't know if you are the one to teach us such solemn subjects."

"Nor do I," said Guillem, with practiced humility. "It may be, young masters, that your learning has already surpassed my abilities. Are you skilled in the mystical herbs that are the path to knowledge?"

"We don't know anything, do we, Lorens?" said the smallest of the three.

"Quiet, Marc," said Lorens. "Leave this to me. We are poor students," he went on. "We cannot pay large fees. A penny in the bag from the three of us to listen to a few words on the importance of learning is one thing, but what do you charge to impart real knowledge?"

"From you, ten pence each," said Lup, breaking in. "And that is only because the master noticed the keen interest and intelligence written across your faces. Usually it is much more. For there are expenses, you know. Rare herbs, and unguents are needed, and sweet incense must be burned for the occasion to be a success. We make nothing for ourselves at ten pence, but the master is a kind and generous man, who seeks to bring wisdom to those who can profit from it."

"And if we decide to accept your most generous offer," said Lorens dryly, "when can we meet? We are not gentlemen of leisure. Our time is not our own."

Master Guillem gave his servant a slightly panic-stricken look. "You will understand, good sirs, that we trespass on the good nature of others for our private meeting places—"

"But if you can present yourself to us at the second hour past compline, when the city is abed," interrupted Lup, "we will have space and leisure to accommodate you."

"Where shall we seek you? Or do you live in this field?"

"It were better if we did," said Guillem solemnly, "but it would be too difficult. We lodge in San Feliu with Doña Marieta. She seeks atonement for her way of life by giving us free lodging. Anyone can direct you to her house."

"The spirits will be strong tomorrow evening," said Lup. "Present yourselves then, and you will be able to learn much."

"I know where it is," said the third young man, and blushed scarlet.

"You, Aaron?" said Lorens. "And do you know what she is?"

"I do," he answered steadily. "But she and her girls still eat bread."

"What do you think?" murmured Lorens, after the three boys slipped into their places around a table at Rodrigue's. The tavern keeper slapped three wooden cups down in front of them, filled them from a jug of his thinnest, sourest, cheapest wine, and stood there, waiting. Long experience had taught him that if apprentices and students and other young wastrels didn't pay before they drank, he could whistle for his money, often as not. After a considerable amount of searching, the three boys pooled enough from their individual resources to satisfy him.

"About Master Guillem? Too much money," said Marc, in depressed tones. "I have trouble enough buying the vinegar Rodrigue sells for wine, without coming up with more for special sessions."

"Learning always costs money," said Aaron.

"Not if your father is teaching you," said Marc. "Otherwise, who would be a weaver?"

"Did you have to be a weaver?" asked Lorens. "Isn't your brother taking over the business?"

"If you want to call it that," said Marc. "But it would have cost my father money to apprentice me outside. He's too cheap to do that." He raised his cup. "Here's to work. I hate it. I'm leaving as soon as I can."

"At least you can leave," said Aaron. "I'm expected to stay in the bakery forever—otherwise they'll say I'm abandoning my parents to starve in their old age."

"Let your sister marry someone who wants to learn the business," said Lorens. "You're not your parents' slave."

"What would you do?" asked Marc. "If you left."

"I'd go north," said Aaron. "To Toulouse or somewhere like that. Where they appreciate poetry and learning."

"Aaron has copied out all the new poems," said Lorens. "And many of the old ones."

"I spend all my money on paper and ink," he said, with an embarrassed smile. "And wine."

"Where did you get the poems to copy?" asked Marc.

Lorens winked. "He didn't. Some came from my father, some from my teachers, and one very fine book from the Bishop himself."

"I was careful," said Aaron. "I returned them as quickly as I could. If they didn't want me to read, why did they send me to school?"

"It makes them feel important," said Lorens. "And they think it's money in the strongbox. My father's the same. But I'm not staying here. No one in this city thinks of anything but the price of wool and cloth, and getting rich. I'm going to Montpellier to study astronomy and astrology, and the Greeks on logic and mathematics. I would speak to Master Guillem about courses of study there, and ask him who are the most learned masters." He raised his cup with a rueful smile. "To freedom."

"My father says that only rich Christians can afford to waste their time on idle pursuits like poetry and mathematics," said Aaron. "He wants me to marry a hard-working girl with a good dowry and settle down. Right now the thought of it makes me sick."

"When you think about it," said Lorens, "my father feels the same. Except for me getting married, since he wants me to be a bishop at least. If I were a count, I suppose, I could spend my time learning frivolous things."

"If you were a count," said Marc, "you'd be off getting killed in some war or other."

"That's true," said Lorens. "What would you like to do if you weren't working for your father? Besides leave the city."

"Create beautiful things," said Marc simply. "I can do it on the loom, but Papa says it's a waste of time and good wool. Not that he uses good wool," he added. A general gloom settled over the three.

"But what about Master Guillem?" asked Aaron.

"We'd need thirty pence for one session," said Lorens.

"It might as well be thirty thousand," said Marc. "I have enough for tomorrow's wine, and that's it."

"I have five," said Lorens. "I'm not sure that I can get any more from my father right now. He's not very happy with me. But I'll try."

"I can pay for all of us," said Aaron. "Let's do it."

"You can?" said Marc, startled. "That's a lot of money."

"What money, Marc old friend?" Another young man in black sat down at the table and gestured to a couple of friends to join them. "A scarce commodity in my life, I can tell you. And that fraud in the meadow had scant hope of extracting my drinking money out of me."

"Evening, Bertran. Why do you call him a fraud?" asked Lorens.

"Weren't you listening to him, Lorens, my friend? I never heard so many half-truths and such contorted logic in my life."

"What do you know about logic?" said Lorens, with considerable heat. "And if you'd been at his first two talks, you would have known what his arguments were."

"I know that when someone offers to teach me the secrets of the Magi, and the Seven Sages and God knows who else, in three expensive but simple lessons, I am being fleeced like a sheep in spring."

"You were listening in," said Aaron.

"You can't have a private conversation in a meadow," said Bertran. "Anyway, knowledge is something you get from a lot of hard work, and from good teachers."

"Whose sermon is that, Bertran?" A laugh went around the table.

"My father's," he said, turning red. "But it's true, even so. And what is this wise man doing lodging at Marieta's?"

"You lads off to Marieta's to learn wisdom?" said a leathery-faced farmer at the next table, and then roared with laughter. "She'll teach you wisdom all right."

"Some pretty fancy things going on there these days," observed another. "I've heard tales you wouldn't believe."

"We've had enough trouble for this year," said the farmer. "And the secrets of the Magi, if you'll pardon me for listening in, that sounds like more trouble to me. If I were you, I wouldn't dabble in those things. Not right now. Let the Magi keep their secrets to themselves."

Toward the end of September, Isaac the physician was awakened one Thursday morning by the sound of his wife's voice berating Ibrahim for making noise when he knew his master was still asleep. Isaac was not deceived. A panic-stricken summons from young Astruch's wife had taken him out after midnight, and kept him out until fatigue and the chill that comes before dawn made his fingers clumsy. He had slept what remained of the night on the couch in his study off the courtyard. Judith wanted him out of his bed, but that room was sacred, and she was reluctant to enter it unless she had an overwhelmingly important reason.

The courtyard was quiet again. He pulled himself out of bed, opened the door, and sniffed. In spite of the perpetual night in which he now lived, Isaac knew that the sun was bright behind a morning mist, and that the cool of the morning would soon give way to another hot day. He could smell the mist and the rising heat and the strong sun before other men saw or felt them. He had just begun to wash himself systematically and thoroughly in cold water, when he heard a creak of the gate, and Judith, out in the courtyard again, making a fuss over young Salomó, the son of Vidal, the banker.

He had engaged Salomó des Mestre for three months to teach his thirteen-year-old apprentice, Yusuf. He had run into the Moorish boy at the beginning of the summer, when the hungry waif had led the blind physician out of the middle of a riot. Yusuf's father had been an emissary from Emir Abu Hajjij Yusuf of Granada; he had been slain five years before in the civil wars between Don Pedro and his brother, Fernando. Yusuf, with Isaac's assistance, had been placed under the protection of Don Pedro, King of Aragon.

Not only was Yusuf clever, but as a small boy he had been carefully taught. He had mastered the basics of reading and writing in Arabic before fate thrust him out onto the roads with no protection but his wits, and he was eager to learn all he could in his new world. But a man without sight could not teach a boy Roman letters, nor the rudiments of grammar of the Latin tongue in which part of the physician's rich store of medical texts was written. Once the boy could read the words aloud, they would work together, but for now Yusuf needed a teacher who could see.

Young Salomó was scarcely more than a boy himself. "How do you like your new teacher?" asked Isaac, a few days after the lessons had begun.

"Well enough," said Yusuf, with all the sophistication of his thirteen years. "He is a pleasant young man, lord, and appears to be very learned. But he understands nothing of the world. He seems much struck by Mistress Raquel," he added innocently.

"Does he indeed?" said Isaac. "And does he impress her as well?"

"I don't think so. He is too young for her taste, I think. I know nothing, lord," he added hastily. "She has said nothing to me, or to him. I judge only from the look in her eyes. And because she keeps herself well veiled when he is about."

Then the momentary bustle was over, and the only sound left was that of Ibrahim, slowly sweeping the courtyard.

Isaac said his morning prayers and went outside.

"Is it too cool to take our breakfast in the courtyard, Isaac?" said his wife, who was hovering at his elbow. "We can set a table by the fire if you prefer."

"Judith, my dear," he said, with amusement, "it is my patients who are sick, not I. It is very pleasant out here, and soon you will be complaining once more of the heat. And besides, I hear our excellent Naomi approaching with a dish that could awaken a dead man's appetite. I worked hard last night and I am very hungry. Let us eat." Naomi set a steaming dish of rice and vegetables down on the table, where the usual plates and bowls of cheeses, fruit, and soft breads already awaited them.

"Were you late in?" asked Judith. "Raquel is still asleep."

This was a much more complicated question than it sounded. First of all, Judith felt aggrieved at people who called out physicians in the middle of the night. Let them say their prayers and wait patiently until the sun rose before sending for her husband. And secondly, she felt their seventeen-year-old daughter had much better get married as soon as possible, and stop going off with her father at all hours to assist him. And she wanted to be sure that it truly was late when they returned, and that Raquel was not using her responsible position as an excuse to lie in bed all the morning.

All of this Isaac knew as well as he knew what infusion was needed to cure an aching head. "Yes, indeed," he said. "It was very late. I'm not surprised that she is still in her bed. But young Astruch's son is mending, I think. It was well that they called me when they did."

"And me, Papa," said Raquel. "Good morning, Mama," she said, giving her mother a kiss on the cheek. "I was too hungry to sleep the morning away," she added, to let them know that she had been eavesdropping, and reached for the tureen filled with rice.

They had scarcely begun their breakfast when someone began to hammer on the gate.

"I'll answer that," said Isaac.

"No, you won't," said Judith. "Whoever that is can wait. You finish your breakfast in peace before you start the day. Ibrahim will answer the gate. If it's that important, he'll come in.''

It was apparently that important. Mossé the baker burst into the courtyard uttering a series of elaborate and almost unintelligible apologies. "Begging your pardon, Master Isaac, sir, and Mistress Judith. And Mistress Raquel. For disturbing your breakfast. Doubtless you were kept out late last night. I know that happens. And I wouldn't disturb you if I weren't that worried, sir, and my wife frantic with grief and upset, so I said to her, I'll go and speak to the physician, Esther, my dear, and he'll know what to do. Only mint tea, that's all, and nothing else—you can't live on that, can you?''

"Mossé, my friend," said Isaac, "who is ill?''

"It's Aaron, Master Isaac. And he's—''

"Tell me exactly what has happened this morning that made your wife anxious about him.''

"Oh. Well . . .'' he said, vaguely, "he never got up. Said he wasn't feeling well.''

"And in what way?''

"Well—'' Mossé stopped and looked over at Judith and Raquel. "He didn't sleep well last night.''

"Come, Raquel," said Judith, "it's late and there is much to be done. Excuse us, please, Mossé. We'll finish our meal in the kitchen as we work.''

"Good," said Raquel. "Don't you find it chilly out here, Mama?''

"Naomi?'' Judith's voice reverberated throughout the house. "Come help us carry these dishes in.'' And Naomi bustled out to transfer everything back to where it came from.

Isaac waited until he heard them leave. "Now, Mossé, sit down, and tell me how Aaron has been. Still those terrible nightmares?''

"Worse than that, Master Isaac. Three nights ago I came across him walking, his eyes wide open, seeing not a thing. And the nightmares haven't stopped. He jumps with fear at noises that aren't there, and sees people in the shadows on the wall. He doesn't eat, and he shouts at his sister and his mother until they are quite terrified."

"What have you done for him?"

"Esther gives him mint tea, and chamomile and other herbs for sleeping, but they won't help. I know it." The baker leaned forward until Isaac could feel the baker's breath on his face. "My son has an enemy. Or I have an enemy. Someone has bewitched my son. Someone who's trying to drive me out of the Quarter. It's an important position, you might say a sacred position, to be baker, isn't it, master?"

"It is indeed, Mossé. And you're a very good baker as well, but before you start talking about witchcraft, I think we should know more about what's wrong with your son."

"Come with me. Examine him, talk to him. You'll be able to find out what spells have been cast on him."

"There could be other reasons for Aaron's behavior," said Isaac. "I can think of a few."

"It's witchcraft," said Mossé firmly. "I know."

"Why are you so sure?"

He looked around the courtyard suspiciously. "Because it's affected me," he whispered. "They want to kill my son and heir, but that only works if I can't have another boy. And they've laid a spell on me to—to keep me from fathering another child."

"There could be other reasons for that, too, Mossé," said Isaac gently.

"At first I thought it was the Lord punishing me because I sent my firstborn son to my brother-in-law Ephraim, when his son died of the Black Death."

"The Lord would not punish a man for helping his wife's brother," said Isaac.

"But I didn't do it out of kindness," Mossé muttered.

"You mean that he paid you," said Isaac. Everyone knew that Mossé had accepted a fat purse for allowing his brother-in-law to take over his eldest boy. Only Mossé believed it was a secret.

"I sold my son. A great sin. But Daniel will inherit a good business, and be a rich man. I did it for him, too."

"But mostly for yourself," said Isaac.

"Yes. And I'm being punished. I should have sent Aaron to him, but I thought Aaron would be an easier boy to teach and handle. And it's all turned out wrong."

"Again, what is it you want me to do?" asked Isaac.

"I want you to lift the spells on Aaron, and on me, and to cast a spell back on the villain who did this. I know who it is, master, and I can get you whatever you need to witch him back."

"Mossé, my friend," said the physician. "I'm a dealer in physics, not in spells. But from what you say, it is possible—even likely—that the lad is suffering from a complaint that I can help ease. I have a few cures to help what is troubling you as well. Put aside the thought that you've both been bewitched, and I will come and see what I can do. Wait here while I gather my remedies together."

Isaac ate a hasty mouthful of rice and took a piece of soft bread stuffed with cheese in hand. Yusuf was snatched from his lesson, and Raquel sent to put together a basket of herbs and potions. Before Mossé had time to decide whether he had won or lost in this encounter with the physician, all four of them were making their way up the main street.

The bakery had been built against the north wall of the Quarter; like several other businesses, its entrance was from the city side through a door in the wall. But instead of going out the gate and around to the bakery door, Mossé turned down the first street before the gate, and entered his comfortable domestic apartments from a door within the Quarter. Mossé's household never needed to awaken Jacob, the gatekeeper, if they wished to leave or enter the *Call* during the night, when the gates were locked. They had only to unbar the small door through the wall that gave the bakery access to the rest of the city.

• • •

When they entered the baker's house they were greeted by a heartrending wail from the upstairs apartments. Esther came running down the stairs and looked wildly at her husband. "He's dead, Mossé," she shrieked. "He's dead. My Aaron is dead."

TWO

Death, and the grief and shock it leaves behind, had become a familiar experience for Raquel in the three years she had been assisting her father. His failing sight, and the death of his former assistant, Benjamin, during the plague, had pressed her sister, Rebecca, into his service during those troubled times. After Rebecca's marriage, Raquel had, as a matter of course, taken over her sister's role as his eyes, and where sight must be married to touch, his hands. Since then, she had seen desolation and despair on the faces of the truly bereft, and their counterfeits on the faces of those who had been rescued from domestic tyranny by the long divorce of death. But the baker was unlike any mourner she had met. He stood back, making no move to console his devastated wife, accepting the loss of his heir with what appeared to be a stoic, almost sullen, fortitude. Mossé was an excellent baker, she knew, but no one had ever considered him a model of fortitude in adversity. There was an awkward pause, and then it was her father who stepped forward.

"Mistress Esther, please," said Isaac, reaching out a hand to comfort the sobbing woman. "Let us examine him first. Sometimes—"

"It's too late, Master Isaac," she wailed. "I know. I've seen the dead before. He's dead. My Aaron is dead. You're too late."

Mossé stood back, silent and impassive.

"If you will come with me," said a quiet voice from the foot of the stairs. "I will take you to him, Master Isaac. Papa," he added sharply, "I will take the physician up. Please stay with Mama." The speaker was a good-looking young man, sturdy in build but graceful in movement, and almost as tall as his brother. His eyes were reddened with tears, but his manners had not forsaken him. "Master Isaac, Mistress Raquel," he said. "And young Yusuf. You are all welcome. Thank you for your haste."

"It's Daniel, isn't it?" said Isaac, quietly. "If you will lead the way, we will follow."

The little procession trailed up the stairs to a small sleeping chamber over the bakery. "He lies in here," said Daniel.

Isaac stood in the doorway, listening, and sniffing the air. "When did he die?" he asked.

"Just moments before your arrival, sir. Even before there was time to arrange his body decently, Mama heard you and rushed down the stairs."

"Were you with him when he died?"

"I was, sir," he said, and fell silent.

"Take me to him," said Isaac. Raquel took her father's hand and led him to the head of the sadly disarranged bed. Isaac ran his fingers over the body where it lay, contorted and twisted, exactly as it had fallen in his death throes. "His death was not peaceful," he remarked.

"It was a horrifying sight," said Daniel in sober tones. "I shall not forget it easily."

"How long have you been here watching with him?"

"My father sent the boy for me in the night."

"Had he been taken ill so early?"

"No, Master Isaac. Aaron had awakened Papa."

"What do you mean?" asked Isaac. "Did he go into his chamber and ask for his help?"

"No. He was wandering through the house, up and down the stairs."

"Ah. While still asleep?"

"Yes."

"That speaks often of great disturbance of mind," said Isaac, "but not necessarily of illness. He had not the smell of illness or death on him when I last visited," he added, almost to himself.

"Papa said that he had done this several times before. You could see that he was asleep, yet he moved about the house as if he looked for something. I confess to you, master, that I would rather encounter an enraged mob than see something like that again." He voice trembled, and he paused to collect himself. "We put him back into his bed, and I sat with him until it was light. He woke up as usual, surprised to see me, but pale and tired. The maid brought us something to eat and drink. By this time the household was all at work."

"Bakers rise earlier than glove makers," said Mossé, who had appeared suddenly in the doorway. "We had to fire up the oven, and get ready for the first bake of the day."

"So at that time, although Aaron was walking in his sleep, he was not doing anything else that alarmed you?"

"That was enough for me," said Mossé. "I liked it not—it resembled too much a dead man rising from his bier and walking."

"And then I went below to speak a few words to my mother," said Daniel, paying no attention to his father's comments or answers.

"Indeed," murmured Isaac. "And what did he eat or drink? Anything of what was brought him?"

"Not a great amount," said Daniel. "The maid brought us a jug of mint tea and a fresh-baked loaf. He had some of that."

Mossé gasped, and struck the edge of the door with his fist. "It wasn't my loaf. You're never saying it was my loaf that killed him," said Mossé shrilly. "You'll ruin me.

My own son killed by my bread? No! You come with me when I buy grain and have it milled. Bring anyone you like. You'll see that Mossé the baker never buys bad grain." He clutched Isaac by the shoulder and gave him a shake. "Every sack of grain I buy I inspect. I can pick out a single seed of cockle in ten thousand of corn. I carry it myself to the mill, and never take my eyes from it until the flour is back in the shop. I never yet baked a loaf that gave anyone bread poisoning."

"Papa, no one is saying the bread poisoned Aaron. After all, I, too, ate from the loaf, much more than Aaron did, since I had been watching for much longer and was very hungry. And I drank from the pitcher. I am in excellent health, I assure you. No, it was not the bread."

"I doubt that it was bread poisoning," said Isaac.

"If I'm not needed here," said Mossé, "I must tend to my ovens."

"Papa! Aaron is dead," said Daniel. "You can wait a moment here to speak to the physician."

"The ovens are hot," said Mossé. "Burning the bread will not bring him back. Tomorrow is time enough to mourn." He turned on his heel and walked down the hall to the dimly lit stairs.

Isaac waited for Mossé to reach the ground floor. "Now, Daniel," he said, "can you tell me how he died? I would not ask if I did not think it important."

"As I said, Master Isaac, I had been out of the room for a while, talking to my mother and to Sara. Then Papa went off, and I came back. Aaron was out of bed, pacing back and forth like a sick animal, and shouting strange disconnected things that I could not understand. Then he backed up to his bed and covered his eyes. He snatched my hand, gripping it until it hurt, and said, 'Look at it. Over there. That thing. It's coming for us.' His face was gray, and drenched with sweat. He began to heave, as if he would vomit, but could not, shrieked at me not to let it catch him, and collapsed. My mother heard the commotion and came in. His limbs were twitching and jerking and he was making strange sounds, then he clenched himself up tight, as he is now, and died.''

"Raquel," said Isaac, "describe him to me more closely."

Raquel started with the top of his head. "It is twisted in an odd angle, Papa—"

"I could feel how he lies, child," chided her father. "And the stiffness of his flesh from the manner of his death. And I can smell a curious odor of something he ate or drank. Yusuf—look to see if you can find a vial, or a cup, or some container. But, Raquel, I need color. I need what my fingers cannot tell me. You know that."

"Yes, Papa. But there is little to say. His flesh is very white—or gray. He is not jaundiced, or suffused with blood, or blue about the lips. Even his eyes are not red or yellowed. He has bruises on his legs and arms, but they do not look new, and he has a burn mark on his hand."

"From the ovens, I expect," said Daniel. "It's very easy to be careless for a moment."

"I can find nothing, lord," said Yusuf. "Except a towel that is still wet from use. It has a yellowish stain on it."

"On the wet part?"

"Yes, lord."

"I shall take this. Otherwise, we can do nothing more," said Isaac. "I suspect many things, but they would be of little comfort to your grieving parents, or to yourself, Daniel."

"I shall walk out with you, master," said Daniel, "and let them wash and prepare the body."

Once they were out on the narrow street, Daniel turned to the physician. "What I didn't like to say in the house, Master Isaac," said Daniel, "was that, in recent days, my brother had been tormented with visions and terrible nightmares. He came to see me in great distress over it."

"For how long?"

"I don't know. Not long, I think. Two weeks, perhaps? Or three?"

"Your father had noticed something wrong as well," said the physician. "He consulted me about it."

"I think Aaron was mad, Master Isaac," said the young man. "He suffered from delusion and terrors—not always, but from time to time. In his disordered state he might have eaten anything."

"You believe he took his own life?"

"Not deliberately. I believe he ate or drank some noxious substance, thinking it healthful food."

"Were these melancholic fits? Was he unhappy?"

"Not at all. Sometimes he felt exalted, sometimes terrified. He never suggested that he was melancholy. And when the fits weren't on him, when he was in good temper, he was more restless than despairing. He had great plans for running away from the bakery, and living the life of a wandering scholar and poet. He dreamed of going to Toulouse. Someone had told him that art and beauty were appreciated there." Daniel stopped at the edge of a small square. "I think my father would have been wiser to keep me in the bakery, and send Aaron to Uncle Ephraim. I could have endured the life of a baker, and stood up to my father better. And Uncle Ephraim would have appreciated Aaron. My uncle is an artist in his way. He creates beautiful objects in leather, even though they are meant to be used every day."

"I know your uncle's work," said Isaac. "From those days when I could still see. It is indeed beautiful, and exquisitely crafted."

"Please don't think I'm complaining," said Daniel. "I cannot count the benefits I have received from being sent to him, although it was a blow for me when I discovered that Papa had sold me, his firstborn, for the money to build a new oven." He laughed, but it was a strained and difficult laugh. "Still—one recovers from these things," he added quickly, shifting his feet uneasily on the cobbles. "Poor Aaron. I enjoy my life at Uncle Ephraim's, but rightfully the experience belonged to Aaron. In this case,

Esau has the better portion, and I fear Aaron has died for it."

"You must not think these things, Daniel," said Isaac. "The artist in you has painted a memorable picture of your brother, cheated of his rights and driven mad because of it, lying dead at the feet of his grasping brother. Memorable, but untrue. We may never know how or why he died, but it was not because of you. Of that I am sure. Now go home and comfort your mother and your sister. They will need you. Where is Raquel?"

"She is standing up the street a little, talking to the boy, Yusuf," said Daniel. "I will fetch her. And thank you for your wise counsel. I have been much distressed by my brother's disordered imaginings and his death. We will meet again soon, I am sure," said the young man.

"Did you hear what Daniel had to say, Raquel?" asked Isaac, after giving the young man sufficient time to get out of earshot.

"Some of it," she admitted, taking her father's arm and moving slowly in the direction of their house.

"Yes, lord," said Yusuf, with more frankness than tact.

"It is unfortunate that he should believe that his brother died because of him," said the physician. "It is a heavy burden to place on his shoulders."

"But didn't he, lord?" said Yusuf.

"Not because of some deliberate action on his part," said Raquel. "But I agree with Yusuf. He is the cause."

"Now here is strange harmony," said Isaac, "when you two agree on anything more complicated than a good dinner." He stopped outside their gate, and slapped his leather wallet. "How very careless of me. I forgot to leave that vial of soporific drops for Mistress Esther. Yusuf can return to his lessons, but we must go back to the bakery and intrude on their grief once more."

"There is no vial of soporific drops, Papa," said Raquel.

"Then we will leave something else, my dear," said Isaac. "And this time we will not disturb the household, but enter through the shop.'' And he headed at a rapid pace for the gate to the Quarter.

Mossé was removing the baked loaves when Isaac returned. ''You again, Master Isaac?'' asked the baker. ''Did my wife summon you?''

''No, indeed. It is my cursed forgetfulness that makes me intrude upon you so soon. Raquel, take the mixture for Mistress Esther, and give it to her. Or to the maid, perhaps. I apologize for disturbing the household again on such a day,'' he said. ''If I might wait here a moment for my daughter to return, we will leave you in peace to get on with your work.''

''My wife and son find it heartless of me, carrying on like this.''

''Doubtless you find solace in work, Mossé.''

''I do,'' said the baker. ''And the wailing of women abovestairs grates on my ears. It won't bring Aaron back.''

''It eases their sorrow, much as working does yours,'' said Isaac soothingly. ''Did anything significant happen in Aaron's life a fortnight ago?''

''A fortnight? When was that?'' He stopped to consider. ''Just before Yom Kippur. Indeed it did. We baked six dozen loaves of special bread for the council. We were at it all the night and most of the next day, for that and for our regular customers.''

''I thought rather of something in Aaron's own life. Did he find any new acquaintances or friends?''

''Aaron never had many friends,'' said his father. ''He was content with his family. And his brother.''

''He was a solitary young man?''

''You could call him that. But it wasn't our fault he was solitary,'' said Mossé. ''We did our best for him, tried to arrange matches—with rich girls, pretty girls—he'd have none of it. But that had naught to do with his death. You just find the sorcerer who laid that spell on him, and accuse him of Aaron's death. Because until you do, he won't lie easy in his grave. He'll keep on walking in the night, just as he did these last two weeks. And I don't want to live with that." And mixed in with the heady scent of baking bread, Isaac caught a strong whiff of fear and loathing.

"I will make what inquiries I can, Mossé. I can't promise more than that. I think I hear Raquel returning."

"And my son with her," said Mossé. "He's a fine lad, you know. Stands to inherit a valuable concern." Then he yelled for the boy, who had fallen asleep in the corner, to stoke the fire and get to work with the bellows, and turned his attention to the next batch of bread.

Daniel walked with them to the door of the shop. "Tell me, Daniel," said Isaac, "who were Aaron's friends?"

There was a silence, a heavy silence. "I'm not the person to ask," said Daniel at last. "We saw each other several times in the past fortnight, but I live with Uncle Ephraim and Aunt Dolsa. I work long hours, and am more familiar with their visitors than with my poor brother's. Mama would know, or the maid. Not Papa," he added with some bitterness, "unless the visitor stopped to buy bread on his way to see Aaron. I must go back to my parents," he said abruptly. "Good day to you, Master Isaac."

Isaac waited until his footsteps receded into the back of the shop, and then started slowly along the cobbled street. "Did you speak to the maid?"

"I did, Papa," said Raquel. "She told me that since she entered the household, Aaron was out almost every night, and often came home drunk with wine. Several times she had to put him to bed and clean up after the wine sickness, and sometimes he gave her a farthing with his thanks. But she has no idea who he drank with. Or where he went. Except that he left through the shop, not through the house door, and sometimes he forgot to lock and bar the door when he returned. Every morning before the master got up she used to go into the bakery to make sure he would find it barred when he came down."

"She seems to have been the only person who knew anything about him," said Isaac.

"She certainly knows more than his family," said his daughter.

Twenty or thirty mourners followed the slow-moving ox-cart bearing Aaron's body up the steep track to the cemetery. Daniel's powerful legs carried him easily up the slope, walking beside the cart. Speaking of it for the first time, years later, as he lay in his wife's arms, the terrifying unreality, the nightmarish quality of the occasion, haunted him still. The world was silent except for the creaking of the cart and the swishing of the ox's tail. The sun beat down from a clear sky, and no one spoke. It was as if the heat had rendered them mute. They crushed the sweet-smelling grass and wild herbs as they walked, and the odor from the plants surrounded them in the warm air, bringing with it flies and gnats that rose silently out of the hard ground to torment ox and man alike. When they reached the cemetery, only the ox seemed to have retained any will of its own. It plodded to a spot under the shade of a tree and stopped. The silence swallowed up the prayers that issued from the mourners' dry throats and tongues, leaving behind a senseless murmur, like the buzzing of bees. When at last the earth was piled up again over Aaron's grave, each man made a polite rush for the fountain to wash his hands, apologizing, giving way, chatting, offering condolences. The spell was broken. The mourners turned their faces gratefully toward the city, hastening almost too precipitately in the direction of cool, shady rooms, and refreshing drinks and food and company.

Only Daniel stayed, trying to say something to his dead brother. But his mind was a blank, and he turned and headed back to the city as well.

Three days later Isaac received an urgent summons from Berenguer de Cruilles, Bishop of Girona, to whom he was personal physician. Ordinarily, this was the least onerous of his duties. Berenguer was a strong, active, healthy man of middle age, who shrugged off illness as other men chased away flies.

But not today. "Isaac, my friend," said the Bishop as soon as the physician entered his study, "I am stricken and out of temper. Something—the heat, or too much aggravating work—has brought on my gout. My toe is as red as a cardinal's hat, and almost as large." Berenguer de Cruilles sat by his desk, with his foot raised on a stool, radiating ill humor.

"I doubt that it's the heat that's brought it on, Your Excellency," said Isaac. "It's more likely to be sweet wine and rich meats. Admit, my lord Bishop, that you have dined well, on rich and spicy dishes recently."

"Sit, friend, sit. Your chair is where it always is. And I cannot control the cooks," added the Bishop ruefully. "Starting in September, they feel I must be built up to withstand the rigors of winter. As a result of their tender care, I can scarcely hobble across the room. No, my friend, don't say it. I am too choleric at the moment to listen to anyone, even you, tell me that I am not forced to fill my plate from a rich dish merely because it is placed before me."

Isaac shook his head with amusement. "You need something to cool and cleanse the blood, Your Excellency. I shall leave the herbs for an infusion with instructions for their preparation. Drink it three times every day. I have here as well a specific for the gout." He reached into the leather wallet that hung from a strap over his shoulder and removed a glass vial. "Put three drops of this into water, and drink it every time your cathedral bells call out the hours for prayer. Starting now."

"That's easy." He poured water into a cup and added the drops. "A bitter drink, Isaac," he said, tasting it. "I prefer good wine."

"Indeed. Which from now on, you will only drink well mixed with water. I will return tomorrow to discover how you are faring, Your Excellency. You are otherwise well?"

"As well as a man can be in this position. Isaac, I am surrounded by restlessness and revolt. No one is happy. The canons want to be bishops, the priests hunger to be canons, or to be given rich parishes, and important positions in court. They are all gone mad with ambition. Even the ones who can barely stumble through a line of holy text believe I owe them advancement to dizzying levels. Because a duke's younger son is promoted to a position far beyond his deserving, the fishmonger's son thinks he should be a cardinal."

"Does he really?"

"Not literally, Isaac. I don't think we have a fishmonger's son—but if we did, and if he were stupid enough, he'd want to be a cardinal."

"Even Monterranes?"

"Francesc? No. Francesc remains loyal, clever and competent, and too aware of the follies of mankind to suffer from arrogant ambition. I thank heaven daily for Francesc. But those cursed seminarians, Isaac. I am doomed to have eternal problems with the seminarians. They are like bees whose hive has been disturbed, flying this way and that, making noise, and creating trouble, but accomplishing nothing."

"What has disturbed them?"

"I wish I knew," the Bishop replied. "They are more agitated than ever these days, and breaking every rule in the seminary on a daily basis. And their masters, instead of dealing with them, send them over to me, with wailing and lamentations that they are beyond redemption." He stopped. "What am I to do? My temper is too short these days to deal with a pack of fools."

Isaac took his friend's lamentation at its face value for the moment. "You can do two things, Your Excellency," he said. "Find someone trustworthy in the seminary, or someone who can be placed in the seminary, to discover what the problem is—and it may be something quite negligible, like a change in cooks, or a minor restriction of liberties—and then deal with it, one way or another."

"A good idea. And I think I can lay my hands on some-one suitable. And the second?"

"Forget the gout, and engage me in a game of chess. You need respite from everyday cares."

"This is what makes you the best physician in the king-dom, Isaac," said Berenguer, and rang for someone to set up the board.

THREE

By the time the dinner break was over for the workers of the city, a small, blue-black cloud was visible on the horizon, tottering, as it were, on the tip of the mountains. After a certain amount of reflection, it moved toward the city, closely followed by its fellows. Before any but the most observant, or the most idle, had noticed any clouds, they had covered the sun. The wind rose, thunder crashed, and a storm broke. Water pelted down from the heavens, drenching everyone and everything that was not covered over. It raced down the streets in the Quarter, pooling into small lakes; it turned fields and paths outside the walls into seas of mud. It rained for close to two hours, and then as suddenly as it had started, it stopped. The clouds shrugged and moved over the next clutch of hills; the sun came out and steam began to rise from the wet earth. Men in waterlogged boots and wet tunics, their hair plastered to their heads, had crowded into Rodrigue's tavern to escape the storm, tossing their various outer garments onto benches where they dripped steadily onto an already wet floor.

In the corner farthest from the crowd, Marc, the

weaver's son, and Lorens, the seminarian, huddled together over a cup of Rodrigue's worst.

"What shall we do?" whispered Marc.

"Nothing," returned his companion. Lorens raised his head confidently and looked straight at the weaver's son. "We did nothing. Aaron did nothing."

"You call what we did nothing?" asked Marc. "Then why did he die?"

"Men die," said Lorens. "All the time. Of fevers, and fits, and other unexplained disorders. It had nothing to do with us. He was a friend, Aaron was, a good person, and an interesting one." He slowed until his speech was heavy with deliberation. "I will miss him sorely, but in no other way was his death a part of us. A sad loss, but otherwise nothing." He drained his cup, and then stared in astonishment at his hand, which trembled so violently he had difficulty in setting the cup down on the table.

"Let me buy you another, young master," said a voice from behind him. "It is cruel weather out there for the time of year." An empty cup appeared on the rough trestle table beside the two that were there.

Lorens turned, startled, and discovered he was a handsbreadth away from the scarred face and twisted smile of Lup, Master Guillem's servant and assistant. "I didn't know you drank at Rodrigue's, Lup," he said. Rodrigue heard his name and looked up. He caught Lup's signal and, without a word, was filling his cup with his better quality, slightly less thin and sour wine. Before Lorens or Marc could protest, Lup was sitting with them, their cups were filled as well, and the jug sat on the table, invitingly.

"It was a sad thing that happened to your friend. Master Guillem was most disturbed. He has been locked in his chamber, praying for the lad, ever since he heard the grim news." Lup raised his cup, as if for a toast, and drank. "What know you of the manner of his death? Had he been ill?"

"Not to my knowledge," said Lorens shortly. "He seemed perfectly well when last we saw him. And that was on our way home from Doña Marieta's."

"You found nothing odd in his manner that night?" asked Lup "Thinking back, it seems to me he was almost distraught—"

"Not at all," said Lorens. "You think that only because he died the next day."

"You are no doubt correct, young master," said Lup humbly.

"There are strange rumors about his death," said Marc. "People whisper about sorcery."

"People always whisper about sorcery when someone dies before his eightieth year, unless it be from a stabbing, or a woman brought to bed with a child," said Lorens.

"You have a clear head on your shoulders, Master Lorens," said Lup admiringly. "The world can use more like you. And your friend here. But alas, I am not here to enjoy your wise conversation. I bring a message from my master. He pities you from the bottom of his heart for the death of your friend, and begs that from this moment you will forget payment for the ceremonies—until you are earning the wherewithal to pay. Except if you have a farthing, or even a penny for the lad, it would be appreciated. The master asks whether we should prepare for you tomorrow evening, as usual?" He filled the cups once more.

The boys looked at each other uncertainly. The thought of carrying on had never occurred to them, not with Aaron dead. Lorens was their spokesman, but in his quiet way, Aaron had been the effective instigator of most of their actions. "It doesn't seem—" said Marc, and stopped. He thought of Marieta's hall, warm and colorful, hung with bright cloths and lit by more lamps and candles in that one room than his father had for their workroom and house together. "But if you think—" He gave Lorens a beseeching look.

"That is very generous of your master," said Lorens, guardedly. "But I do not think—" He looked over at Marc, and shrugged his shoulders. "Give him our thanks, and tell him that we will see him tomorrow."

"My master will be pleased with my news," said Lup. And he departed, leaving the jug of wine, paid for, on the table.

The suburb of San Feliu had begun in the shade of the north wall of the city of Girona. It had spread slowly north and eastward, as all manner and condition of the citizenry, and particularly those who worked with their hands, built themselves houses in the unprotected spaces outside the city. Along with being home to the discreetly managed premises of Doña Marieta, it was also where Isaac's daughter, Rebecca, lived with her Christian husband, Nicholau Mallol, and their two-year-old son, Carles. Nicholau scraped out a living for them as a scribe, working when he could for the cathedral and church courts. Their house was a routine stop on Isaac's daily round of visits to his patients, for the simple reason that otherwise he would never have spoken to his daughter, nor met his son-in-law, nor been a part of his grandson's life. Rebecca's conversion and marriage had been a blow from which her mother had not recovered; from the day her eldest daughter had left home, Judith had attempted to wipe her very existence from her memory. So Isaac visited, and never spoke of his visits, but persisted in reminding his wife from time to time that she had a grandson, and a daughter who still loved her mother.

And on this particular morning, later in the same week, he had been at the Bishop's palace, where Berenguer still swallowed bitter medicine against the gout, and drank water instead of wine, and ate herbs and grains and other fruits of the earth instead of rich meats and sauces, and complained about the rigors of administration and the helplessness of the people around him.

"One day soon, Isaac my friend," he said, "I am going to place a few of my most treasured books in a sack, along with an extra pair of stout sandals, and retire to the mountains, to the highest and most remote monastery that will accept me."

"Doubtless it would be very helpful for the gout, Your Excellency," said Isaac. "A diet of herbs and bread and water, and a regime of prayer and hard work would be very good for you. You must be improving rapidly to consider it." He laughed and turned to go.

"Where are you headed in such a hurry?" asked Berenguer. "Isaac, Isaac, I am infernally restless, confined here to my study and my bedchamber, listening to reports of the world outside my door, and helpless to act."

"I am off to visit Rebecca."

"Then of course you must leave. Pray give her my best wishes, Master Isaac," said Berenguer warmly. "She is an intelligent, resourceful woman, a true daughter of her father. She deserves a good life," he added thoughtfully. "And I have been considering what I could do for her. No," he said. "Do not interrupt me. I have observed her husband recently. He does not clamor for favor and preferment, although he has better reason than most."

"I'm not surprised," said Isaac. "He is modest about his abilities."

"I agree. But he is a good man, and an excellent scribe, clever and precise. I have in mind a minor reorganization in the work of the court, from which, if he wishes, Master Nicholau could benefit. But say nothing to your daughter, since there are a few political hurdles to overcome before it can be accomplished."

"I am sure they would be most grateful. As it is now, the work is shared out in such a way that he is idle more than he would like."

"Idle, and unpaid," said Berenguer.

"Indeed, Your Excellency."

"This post brings an annual stipend," observed the Bishop. "There now. For a moment I had forgotten my wretched toe in the pleasure of considering what I can do for your daughter. A most potent, but selfish, argument for unselfishness. Tell me, Isaac. You are skilled in logic. If I do a kind act, not because it is better to do it than not to do it, but because it makes me believe falsely that I am better than other men, does that negate the virtue of the act?''

"As you well understand, my lord Berenguer," said the physician, "being equally skilled in logic and the other arguments of the Greeks, you are deliberately confusing a virtuous act with its causes, some of which are virtuous and some not. These things must be carefully divided up and considered separately," said Isaac.

"And the importance of each act and cause weighed against the rest. An excellent point, my friend. We could construct an argument from this case that would take us three days to resolve. But do not let me keep you. Visit your good Rebecca, and we will save the disputation for another gouty afternoon. As an alternative to chess, per- haps.''

"Your guardian, His Majesty Don Pedro, asked after you in his latest letter to the Bishop, Yusuf," said Isaac, when he rejoined his young apprentice by the door to the Bishop's palace.

"Soon, lord—very soon, I will be able to write to His Majesty and send him my most grateful thanks for his protection," said Yusuf.

"Not if I keep interrupting your lessons," said Isaac. "But let us hasten to Rebecca's, so that we may be home in time for dinner." And resting his hand lightly on Yu- suf's shoulder, he walked quickly down to the north gate of the city, and out into the streets of San Feliu.

"What news do you hear from the town?" asked Isaac, once they were comfortably seated in Rebecca's small, neat house. "Between this new outbreak of the fever—''

"And the Bishop's gout," said Rebecca. "Everyone has heard of the Bishop's gout. His roars can be heard from the palace to the court.''

Isaac laughed. "Let us not forget the Bishop's gout. I feel I have been trapped inside the sickrooms of the city, and cut off from news.''

Nicholau looked up from the toy he was mending. "The

latest news comes from the wool exchange, Master Isaac. Concerning Pons Manet.''

"The wool merchant?"

"The same." He set down the toy. "There are three sets of rumors, I believe, all about Master Pons's plot to seize a council seat."

"But is that not assured at the moment?" asked Isaac.

"It matters not. They prefer to have him plotting, or bribing his way to head up the exchange, or the council itself. They would have him ambitious to become a duke, if it were possible that someone who began life so poor could raise himself to that level. But it is generally agreed that powerful interests, although there is no agreement on who they are—"

"Nicholau," said Rebecca. "Papa cannot stay all day."

"Leave him, daughter," said Isaac. "He is telling this very well."

"—that powerful interests are determined to stop him. And that he has been threatened with death, if he persists, or perhaps a loathsome disease. And this punishment is to be accomplished by witchcraft."

"What gave rise to the rumors?" asked Isaac. "I like them not."

"There can be nothing in them, Papa Isaac," said Nicholau, with more confidence than he felt. "But I saw him yesterday, and he does look like a man with a sentence of death on him. Pale, distracted, ill."

"And who is the witch who will inflict these punishments on him?"

"Speculation abounds. No one knows, of course, but names are whispered. In spite of my jests, Papa Isaac, I worry seriously, as do many people, that some innocent woman will be accused. It takes only one malicious gossipmonger to point a finger at a woman she dislikes to bring her to ruin. Imagine if one our neighbors envied Rebecca her beauty—"

"Nicholau, don't say that!" said Rebecca. "You frighten me."

"Calm yourself, Rebecca," said her father. "Nicholau meant nothing by using your name. But such talk is worrisome." He paused. "I wonder what is wrong with Master Pons? He has always been hale, energetic, and hardworking. Charitable and honest, too. It seems hard that he should be the subject of such baseless and unpleasant rumors."

"They will probably die down as soon as some other subject of speculation arises," said Nicholau. "The gossips of the town can only keep one scandal in their heads at a time, fortunately."

"True," said Isaac. "Now that I have had my full measure of news, I must go, or Yusuf and I will get no dinner this day."

FOUR

More than ten days had passed since the death of the baker's son, and life was resuming its ordinary rhythms even in the household of Mossé the baker. Clothes were washed and hung out on branches and on balconies to dry in the sun. Meals were cooked, floors were swept, and the task of preserving this year's bountiful harvest had begun. Herbs and fruits were drying, or being laid down in oil or brandy or salt for the winter ahead.

The Bishop's gout began to improve, and a mysterious fever that had attacked many of Isaac's other patients disappeared as unaccountably as it had arrived. With luck, it would be some time before the winter crop of coughs and aches would appear, so that except for two or three of the truly ill, who needed to be coaxed back to life, or eased with soothing compounds through the rigors of their final illnesses, the physician had little to concern him. Yusuf took advantage of the lull to turn his attention to young Master Salomó's instruction, and had just succeeded in penning a brief, legible message to his guardian, Don Pedro of Aragon.

"It doesn't look very elegant," said Yusuf, staring gloomily down at his finished work. A breeze—for they

were sitting in the courtyard under the grape arbor—
tugged at his paper, and caused him to add a further blot
to it as he reached, pen in hand, to keep it from blowing
away. "Not nearly as elegant as your hand, Master Salomó. I cannot make my fingers obey me in forming these
strange shapes. Perhaps you should copy it for me, and
then I will take it to the Bishop."

"No, Yusuf," said the familiar voice of his master.
"His Majesty will derive more pleasure from your unaided
efforts than from the accomplished hands of those who
have had many years of practice and instruction. But I
congratulate you, Master Salomó, for stuffing several
years' worth of learning into the lad in a few short weeks."

"Thank you, Master Isaac," said the young man, with
embarrassment. "You are most generous in your praise.
But I had little to do with it. Yusuf has a quick wit, and
a natural aptitude for letters. If you have time to listen, he
will read to you from one of your books—whichever one
you like. His reading is more polished than his writing."

"Excellent," said Isaac. "I shall sit by the fountain in
the sun, and devote myself to the pleasure of listening to
your pupil."

The physician sat down wearily, for he had been up
most of the night, and gave himself up to the sensuous
pleasures of his courtyard: sun on his back and shoulders,
the gentle splashing of the fountain, the rustling of leaves,
and the warm scent of grapes as yet unharvested on the
vine. Feliz the cat jumped on his lap, and its purring mingled with Yusuf's clear voice as he read, slowly and carefully, through a page of *Materia Medica,* stumbling
occasionally on the long words.

And later, at Doña Marieta's house in San Feliu, another
Tuesday evening came and went, with two young men in
attendance, instead of three.

On Wednesday morning, Martin, youngest son of Ramon,
the weaver, tugged at the bell to Isaac's house with great

urgency; Ibrahim went to the gate and peered through the ironwork at the thin, dusty-looking boy.

"What do you want?" he growled. He was, by nature, suspicious of boys.

"Sir," said Martin, clutching the grille, and speaking as rapidly as he could, "You must come with me right now. Father said to run to you as fast as I could before he dies," he gasped.

Ibrahim looked down at him in astonishment. "I must come?"

"He's dying," the boy repeated in frustration. "In the town, sir. A terrible disaster."

Ibrahim continued to stare, speechless, at him.

Martin was becoming frantic. "To my brother, sir, a great sickness, and my other brother says the judgment day is on us. And so does Bonanata. What shall we do?"

Ibrahim backed away in great alarm. Out of the jumble of words, his slow-working brain had caught "death" and "disaster" and "judgment day." "You want me?" he asked.

"Aren't you Master Isaac, the physician?"

He stepped back again. "Mistress!" he called. "Master! Mistress Raquel! Come quickly! Disaster—"

Raquel raced down the stairs, followed closely by her mother, and almost collided with her father. "Papa. What has happened?"

"I don't know," he said. "Ibrahim, what are you talking about? Who is here?"

"It's a lad, Father, of ten or eleven years," Raquel said. "Ibrahim, open the gate to him."

Ibrahim unlocked the gate and pulled it slowly open.

"Twelve," said the boy, indignantly, in his normal voice. He walked in and looked around the leafy courtyard with an air of profound approval. "I was seven in the year of the Black Death, and I know my numbers."

"And who might you be?" asked Isaac.

"I am Martin, sir," he said, approaching Isaac and bowing. "My father is Ramon the weaver, and my brother

Marc is very ill. Papa says you are to come at once. If you can," he added, somewhat abashed.

"Tell me something of his illness, if you can, so that I know what to bring with me," said Isaac.

"He awoke this morning with a great thirst, and raved and saw things that are not there. Now we cannot wake him, and when he breathes, he makes strange sounds."

"When did this start?"

"He was in good health last evening. He ate a large supper."

"Then quickly, Raquel. Fill the basket." The two disappeared into Isaac's study and workroom, where he kept his supplies of herbs, and barks for infusions, and essences to be given as drops, and poultices for wounds and burns and infections, all carefully arranged on shelves so that, sightless though he was, he could pick out anything that he needed.

"What do you need, Papa?"

"Emetics, and stimulants. Then tisanes to calm the stomach and cleanse the gut and cool the blood. It would be well to include soporifics if there are spasms. We cannot tell how accurate the lad's descriptions are."

"He has been poisoned?"

"Most likely. What I am sure of is that he is very ill, because Ramon is not one to throw money away on physicians without cause. His thrift is legendary. But poison or contagion, the treatment may keep him alive long enough for his body to recover itself. Where is Yusuf?"

"He is at the market, Isaac," said Judith. "He asked leave to go before his lesson. I did not know you would have need of him."

"I would have wished—but never mind. He will learn these things in due course."

Marc was in a pitiful state by the time Raquel and Isaac reached the weaver's small house by the river. He lay in a tiny, curtained-off sleeping chamber, whose three walls were lined with narrow beds. He was collapsed in a tangle of bedclothes, his chest heaving in an agonizing fight for each breath. A helpless-looking young man of about twenty sat on the bed across from him, listening to his labored breathing, and doing nothing.

Raquel led her father into the cramped room. "He lies on the bed to your left, Papa," she murmured. "He is very pale—"

Isaac raised his hand to silence her, leaned down until his head was on Marc's chest, and listened to his breathing for almost a minute. "Now tell me, my dear."

"He appears to be without consciousness, Papa, but— there. He tried to open his eyes. I think he may hear our voices."

"Speak to him, Raquel. Call him by name. And young man, bring us a basin, and a jug of water, and towels," said Isaac. "And a cup. Quickly. When you come back, you can tell us what you know of this illness."

Marc's brother fled as if pursued by wild beasts, and returned almost instantly with the required materials clutched in his arms. Raquel relieved him of the jug, which she set on the floor, and the cup, which she placed on a stool. She stacked the towels and basin on the bed beside her.

While this was going on, Isaac ran his fingers down Marc's body, looking for swellings, and feeling for a pulse; once more he laid his ear on the young man's chest, listening to his heartbeat and his breathing, and he sniffed the air for further signs of the nature of his illness. "Put four drops of the blue mixture into a spoonful or two of water, my dear," he murmured. "And we shall try to rid his body of what troubles it."

It takes skill and great determination to induce an intermittently unconscious man to drink a bitter-tasting, powerful emetic without causing him to choke. Isaac and his daughter turned the brothers out of the room, dragged Marc to a sitting position on the edge of the bed, and started to work.

Some half hour later Raquel set down the basin. "If

there is anything in the young man's stomach now, Papa, I will give up trying to cure people.''

Isaac continued to hold him upright. "Has he opened his eyes?" he asked.

"He is trying to, Papa, but it seems difficult for him."

Marc's eyes opened at the sound of Raquel's voice, but then his head lolled against the physician's chest, and his eyelids drooped again as his body demanded sleep. "I think you are probably correct, Raquel. What he needs now is a stimulant to drive this fatal drowsiness from his body. Six drops, to begin with. In a little water."

And with infinite patience, while her father held him sitting upright, Raquel coaxed tiny amounts of the liquid into the barely conscious man's mouth, and held it closed until he swallowed, talking all the time. Twice he began to choke, and was thumped back into breathing, but at last it was all consumed. Raquel washed his face with cold water. His eyes opened and closed again. Isaac continued to hold him upright. Raquel washed his face with cold water again. His eyes opened, and focused on her. He glanced down, realized that he was sitting on the edge of his bed wearing only his shirt, and blushed.

"Ah," she said. "Papa. He's awake. And aware of us."

"Good," said Isaac. "Now—another six drops in more water and then I would speak to his father. Young man," he called to Marc's older brother, "take my place here. Hold your brother upright, and try to keep him awake. Talk to him. Make him answer you."

"Drink this," said Raquel, holding the cup to his lips.

"It tastes foul," said Marc, his voice slow and thick.

"Good," she said. "You can speak. That means you're recovering."

"And Raquel, if he begins to fall back into his former state," said Isaac, "give him another six drops. I will be below, talking to the father. Is the lad who brought me here still around? Martin?"

"Here, master. In the hall."

"I would speak to your father. Take me to him, please."

● ● ●

"They say," said Martin as they walked down the narrow stairs, "that you can fly."

"Do they indeed," said Isaac. "I'm afraid it isn't true. As you can see, I walk on two feet, like other men—and long distances, some days, when many of my patients are ill."

"Then you're not a magician?" he asked, in a bitterly disappointed voice.

"No. I'm not a magician. I have some skill in medicine, which I learned quite honestly from my elders, who were even more skilled than I."

"Here is my father," said the boy, clearly no longer interested in their guest. Physicians were much less intriguing than magicians.

Isaac reached out a hand and felt the doorway. He took a step forward and stopped to acquaint himself with the room. It smelled of new wool, and the air that touched his cheek was thick with small fibers. The thump of the loom echoed between walls and ceiling, speaking of the room's generous dimensions, in comparison with the cramped quarters in the rest of the house. The weaver sat like a spider in the spacious center of his universe—his workroom. "Master Ramon," he said. "I come from your son's bedside."

"Does he still live?" said Ramon, and threw the shuttle across and through the weft.

"He was near death when I arrived," said Isaac, "and is still in grave danger. But I think he will recover. Someone must sit with him and administer stimulants until he is alert and capable of moving about. Do you have a reliable servant?"

"Bonanata? She is a good girl, but whether she could nurse the sick, that I can't tell you. And who is to prepare our dinner if Bonanata is not in the kitchen? Since my wife died in the Black Death we have had to shift for ourselves."

"Perhaps you could leave your loom for a few hours to

attend to him, then," said Isaac sharply. "Your sons seem ill equipped for the task."

"I cannot leave my loom for a whole day," said Ramon. "Nor half the day, neither. Nor can I excuse my son from his work for that time. Martin will leave his sweeping and sorting, and tend to his brother. If he lives, he lives. We are in the hands of God."

"You are not concerned about your son?"

"I sent for you, didn't I? But Marc has ever been more trouble than his brothers. Not that he isn't good at his loom," he added grudgingly. "And he can dye fleeces in colors so excellent I could sell cloth made from them to the court. But who in this city wants goods of that sort?" He picked up his shuttle once more. "But discontented. Always wanting to waste money, to go off and do something foolish. It's wearying living with one who complains all the time." The loom thumped and Isaac left the room.

He mounted the stairs once again, exhausted, not from his efforts, but from the folly and heartlessness of mankind, and felt his way to the tiny bedchamber.

"Papa," said Raquel. "He is so much better; he has been talking and trying to walk about the room."

"Walking in this room was always difficult," said Marc. "There is scarcely room for a flea to make its way between the beds."

"Excellent," said Isaac. "If you're well enough to be witty, you are on the mend. Take one more cup of the mixture that Raquel will give to you, and move about until your limbs feel active again. In a while you may eat a little, but wait until tomorrow before you resume your usual life. You may tell your father that I advise against working too soon. In the meantime your brother will amuse you."

When Isaac and Raquel returned from the weaver's tiny house, Yusuf was waiting, pale with apprehension. "Lord," he said, "please forgive me. I did not think that you would need me."

"I would have sent him to the weaver's," said Judith apologetically, "but we heard your voices."

"We saved the life of the weaver's son," said Raquel, with a touch of self-satisfaction in her voice. "He was sunk in a very deep sleep, so deep he could scarcely breathe."

"Raquel," said her father, "do not boast of achievements until they are certain. When we hear that the young man can run or dance, then we can rejoice. You did well, but his life is in the hands of the Lord."

"Yes, Papa," said Raquel, with a touch of mutiny in her voice.

"And it was for your instruction that you should have been there, Yusuf," said Isaac, severely. "You might have been useful, but I wanted you to observe what can be done in such cases."

"You stink to the heavens, Raquel," said Judith. "Your gown is all spattered. And your tunic, Isaac. You must both change."

"He was sick all over me," said Raquel. "It wasn't my fault."

"I did not say it was," snapped Judith. "Change your gown."

"Wait," said Isaac, "wait." It was as if the weaver's meanness of spirit had infected them all, and was now darkening the courtyard with a cloud of ill temper. "I was ungenerous," he said. "Raquel labored mightily and saved the life of a most gentle and worthwhile young man. Her gown was dirtied in the noblest of causes. And had you been there, Yusuf, you would have learned much, as well as being of use. But tell me, how did you spend your morning?"

"I met a friend," said Yusuf.

"Did you?" asked Isaac. "An old friend?"

"No—a new friend. He is from Valencia, and he speaks my language. He was in the market buying incense and medicinal herbs for his master. His name is Hasan."

"A slave?" asked Isaac.

"Yes," said Yusuf in a troubled voice. "Traders stole him from his family and brought him to Barcelona."

"Yusuf, it is not fitting for you to be consorting with slaves and such—"

"Hush, Judith, my dear," said Isaac. "These have been troubled times, and many blameless creatures from honest and respectable families have been stolen and sold into slavery."

"His master is a scholar," said Yusuf. "From Montpellier. He can call up spirits, he says. Or that is what his master tells people. Hasan has never seen one of these spirits."

"Poor child," said Raquel. "What a fate."

"He didn't seem too unhappy," said Yusuf. "But that's because he is saving up his money to buy his freedom. He is sure he will be able to return to his family." He paused for a moment. "I don't think he knows how difficult that can be."

"Where is young Master Salomó?" asked Isaac. "Shouldn't you be having a lesson?"

"He excused himself from attending today," said Judith. "He feels somewhat ill."

"Then Yusuf can read to me on the uses of plants in medicine," said Isaac, "until dinner. After dinner I would like you to visit the weaver's house, and find out how young Marc is faring. I will tell you what to look for."

"Yes, lord," said Yusuf, his face grave with new responsibility. "Is Mistress Raquel not to come with me?" he asked with apprehension.

"It is not fitting that Raquel should visit a household of four men and one female servant, with only you as her guardian," said Isaac. "Do you not agree, my dear?"

"Four men?" said Judith. "Living alone together? How old is the servant?"

"She looks to be twelve, Mama," said Raquel. "Although she may be thirteen."

"You are not to set foot in that house without your father by your side at all times." At that, Judith set off to see about dinner. "And change your gown," she called from the stairs.

FIVE

Thursday morning, Isaac walked down the broad cobbled street outside his courtyard gate unaware of the sunshine, the growing bustle, or even Raquel and Yusuf beside him. He was concentrating on the troubles of a young mother whose delight in her infant had suddenly faded into weakness and lethargy. She was neither feverish nor melancholy, in the usual way, nor was her strength being taxed beyond endurance. But the evening before, she had caught the sleeve of his tunic in his hand. "It is as if there is a voice in my head, telling me my baby cannot live," she had whispered to him. "I do not really hear it," she had added quickly. "I am not mad, like poor Teresa who hears voices, but I cannot erase it from my thoughts. Master Isaac, I have been cursed." Tears trickled over her cheeks.

The birth had been easy, the baby strong and healthy, and the woman's family was lavishing on her all the care they could command. Young mothers often worried, but she had every reason to be well and happy. He did not like this talk of being cursed. He did not like it at all. While brooding over it, Isaac reached the gate of the Quarter before he realized he had left his own courtyard.

"We will stop at the weaver's house," he said.

"Yes, Papa," said Raquel vaguely. She had her own preoccupations. Yusuf had come back with his report the previous evening well pleased with himself. Marc was well, although his head ached, and the two of them had strolled along the riverbank in the late afternoon, talking of his restlessness and discontent, and then of art, and beauty, and the wider world outside Girona, until evening approached. "The dust and noise in the house seemed to oppress him," Yusuf had said, "but he was well and cheerful outside."

Yusuf is taking over my role in Papa's life, she reflected. He can go where I cannot, and as soon as he learns what I know, Papa will no longer need me.

Mama talked of her marriage daily now. It was all very well for Papa to tell her mother that he wouldn't listen to another word on the subject until next year, but that didn't stop her when they were alone. She knew all the men in the Quarter, and there wasn't one she wanted to marry. The thought of leaving her family to go to some stranger considered suitable by her mother filled her with dismay and fear. Today she would talk to him about it, she resolved, just as they arrived at the weaver's little house, and Yusuf knocked confidently on the door.

They heard running footsteps, and the heavy door was pulled open. The little maid, her face buried in her grubby apron, and her shoulders heaving, stood in the doorway. She tried to speak, but her words were lost in a wrenching sob.

"Bonanata?" said Raquel. "What's happened?"

She took a gasping breath and emerged from her apron. "It's young master Marc," she said. "He's dead."

"Well, Master Isaac," said a hostile voice from the dark passage behind the maid. "You have succeeded. My son is dead."

"Succeeded?" said Isaac. "What the devil are you talking about? Succeeded in what?"

"You know better than I, physician," said Ramon.

"I know nothing. I stopped at your door for a moment to inquire after Marc. You say he has died?" He stopped for a moment. "I'm astonished. I had thought that he was recovering well," he added in a puzzled voice, "but there is nothing more uncertain in this world than life. I am very sorry, Master Ramon. He was a most worthy young man."

"Sorry is no help to me," said Ramon, his voice rising. "He's dead now, and a pretty penny it's cost me to raise him and teach him to weave with artistry and craft. I was given black counsel the day they told me to send for you."

"How did he die?" said Isaac, ignoring the weaver's last comment. He planted his staff firmly on the doorstep and leaned on it. He was intent on an answer, in the house or on the threshold.

"You know well how he died. It was that one, standing beside you, all innocent. She gave him those potions that you concocted, sir, and evil they were," he said. "He took them and never recovered. It was a horrible sight, his death, the like of which I hope never to see again."

"But Mistress Raquel gave him those in the morning, and he was in good health all the afternoon," said Yusuf. "I was with him. You cannot accuse her. I am more likely to have been at fault than she is."

"I know that," said Ramon impatiently. "I'm talking about the mixtures that murdering witch brought with her last night."

"Last night," said Raquel, breaking in indignantly. "I wasn't here last night. I was at home, with Mama and Papa."

"She was indeed," said Isaac grimly. "And I, and all my house, and Jacob the gatekeeper can attest that my daughter never set foot past our gate, nor outside the Quarter yestereve. I want to know who came to this house pretending to be my daughter."

"So you say."

"So everyone says, and will say, because it is the truth."

The weaver turned his head and shouted into the darkened hall. "We'll see," he said. "Martin!"

Isaac heard the boy's light footsteps coming down the stairs.

"Martin, who was that lady who came to see Marc after sunset? The physician's daughter?"

"No, Papa." His voice quavered, he gulped and then carried on firmly. "She was nothing like the physician's daughter. She was not near so tall, and her voice was very different."

Ramon paused to consider this. "If it were not Mistress Raquel, then I don't understand—" he said at last, with a baffled air. "It may be best to speak of this in private. Follow me, Master Isaac."

And once more Isaac found himself in the weaver's workroom.

"Well," said Ramon, "someone came to the door after sunset. It was a lady in a dark gown—brown it was, and a fine wool—and veiled. She asked to see Marc. I thought it was young Mistress Raquel. Who else would it be? No young lady had ever come asking for my son before this. She said she had some remedies for him, and Martin took her to the chamber where he lay. I listened at the foot of the stairs and, after a while, heard chanting coming from the room, and smelled incense."

"That was all you heard? Did they speak?"

"No more than a few words. I couldn't make them out. And the chanting was enough to send shivers all over your body, Master Isaac—high-pitched like, and strange. She was there a good while, I'd say. After she left, I went in to see him, but he was sleeping. So I left him to his rest, had my supper, and went to my bed."

"It could not have been my daughter," said Isaac firmly. "First of all, I would never send her out alone to visit a patient, and certainly not at night. And my daughter would never try to heal a sick man with chants and incense."

"Well—if not your daughter, then some woman came

here last night and wrought a spell over my son, and he died.'' He moved closer, until Isaac could feel hot breath on his face, and then prodded him in the chest with a finger. ''You could have sent someone else. Marc died from witchcraft, and I want to know who was responsible for his death. You find out, Master Isaac, or by all the saints in heaven I'll know you had something to do with it. My boy will never rest in his grave if he died from the sorcerer's art, and stays unavenged.''

''Why sorcery, Master Ramon?''

''Why else was there chanting and incense?''

''They could have been praying, Papa,'' said his older son, pushing aside the curtain that screened off the work-room and walking quietly in. ''But, Master Isaac,'' he went on, ''I believe that it is possible that it was sorcery.''

''Why do you say that?''

''There was nothing natural about his end. When I came to my bed, he was sleeping restlessly, like a tormented soul, thrashing about, and muttering in his sleep. And when he woke, he screamed, and said that he could see into the pit of hell itself, and there were demons, horrible red and yellow demons leaping up from the flames and crawling all over him. He said it over and over, and tore at his flesh like a madman. By then, Martin was awake, and we tried to hold Marc down to keep him from injuring himself. We called for Papa, and asked him to go for the priest, but by the time he roused himself enough and left, it was too late to do anything. Then Marc stared up at me, and said I was the devil, and Martin was my helper, and he begged us to stop tearing him apart. Then he screamed and screamed, and died. I have never seen anything like it.''

''And so, my Lord Berenguer, I thought I should hasten to tell you of this before the weaver's accusations are the common talk of the town. Perhaps one of your priests could visit the man, and calm his fears.''

It was late in the afternoon of the same day; the autumn

sun slanted into the Bishop's study, picking up dust motes in the air, and suffusing the bowl of fruit on the table with a warm glow. The Bishop of Girona sat with his foot up on a gout stool, tapping his fingers on his desk. "That fool of a weaver should know better than to worry about the visions of a dying man. They are more likely to proceed from fever than from a glimpse of the devil come to collect his own."

"Indeed, Your Excellency, I agree completely," said Isaac. "But I failed to convince the weaver of that."

"I knew young Marc," said Berenguer. "A pleasant lad, a good and virtuous young man, as far as I know. And a better craftsman than his father, with more sense. He favored his mother, who was an excellent woman. One wondered at the time," he added wryly, "why our heavenly Father decided to take that worthy soul and leave a lesser man behind. Perhaps it was to give him time to prepare himself for paradise. And if that was the reason, one suspects that Ramon will die a very old man."

"Doubtless the Lord had His own purposes, my lord Berenguer," said Isaac.

"Indeed. Well—I don't like this, Isaac my friend. Ramon can stir up a great deal of trouble. I will send someone to reassure him and see if we can quell this talk of sorcery."

"That would be an excellent thing, my lord Berenguer."

"But I confess to you, Isaac, that I am much concerned over the young man's state of mind before he died."

"The visions?"

"Not that. Certainly, we cannot see the state of another's soul, but I find it difficult to believe that those visions mean that he died in mortal sin. What disturbs me is the unhappiness and rebellion he spoke of to young Yusuf. It mirrors what I see in the seminary. That means it is everywhere," he said gloomily, "and I want to know where it's coming from."

"But, Your Excellency, youth always dreams, and rebels at being put in harness. Perhaps you are fretting about a problem that will solve itself in time. The gout does that to you, if you remember.''

'' 'Struth, Isaac, it's bad enough to have the gout, without being told it's responsible for discontent in the seminary. And I know that youth rebels. I did myself, and no doubt so did you. But this seems somehow different.''

"Did you ever place someone among the seminarians to test their present humors? You had spoken of it, I remember.''

"Isaac, you are too modest. You had spoken of it, and an excellent idea it was. But I had no need to search for anyone. I have a young cousin in there, older by some years than the rest of the lads, placed through my influence, I have to admit. I sent for young Bertran, and gave him his commission. He was a young officer when he changed from swordplay to prayer. He knows how to follow orders, and how to hold his tongue.''

"Useful qualities. Has he learned anything?''

"Only that there are things to be discovered, things that are being kept from those who are not initiates into an inner group.''

"The very existence of an inner group will sometimes cause dissension,'' observed Isaac. "But that seems a long way from the death of poor Marc.''

"Perhaps not,'' said the Bishop. "Do we know who his friends were?''

"Marc is dead,'' said Lorens desperately. "I will be next.''

"May God protect you,'' said Master Guillem, crossing himself.

"The way He protected Aaron and Marc?''

"That is a blasphemous thought,'' said Master Guillem, looking nervously around. They were standing in the meadow, well out of earshot of the rest of the curious world. A stray breeze caught the skirts of Master Guillem's long tunic, giving his figure an air of comic gaiety. Nothing could be further from the truth.

"No,'' said Lorens. Despite the warm sun on his shoulders, he shivered uncontrollably, like a man trapped in a snowstorm. "It is not blasphemy. It is a question."

"Your friends had not your strength," said Master Guillem. "They faltered in the search, and became vulnerable. I blame myself for not protecting them."

Lorens jumped on the word. "Protecting them?" he asked. "Can you protect people? How is it done?"

"There are some powerful protective spells that can be woven," he said slowly, almost reluctantly. "To keep the demons from attacking your body in their search for your soul."

"Then weave them, sir, I implore you," said Lorens.

"It is not so easy," said Master Guillem. "And that is why I have not spoken of them before. To be effective your body must first be rubbed with a certain mixture of oils and unguents and spices. Your spirit must then be fed and strengthened with the odor of incense—a particular incense. I have none of these in my possession. And they are very costly. I know of an apothecary in Barcelona who can supply them, but they must be fetched. For that I need a trustworthy messenger, and a sturdy mule, or even better, a swift horse. That alone takes more money than I have. My pupils here in Girona give me but little for their instruction, and I am not a rich man. And then there is the cost of the ingredients."

"Perhaps I could ask my father for the money," said Lorens.

"And who is he?" asked Master Guillem innocently.

"Master Pons Manet, the wool merchant. How much do you require?"

"All those ingredients of which I spoke—and the horse and his rider and their keep for two, no—three, days . . ." His voice trailed off as he worked sums in his head. "It could all be done for fifty silver groats."

"Fifty groats!" said Lorens. "That is more than it costs my father to maintain his household for a year."

"I doubt that, young master. Not if he is the person you say. But if your father will not help, then I will do my best with what is available here, in the markets and in the fields. And we will pray most earnestly for the protection of God.''

Lorens stared at the scholar's face as if the older man had just pronounced a sentence of death on his head.

But for most of the world—with the exception of Lorens, and Marc's brothers, and their heartbroken little maid—the week seemed to proceed quietly enough to its end. In spite of the farmers' annual dire predictions of disaster, in the orchards, fruit trees drooped almost to the ground with the weight of their burdens, and in the fields, the ears of grain that fell to the scythe were plump and golden, and gardens everywhere were bright with greens and sturdy autumn vegetables. But unease permeated the very stones of the houses in the city. The streets should have been bustling with preparations for the autumn fair, and the merchants busy counting up profits to come as a result of a good harvest, and the shops filled in anticipation of prosperity. But instead, men glanced at the clear sky and shook their heads, as if this sunny weather was there to deceive them, to lure them into thinking all was well. ''Men remember the plague,'' said the armorer to the silversmith. ''Times were very good just before it struck.''

''No, they weren't,'' said the silversmith, who had an excellent memory.

''Exactly,'' said the armorer, shaking his head and paying no attention. ''And we will pay dearly once more for this bounty.''

On Monday, Isaac had just returned from a round of late-afternoon visits when a messenger arrived at his gate, requesting his attendance at the house of Pons, the wool merchant, on a matter of some urgency. The messenger could tell him nothing more. His master was not in his bed, and although he did not look well, he couldn't really say that he seemed particularly ill.

"Very well," he said. "I shall come shortly. Raquel? Yusuf?" he called.

"Yes, Papa?" said Raquel, yawning. In the past week too many patients with trifling complaints had sent urgent summonses to the physician to come out during the night, and she was suffering from lack of sleep.

"We must go out again," Isaac said briskly. "Put together an ordinary basket until we know what more is needed."

"Who are they?" asked the messenger suspiciously. "The master didn't ask for three physicians."

"My daughter and my apprentice. I am blind, as you no doubt know, and they are my eyes."

"You won't need them," said the messenger. "My master said you were to come alone, and quietly."

"That may be," said Isaac, "but they are coming."

"As you wish."

The room Isaac was ushered into was large enough for his footsteps to throw back a slight echo. His guide led him to a bench made comfortable with cushions, and left. Raquel and Yusuf followed with a gentle rustle of leather boots and woollen cloth, and took up positions behind him. In a moment another person entered.

"Master Isaac. I am Pons," he said simply, in a pleasant, not-quite-cultivated voice. Men credited him with little breeding and an impoverished upbringing, but Isaac noted the cordiality in his words and tone. "I am most grateful to you for coming in such haste," he added. "And I see that you have brought your assistants with you. Their fame has traveled the country almost as rapidly as yours."

"Thank you, Master Pons," said Isaac. "I hope we can help you."

The merchant paused, as if uncertain. "The most gracious favor you could grant me, Master Isaac," he said at last, "would be a few moments of conversation with you alone. I have things to impart that I could not easily say in front of a gently raised maiden and a young boy. Whenever their assistance is needed, I will send for them. Will you grant me this?''

"Certainly, sir."

"See that they are refreshed," said the wool merchant to someone behind him, and footsteps bustled away. "Let me take you to my study."

"You are ill, Master Pons?" asked Isaac tentatively as he sat down in the merchant's quiet sanctuary. It smelled of leather and wax candles, and sweet scented wood—the room of a wealthy man.

"I am certainly weary in body and spirit, good sir, but I doubt that you would call me ill." He fell silent; outside, a breeze rattled some branches, and a flock of birds began to gather nearby, with much chirping and calling. Isaac waited. "Before I explain why a healthy man needed an eminent physician to hasten to his side, let me offer you some wine."

"Please. A little, mixed well with water," said Isaac. "It is a thirsty walk on a warm, dry afternoon."

"Of course."

There was a further pause, as his patient—or his host—fussed over the pouring of the wine, and the adding of the water, and the exact placement of the goblet at Isaac's right hand. "I confess I have difficulty in knowing how to begin, Master Isaac," he said.

"Ask whatever you wish," said Isaac, "and we will continue from there."

"Of course," he said, fell silent for a moment, and then drew a deep breath and began to speak very quickly. "Well, then—I need to discover if you have remedies for illnesses caused by magic and sorcery."

This was not the question that Isaac expected from a hardworking and canny merchant. He, too, paused to put his thoughts in some order. "For that, Master Pons," he said at last, "I fear you need a man of religion, not a physician. I might suggest that you consult the excellent Bishop Berenguer, who would, no doubt, be very interested in what you have to say. But if you will tell me what your symptoms are, then whatever may be their cause, I can attempt to alleviate them for now.''

"The problem, Master Isaac, is that the illness is not mine, nor has it happened yet. I want to know how to prevent it. You are reputed to be a very wise man, skilled in all branches of healing, of sickness both of body and soul.''

"Illnesses caused by spells and demons are out of my sphere, sir,'' said Isaac. "For those, you must pray, and seek a priest to guide you. But if I am not too bold, Master Pons, I can discern from your voice that you yourself are not well. You cough, and do not breathe with the ease you should. Are you sure we do not speak of you? There is no shame in it.''

"No doubt all these things are true,'' said the merchant. "But my bodily weaknesses come from lack of sleep, not sorcery. Worries attack me from every side.''

"What kind of worries?''

"I confess to you in all confidence that during these last two or three months I have been living in my own private hell here on earth. I have not spoken of this—'' His voice drifted off into silence. He coughed and suddenly began to speak again, with energy. "It started when someone— and I still have not discovered his identity—accused me not long since of having a Moorish concubine—''

"And do you?''

"No,'' he said. "I am well content with my good wife, Joana. I have no need of other women, and I recoil from the thought of purchasing forced love. My sins are of another sort—anger, and the perennial trap of the merchant, avarice. But that is not all. Another person—who was, no doubt, paid to lay the complaint—accused my eldest son, a gentle and most law-abiding man, happy in his marriage, of raping a Jewish woman. I could not—still cannot— believe it.''

"What evidence did he bring forth?''

"No woman complainant was produced, but the ac-cuser—a man—insisted that only shame prevented her from coming forward. The fines for adultery with a woman outside one's faith are very high, as perhaps you know. And I felt it best to settle—innocent as we both were—before the question of imprisonment could arise. I took care of both accusations before they became public, but they cost me, not only in money, but in worry. If there are more of them, they could bring about my ruin, or my imprisonment, or both.''

''I sympathize, Master Pons. A patient once threatened to accuse me of taking a Christian mistress, and I remember with great clarity the anger and concern—indeed, the fury it engendered in me. It was a difficult time.'' Not the least, he reflected silently, because for a while Judith had believed the accusation to be true.

''I, too, raged like a madman, Master Isaac, until reason prevailed. And then someone—a member of my family dear to me—came to me yesterday and asked for an enormous sum. He needed it to protect himself from death by sorcery. Three attacks on my family's reputation and wealth in such a brief space of time cannot be coincidence, do you not agree?''

''It seems unlikely,'' said Isaac. ''But how can I assist you?''

''It occurred to me that if some evil man, some sorcerer, is trying to destroy me thus, that one could enlist the help of a wise man of benevolent disposition to fight his wickedness.''

''Master Pons, I would be the last in this great kingdom to deny the power of evil in this world,'' said Isaac, ''but there are remedies for it that are better than attempting outright war against it. In my experience, simple prudence can go a long way toward thwarting evil.''

''What do you mean?''

''Evil uses more than threats and maledictions to inflict its harm,'' he said, leaning forward. ''It borrows arrows from the archer and poisons from the earth. They are faster than spells and more efficacious, I suspect. If I were you, I would keep my dear relation close to my side, and place a careful watch on what he eats and drinks.''

"At the moment he lodges in the safest place in the world, but I will think about how to keep him even safer.''

"And I would lead a very careful, very virtuous life, with unimpeachable witnesses to all my actions. Time will make your enemies impatient, and they will begin to reveal themselves.''

"There is something in what you say,'' murmured the wool merchant. "It is difficult, though.''

"And as for you, you need to strengthen yourself to bear these burdens. First, you must sleep, and this is my prescription. From the time the sun sets, I counsel you to avoid foods that heat the blood and increase choler. They feed your anger. Anger in some men kills sleep more certainly than worry. Take soup, and fruit, and bread for your supper. And when you are prepared for bed, put on a warm robe, drink an infusion of the herbs we will leave for you, and kneel. Then, with your head dropped down easily, and your shoulders relaxed, and in a soft murmur, recite your prayers ten times over. Get into bed, and you will sleep.''

"Tell me, Master Isaac, is it the herbs or is it God who will cause me to sleep?''

"That I cannot say, Master Pons,'' said Isaac. "I am only a physician. But I know that if you do what I advise, you will sleep.''

SIX

"It is a curious world we live in, Judith," said her husband, when the supper board was cleared and the household had quieted for the evening.

"It is?" she murmured vaguely, pulling the candle nearer so that she could see her work.

"Do you remember that man who threatened to denounce me for having a Christian mistress?"

"Remember!" She set down her embroidery with an indignant rustle. "That was a foul act—blackening your good name so he wouldn't have to pay a reckoning of half a sou. Half a sou, and you rescued him from certain death, all those visits, not to speak of the herbs and compounds you prepared for him. And he could have well afforded three times the sum," she added. "Saying you were a lecher and a spendthrift like Assach Abnelfalir with his Moorish slut and all those children. No one denounces him. I wonder his wife doesn't die of shame." She picked up her work again. "I rejoiced when I heard of his death. He deserved the most miserable of ends."

"Now, Judith," he said, "a man's death should not be a cause for rejoicing. Not usually, anyway," he went on as a few counterexamples leaped into his mind. "I was called out to the house of his younger brother today. He seems to be as unlike the elder as a rock is to a fish. By all accounts, he is a very good sort of man."

"That's not easy to believe," said Judith. "I'm surprised you consented to see him."

"But the interesting thing is that he, himself, has been formally denounced—not merely threatened with denunciation—for keeping a Moorish mistress. It is not true, he says, but it has cost him dearly. Of course, such denunciations are not an uncommon weapon in the hands of malicious men."

"I am sure he deserved it," said Judith. "It's a hateful family."

"I think he did not, my dear. When his brother died, he worked night and day to create a thriving business out of his brother's casual trade in fleeces, and earned enough to keep the widow and her orphans, as well as his own family. He is prosperous now, but his life was very difficult. Or so one hears."

"It was probably the widow who accused him, then. Wanting to put the property back in her own hands."

"I think not. The Black Death took her and her two sons."

"Oh. Does he know what his brother did to you? And he had the gall to send for you?"

"Certainly not. And you must not speak of this to anyone, my dear. I would not have told you, except that you are, so to speak, an interested party. I fear you suffered a great deal because of that episode."

"We shall sup late today, Judith," said Isaac at breakfast the next morning. "We have a patient to see in town, and it is most convenient for him and for me if we go after the day's business is finished."

"Papa, we cannot go this evening," said his daughter, waking up with a start to what was going on.

"No, Isaac," said Judith. "You cannot. You have forgotten."

"Forgotten what?"

"Blanca's wedding," said Raquel. "Papa, she is being married today, and Master Mordecai holds a great wedding feast, with musicians, and singing and dancing and everyone will be there. You must come. How can we go, if we are in the city with a patient?" Her voice, usually calm and low-pitched, rose in anguish. "I have a new silk gown."

"In that case," said Isaac, "We will have to see my busy patient this morning, even if it means that Yusuf cannot come, for it would be unforgivable if I kept you from showing off your new silk gown."

"Why can Yusuf not come with us?" asked Raquel.

"I am sending him to the weaver's house to talk to the lad, Martin, and the little maid, Bonanata. I would like to know some more about poor Marc."

"They tell me that your house was untouched by the Black Death—one of the few, Master Isaac," said the corn merchant.

Raquel sat in the back of the room, her face half-hidden by her veil, and studied the new patient. He was red of face and well padded in the belly, but at the moment she could see no reason for him to require a physician with such urgency. But, she reflected, with a touch of pride in her diagnostic abilities, if he continues in his way of life he will succumb to an apoplexy.

"We were very fortunate, although not entirely untouched. I lost my assistant to the plague."

"That is a small loss, compared to your own life and the lives of your closest kin, Master Isaac," he said dismissively. "I want you to do the same for me—protect me and my family, and, if you can, those who assist me here, when the plague breaks out again. Whatever you took yourself, and gave to those who belong to you, whatever it costs, that is what I want for me and mine." He pulled a small chest across the table until it was in front of him, opened it, took out a gleaming gold *maravedí*, and let it fall on the table. "This piece of gold I give you as an earnest of my good intentions, and to assure me that you will come when I ask for you, when the illness strikes the city."

"Keep your gold, sir, for the moment," said Isaac, "and let us talk further. Why do you believe the Black Death will strike now? It is five years since the disease was at its height, and for the last two summers the city has been virtually free of it. It seems unlikely," he added cautiously, "that it will arrive again during the cold of winter."

"That's not what everyone says," said the corn merchant, "even some of the wisest I have spoken to. It was treachery and sedition and civil war that brought it on us the last time, and things are worse now."

"Worse?" said Isaac. "Worse than civil war?"

"Yes, worse. Now it is sorcery and witchcraft," said the merchant. "Opening the gates of hell and allowing evil to come pouring out. God will punish us with plagues, as He did before." A cold sweat had broken out on his brow, and he passed a kerchief over his face to mop it up. "Everyone else is looking to find the witches, and hang them before they can do any more harm. That's all very well, but I recall men saying that because of your wisdom and learning, you escaped the plague, you and your patients—or at least the ones who obeyed you."

Isaac paused warily, fully conscious of the danger of his position. There was no point in telling a frightened man—and he could hear the terror in his voice—that he had no magic potions against the contagion. He would believe that the physician was hoarding them for his friends and relations. On the other hand, he thought the chances of it striking again in the fall of the year, when he had heard no rumors of its appearance elsewhere in the kingdom, were very slight. "Before I can answer you," he said gravely, "I must confer with my daughter about what herbs and simples we have ready on hand, and what must be gathered and prepared. If you will excuse us for a moment—"

"No, no, sir. Don't stir. I shall leave you here, since I

have orders to give to my clerk before the morning grows any older," said the corn merchant.

"Quickly, Raquel," said Isaac, as soon as the merchant's footfalls had disappeared in the distance. "Tell me about him."

"He seemed more likely to take an apoplexy than the plague, Papa," she said, with a frown of concentration. "Thick, curly white hair, a ruddy face, rather fat. From the dark rings under his eyes, I would surmise that he sleeps uneasily."

"Excellent," said Isaac.

The corn merchant bustled into the room again with a flurry of documents, bumped against a table, and seated himself. "Were you able—"

"Indeed, sir. For the time being I have all that is needed. To strengthen your constitution before an outbreak of disease, I will send you drops to be taken, three in a cup of water, before each meal. I will also send herbs for an infusion to be drunk before bed. Each day, take a long walk where the air is abundant and good, even if it means sacrificing a few hours usually devoted to profitable labor. This is most important. Eat a light supper, and drink only one cup of wine, mixed with water, in the evening. Should you discover that you have walked or talked with someone who has taken the plague, then before you enter your house, strip off your clothes, wash your body and your clothes well, and put on fresh garments. It seems likely that the contagion hovers about those who have the disease, and can fall upon anyone near to them. But it can be washed away. For the herbs and the drops, you owe me five pence. There is no need to pay me now. And I will return when you ask, gold or no gold."

"What are you sending him, Papa?" asked Raquel, once they were out of earshot of the corn exchange.

"Drops to aid his digestion, and herbs to help him sleep," said Isaac. "They won't hurt him, and he'll feel better. Exercise and moderation in eating will help his apoplectic tendencies. I would have charged him less, but he

wouldn't have believed that the remedies had any power
if I had.''

"And the washing?''

"It can't hurt, my dear, and it may have been what kept
us safe. That and the mercy of heaven.'' He continued on
at a faster pace. "What concerns me, though, is this talk
of sorcery. I knew that it was about the town, but I had
not realized it had spread so far so quickly. I think I will
speak to His Excellency about it before—''

He was interrupted by a high-pitched screech coming
from somewhere ahead of them—a woman's voice, rever-
berating with rage and hysteria. "There she is,'' she
screamed, "the whore who put a spell on my husband.
Kill her!''

Doors opened, feet pounded on the cobbles, drunken
laughter erupted from a tavern. A man with a deep voice
shouted, "Go to it, Mother.''

He was answered from above—from the hill, or a window, "Dunk her in the river!''

"The witch?'' yelled the deep-voiced man.

Someone else—with pretensions to wit—responded at
the top of his lungs, "No—the wife. Cool her off!'' A
roar of laughter greeted the sally.

"The witch is escaping!'' yelled another, and Isaac
heard the sound of a cobblestone hitting the side of a wall.
A terrified voice screamed for help; the crowd roared
louder.

Raquel seized her father by the arm and tried to drag
him back in the direction of the Quarter. "Wait, Raquel,''
said Isaac. "That woman is in danger.''

"No, Papa,'' she said. "The crowd grows much bigger,
and angry. And it is between us and that poor woman. We
can do nothing to save her. They will turn on us.''

Raquel's point was so accurate that it was not worth
debating. He allowed her to pull him quickly back toward
the Quarter.

A frightened Jacob was holding the gate open a crack.
He widened it enough for Raquel to pull her father

through, and closed it again, keeping his eye to the peep-hole. Suddenly the roar of the crowd ceased, and in the unnatural silence that followed, they heard the sound of horses, and the loud voice of authority.

Yusuf was waiting for them when they returned to Isaac's house. He sat in the courtyard in the golden October sun with a book on the table in front of him, ignoring the tumult outside the walls. As he read, his finger moved along the page, and he repeated the words in a soft murmur.

"You are back and already at work," said Isaac. "Excellent. Soon you will be accomplished in grammar. Did you encounter a crowd as you came in?"

"No, lord," said Yusuf, rising to his feet. "I came in at the north gate, and it was very quiet there for the time of day."

"Good. There is a little trouble at the other end of the city. What did you learn of Master Marc's habits?"

"From his brother, very little," said Yusuf. "Martin is sure that he had friends, but he does not know who they were. He never spoke of them by name. Bonanata told me that on many occasions he came home very drunk with wine. She sleeps in the kitchen, on a little bed behind the stove, and Marc used to come in through that door. She said that one night he was so drunk, and suffering so much from the wine sickness, that she had to clean him up and put him to bed. He gave her a penny the next day. It was the most money she'd ever had in her life."

"Who were his drinking companions?" asked Isaac. "Were they and the friends Martin spoke of the same people, do you think?"

"I don't know, lord," said Yusuf. "She said he drank in a tavern close by, and that means Rodriguc's or Tia Josefa's. I could find out which one this evening."

"But the wedding!" said Raquel.

"Excuse me, mistress," he said in a troubled voice, "but perhaps there will be some who do not wish me to be at the wedding. I would rather go to Tia Josefa's and Rodrigue's.''

"Would you really?" asked Raquel.

"I would."

The wedding had been anticipated for weeks, and the preparations for it had gone on for almost the same amount of time. Mossé's giant oven had been working night and day, for in addition to his usual bread baking, it was called upon to roast the meats and bake the cakes and pastries for the wedding feast.

The bride was decked in silk of brilliant hues, cut with fashionable elegance and sewn by the finest seamstresses in the town. The solemnity of the ceremony was much enlivened by the undisguised glee of the main participants, for, as the gossips knew very well, Blanca and her love had chosen each other long since. It had required a great deal of tact and skillful maneuvering on her part to convince Mordecai that he himself had decided that this pleasant but undistinguished young man was a good match for his beautiful—and wealthy—daughter. But the couple was wed, as most are, without incident. Some two hundred wedding guests poured into the hall by the synagogue— for even Mordecai's house, spacious and comfortable though it was, could not accommodate so many. They gasped in polite astonishment—in a most satisfactory manner—at the tables heaped high with magnificent and savory dishes. The wedding feast had begun.

The guests picked the bones clean of nearly fifty baked and boiled and stuffed carp, and almost as many fowls, and the better part of six whole lambs, as well as mountains of rice and a host of lesser dishes. When the remains, filling all the baskets in the merchant's house, had been taken away to be shared with the less fortunate of the community, the singer began his wedding song. It started by extolling the sweetness of love, and became bawdier and noisier with every verse. The bride tried to hide her blushes behind her husband's sleeve, and the hall rang with laughter.

The call went out for everyone to ready themselves for dancing, and Mordecai ordered up another cask of wine. The young women formed themselves into one group, the unmarried men into another, and the musicians started with a slow and stately measure. Mordecai smiled broadly and sent a message to the musicians. They quickened their pace; the melodies grew more and more passionate and frenzied, until the dancers, tired in the legs and weak from laughter, began to stumble. The music stopped at last, the dancers sat down, and Mordecai himself carried a jug filled to overflowing to the sweat-drenched musicians, who needed little encouragement to drink deep.

During the dancing, the servants had been piling the tables high with delicacies, and everyone rushed to attack the sweetmeats, and little cakes, and heaps of fruit. It was a splendid wedding.

In the general movement, Raquel slipped into a place next to Dalia, sister of the bride. "You must miss Aaron," she began innocently.

"Everyone misses him," said Dalia, nibbling on a little pastry. "It is always sad when someone dies so young."

"But weren't you and Aaron . . ." She let her voice fade invitingly.

"Me? And Aaron?" Dalia laughed with genuine amusement. "I can do better than Aaron, Raquel. And he had no more interest in me than he had in my grandmother. I used to tease him sometimes, but only because he was so serious all the time."

"Perhaps he was shy," said Raquel. "His mother is sure that he was in love with you."

"Well—she's wrong." Dalia's voice was firm and assured. "You can tell these things, you know," she added, with an air of sophistication not quite justified by her sixteen years on the earth. "When a man is interested in you, you can tell by how he looks and—everything. And he wasn't. And I never saw why I should be interested in someone who didn't particularly want me, no matter what old mother Esther might have thought.'' She tossed her head, and her thick, black hair, worn loose except for a silk veil caught in a twist at the back, shone in the brilliance of a hundred candles burning in that end of the hall.

''Was he in love with someone else?'' asked Raquel. If anyone knew what was going on in his heart, it would be Dalia. Her sharp ears heard whatever it was possible to hear, and her clear eyes saw everything.

''Not in the Quarter. Or out of it, as far as I know. I don't think he was interested in love or marriage at all. Just in his silly books. Now his brother, Daniel—there's someone worth breaking your heart over.'' She grinned, with the good-natured expression of a young woman who has so many admirers she can afford to point out worthwhile specimens to a friend.

''Are you and Daniel—''

''Me? Not at all. If I could have anyone I wanted, I'd rather marry Jahuda,'' she whispered. ''But Papa knows a goldsmith in Barcelona who is in need of a wife. Papa says he is handsome, and kind, and very rich. I would have ever so many servants and everything I wanted.'' She stared off in the distance, no doubt with visions of silk gowns and brilliant jewels dancing in her eyes. Then she turned back to Raquel with a tragic sigh. ''But Jahuda is so tall, and when he looks at me with that dark, piercing look, I shiver inside,'' said Dalia, and giggled.

Raquel, who had known Jahuda Salomó all her life, stared across the room in disbelief. There he was, lanky, and indeed glowering, as if he had been studying the world and had found it not worth the effort.

The musicians laid aside their cups once more and picked up their instruments. A fast and lively tune cut through the ever-increasing noise and laughter. Two girls stood up, and looked at the rest, who were all gathered at one end of the banquet table, and three more giggled and stood. ''Come on, let's join them,'' said Dalia. And Raquel and Dalia joined the others, dancing, laughing, and shaking their carefully curled or already curly hair at the admiring throng. Raquel noticed that Jahuda never took his eyes off Dalia.

There's someone doomed to disappointment, she thought. It sounded to her as if the twin inducements of the goldsmith's establishment and her father's approval would win Dalia any day over the sulky charms of Jahuda. But it was interesting about Aaron. And if anyone would know, it would be Dalia.

Even Judith was feeling mellow and expansive by now. She watched her daughter dancing with the other unmarried girls with a glow of maternal pride, and a certain amount of self-satisfaction. Raquel was beautiful, she thought, no doubt about that. She was taller and more graceful than the curvaceous Dalia, who stood next to her in the dance. Dalia's huge eyes, full red lips, and glossy hair drew every eye. They were showier than Raquel's finely sculpted features and more muted coloring, but Raquel's looks would keep. Whereas Dalia had better marry now, for in a few years her bloom would be gone, and it would take all the dowry even Master Mordecai could raise to find her a good husband.

"Your Raquel is a real beauty," said the woman beside her. "We'll be dancing at her wedding soon, I hope," she added inquisitively.

"Isaac cannot do without her for at least a year," said Judith. "But we have had many approaches. He is concerned to find her the best possible husband."

"You tell your husband," said the gossip, "that concern or no concern, you let a girl stay unmarried for too long, she'll find her own husband. And he might not like that."

Judith fixed her with a cold stare and the woman turned scarlet.

Whether maliciously or forgetfully done, it was a most unfortunate thing to say to someone whose eldest daughter had run off with a Christian. She swallowed much too much wine, coughed and gasped, and then frantically changed the subject. "Although I have heard it said there will be no more weddings for some time in the community."

Before Judith could respond to this remarkable statement, she noticed a newcomer at the door beckoning to Mordecai, who hastened over to speak to him. He shook his head thoughtfully and went back to the table. Soon he was deep in conversation with Astruch Caravida and Abraham Ravaya, grave men of importance on the council. A murmur began at that end of the hall, and moved swiftly through the crowd still seated at the tables, a murmur that was very different in quality from the noisy convivial conversation of a few moments before. Suddenly realizing her rudeness, even if the woman had provoked her, she turned back to ask her why.

Then Alta, wife to Bonastruch, another member of council, sat down beside her. "Did you hear about the riot today outside the main gate?" she asked.

"Surely not a riot," said Judith. "Isaac and Raquel were there when it started. He called it an unpleasant incident that was quickly over."

"That may be, but a woman was accused of witchcraft, and stoned."

"Was she badly injured?"

"She was. And now she's dead."

"It's what I was telling you about, Mistress Judith, Mistress Alta. It's what I heard," said the gossip. "There are sorcerers and witches everywhere, and unspeakable deeds of wickedness going on. It is the talk of the city that it will bring back the Black Death, and the whole city will be destroyed, and if we're not careful, we will be, too. If I were you, I wouldn't let your Raquel go outside the walls of the Quarter with her father, not these days." She looked more excited than frightened, and drained her cup, looking about for the serving lad with the jug.

Judith nodded and turned to Mistress Alta, who was asking after Mossé and Esther. She listened to her, nodding attentively, but her mind was fixed on what she had just heard.

SEVEN

Judith followed her husband into the middle of the courtyard, and then laid her hand on his shoulder. "Isaac,
wait," she said, in a tight, uncertain voice. "Please stay a
moment."

Raquel, exhausted from too much dancing and giddy
with laughter and wine, had said her good nights as soon
as they walked in, and climbed the stairs to her chamber.
A grumbling Ibrahim had retired into his little room to wait
for Yusuf to return; they were for the time being alone in
the courtyard. The moon was making its way across the
heavens in a series of erratic flashes between fast-moving
clouds. Judith studied her husband's face in its intermittent
light.

"Certainly, my love," murmured Isaac. "What is troubling you?"

She shivered, although the night was mild, and wrapped
her cloak tightly around her. "Nothing is troubling me,"
said Judith with an attempt at her accustomed certainty.
"But—"

"You only speak like that when you are worried," he
said. "Tell me."

"It is Raquel," she began.

"Not now, Judith." Isaac turned and headed in the direction of his study. "I will not stand out in the damp of night to listen to the same arguments about Raquel's marriage, even if we have come from a wedding, and you have spent the evening gazing at a bride in all her finery," he said when he reached the door. "I knew this would happen."

"Then you were wrong," she said tartly. "Don't go in. Please. I promise, at this moment Raquel's marriage is the furthest thing from my mind. Are you listening to me, Isaac? There are much greater dangers out there than an unsatisfactory son-in-law. This talk of witchcraft and sorcery in the town terrifies me."

Isaac walked back in the direction of her voice, and caught her by the hands. "Why, Judith? I am as careful as a man can be, and we have powerful protectors. It is unpleasant—a terrible thing—but unlikely to affect us directly."

His deep, reassuring tones failed, for once, to ease her fears. "Oh, Isaac," she said desperately, "you don't understand. That woman you spoke of this morning is dead."

"I heard. At the wedding," said Isaac. "From Astruch."

"They have already killed one woman as a witch. It won't stop there. And Raquel is beautiful. My dear, dear husband, you are very wise and clever, but you cannot see how beautiful she has grown. Think of me on my marriage day. She has every quality that was beautiful about me, and with it, all that I lacked, Isaac."

"My dear, you—"

"No, please. Let me speak. In addition, she is skilled, and she goes freely about the city helping you, entering houses, and bedchambers, and administering potions and infusions. She arouses jealousy in women and desire in men. I watched our friends watching her at the wedding, and I saw it. And she is a Jew, Isaac. What more will a frightened Christian look for when the hunt is on for witches?"

Isaac sat down heavily on the bench under the arbor.

"You have left me with scarcely enough breath to speak," he said. "I confess to worrying that innocent women might be accused of witchcraft, but I refused to consider that it could touch our Raquel. Not even when the weaver made his foolish accusation. And not because I don't believe you, Judith, with all my soul, but, coward that I am, I cannot face that possibility."

"You are no coward, husband," said Judith, speaking in her soberest and most matter-of-fact voice. "You are, in fact, the bravest man I know. And I don't suppose the danger will come tonight, or tomorrow. But, Isaac, I beg you, keep your ears open when you are outside the Quarter. Listen for murmurs against her. Tell Yusuf he must watch for people noticing her."

"I doubt that Yusuf can see what you, in your wisdom, see," said Isaac thoughtfully.

"Yusuf has been much in the world, Isaac. He knows more than he judges it wise or polite to say, and rest assured, what there is to see, he sees. And Raquel is no fool. She always wears her plainest gowns when out with you, and carries herself with great modesty, but she must remember to keep closely veiled, and you must be prepared to bring her home and lock our gates against the mob outside our walls at the first sign of danger."

"And inside the Quarter?"

"The Lord save us if we must fear for her life inside the Quarter," said Judith. "No one else will."

"I will be vigilant," said Isaac. "On my life, I swear I will be vigilant."

A gentle knock at the gate cut short their conversation. "Ah," said Isaac, "Yusuf has completed his mission."

"I will open it," said Judith. "To judge by the snoring coming from Ibrahim's chamber, it will take more than that feeble summons to awaken him."

"Good evening, mistress," said Yusuf, in tones of badly concealed surprise. Mistress Judith was not in the habit of acting as her own gatekeeper.

"Your master is eagerly awaiting your news, Yusuf,"

she said, in a manner just disapproving enough to remind him how long he had been in gathering it. "Isaac, I shall leave you to your discussions." And with a rustle of silk, she was gone.

"And what have you discovered, Yusuf?" asked Isaac. "Come inside. We will sit in the kitchen. There may be something for you to eat."

Knowing that Yusuf would not have eaten, and fearing that Mordecai's provisions at the wedding might have been inadequate, Naomi had left her staple emergency dishes: a pot of spicy lentils keeping warm on the dying fire, and bread, fruit, and cheese on the table, under a linen towel, enough for everyone in the house to have a late supper. Yusuf uncovered the little feast, poured a splash of wine into a cup of water for his master, and settled down to talk and to eat.

"First I went to Tia Josefa's," said Yusuf, spooning lentils onto some bread and doubling it into a messy roll. "Because it is closest to the weaver's house, and I thought it likely to be the place a young man would choose to drink in."

"Why is that?" asked Isaac, knowing the reason perfectly well, but curious to test Judith's assertion.

"Because it is full of—" With the word trembling on his tongue, Yusuf considered to whom he was speaking, and altered his sentence. "Women, who drink there of an evening."

"Whores," said Isaac. "It was when I was a young man, as well. Tia Josefa doesn't change."

"Yes, lord. And all I got from them was rude and coarse talk. But they assured me that Master Marc was not one of their customers, nor did he drink there alone or with friends. And Tia Josefa said the same, and also said if I wasn't going to drink her overpriced, watered wine, I could go spend my evening elsewhere. So I left."

"She didn't describe her wine that way."

"No—but the girls did," said Yusuf. He thanked his fates that his master could not see his scarlet cheeks as he recalled the teasing those women inflicted on him, pinching him, and praising his pretty face, and trying to snatch up his tunic. He had fled the battlefield with the speed of an unarmed soldier facing a thousand ferocious opponents.

"And then?"

"And then," he said, in muffled tones, through a mouthful of bread and lentils, "I went to Rodrigue's. This time I bought a farthing cup of wine, which I did not drink, and found the potboy. I gave him another farthing—"

"Which means I owe you an obol, Yusuf," said Isaac. "So far."

"—and he was mine for life," he added triumphantly. "He knew Master Marc well. It seems he and two friends came in to Rodrigue's in the evening whenever they had the money. They used to sit by themselves in the corner and moan about how hard their lives were. I think the potboy feels they had an easy time of it compared to working for Rodrigue and his wife." Yusuf paused to fill up another piece of bread. "Especially his wife."

"I have no doubt he was right," said Isaac.

"So I asked him who they were. He said one was a seminarian. And the other was Aaron, the baker's son." Yusuf stopped on that triumphant note.

"That is interesting. So Marc spent his evenings with Aaron," murmured Isaac.

"And a seminarian," said Yusuf, somewhat disappointed that Isaac had not reacted more strongly to his news. "His name is Lorens. His father is a rich man, but the potboy didn't know who. He asked his mistress once, but she boxed his ear and called him a nosy good-for-nothing."

"A rich man?"

"Yes. But Lorens never had any money, because his father is mean and tightfisted, apparently. But lately Aaron had all the money they needed, and they spent many more nights in the tavern, getting very drunk."

The mystery of Mossé's strongbox is solved, thought Isaac. Judith had suspected that their sons were helping themselves to its contents. She was right, except that it was Aaron, alone, using the money to get himself and his friends senseless with cheap wine. "You have done well," said Isaac. His fingers searched the table delicately until they found the fruit bowl. He took a pear, and a knife, and began to peel the fruit.

"Allow me, lord," said Yusuf.

"No, Yusuf. For the moment it amuses me to try." He finished peeling it and began to cut off slices to nibble slowly on. "They seem to be an unlikely trio of friends," he said at last. "I wonder what they had in common besides a dissatisfaction with life and a fondness for bad wine?"

"I don't know, lord," said Yusuf. "But I shall try to discover it."

The morning chill had still been in the air when Isaac made his way up the hill to the Bishop's palace. He had spent the night before in worried and, he felt in disgust, fruitless thought, and now he had very little in the way of coherent proposals to put in front of Berenguer.

"Oh, I heard about it," said the Bishop. "The perpetrators had melted into the walls by the time the officers arrived, but the woman was there, on the cobbles, bleeding. They conveyed her to her house, and did what they could for her. She never came to her senses," he added grimly. "Otherwise she might have told us something."

"A woman accused her of bewitching her husband," said Isaac. "I myself heard the accuser speak."

"We know who she is," said Berenguer. "She shall be called to account for it."

"Will that do any good?" asked Isaac.

"Not to the unfortunate who lost her life, but it might make the rest of them think a moment before hurling baseless accusations."

"No doubt it will, Your Excellency."

"There is much doubt that it will, Isaac, as you know,

but she shall be prosecuted. And now all women must be wary—it is a dangerous time.''

''It is, Your Excellency,'' said Isaac. ''I fear for my daughters.''

''Rebecca will be safe if she stays close to home,'' said the Bishop. ''As will Raquel,'' he added casually. ''Women who must be often abroad are in the most danger, I believe. Do you not agree?''

''There are not many who can instruct their fellow men with such delicate courtesy, Your Excellency,'' said Isaac wryly. ''I do agree. But I will not find it easy to lock Raquel up within our walls.''

''And if things become worse, Isaac, my friend, Lady Elicsenda will keep her safe at the convent for as long as required. It would take a brave witch-hunter to tackle the abbess. I urge you to consider her offer.''

Silence fell between them. ''It is a most gracious offer, Your Excellency. I shall consider it,'' said Isaac at last. ''I fear, however, that my good wife will take the suggestion very ill.''

''But if things become worse—''

''If things become worse, she may indeed think better of hiding her daughter amongst the nuns.''

''We will talk further of this,'' said Berenguer.

In spite of an uneasy sense of threat hanging over their world, everyday concerns occupied all those in Isaac's house until sundown on Friday. Under Judith's sharp eye, the Sabbath was observed with more exactitude than in the houses of some of her neighbors. Even Yusuf worked at his peril. On one Saturday morning, Raquel had had the temerity to point out that in Benjamin Adret's household, the Moorish slave worked on the Sabbath, and to suggest that he might make himself useful. Judith had glowered, said, ''Yusuf is not a slave, and even if he were . . .'' and that was that. One day a week, then, he was free as a bird.

He had developed the habit of slipping away from the calm and quiet of the Quarter into the bustle of the market,

where he spent a few coppers, gossiped, and watched the
world. In the market he had first met Hasan, and it was
for Hasan that he was searching on this particular Sabbath
morning. Hidden in his basket was a sumptuous meal of
leftovers stuffed into a loaf, and honeyed cake, wrapped
closely in a napkin, enough for two hungry boys. Naomi
had developed a soft spot for Yusuf, who so obviously
adored her cooking, and whose appetite seemed unlimited.
And Yusuf had come to realize that Hasan was fed rather
sparingly in his own household.

The market was crowded. In less than two weeks the
fair would start, and the excitement it generated was already in the air. Yusuf stationed himself on the steps and
searched the throng for his new friend. "Hola," he called
shrilly, when he saw the boy at the nutseller's stall, in front
of great baskets of almonds and hazelnuts. "Over here,"
he added in his own tongue. Hasan paid no attention.

Yusuf ran down the steps and ducked through the
crowd. "Hola," he said as he drew closer. "I came looking for you."

Hasan continued to fill his basket, but he shook his head
as he examined the almonds, as if he had found some
serious defect in them. Yusuf stopped dead, and slowly
backed into the crowd behind him.

A short, sturdy woman was bearing down on the slave
boy. She was dressed in black, with a veil pinned loosely
to her carelessly dressed hair. As soon as she was close
enough, she reached out and cuffed Hasan on the ear. "Do
you think I have all day to wait for you to count out the
nuts? Stupid boy!" She glanced at the sky, where the sun
was breaking through the morning clouds. "I have other
errands to attend to. Here." She handed him a coin. "Buy
the fish and take it back along with these. And mind it's
fresh, and that you get enough. Bartolomeo is a thief and
a cheat." She handed him a tall basket filled with pur-
chases. "Tell them at the house I will be back later."

"Yes, mistress," he said.

She cuffed him once again for good measure, and disappeared into the crowd.

"That is your mistress?" asked Yusuf, who had sidled over as soon as the women seemed well out of sight.

"No. That is the woman who owns the house where my master lives. I think he pays the rent by lending her my services. If she had seen me speak to someone, she would have been even worse," he added. "That is why I did not answer you. I am sorry."

"It's Marieta, isn't it?" said Yusuf.

"You know her?"

"Everyone in Girona knows her. Or of her. Do you really live in a brothel?" asked Yusuf incredulously.

"Why are you so surprised?"

"Because you said your master was a scholar," said Yusuf. "I have been too many months among respectable people," he said, shaking his head. "I think of scholars now as good and law-abiding citizens, like my master."

"I have never met one like that," said Hasan, in amazement. "All the scholars I have known are on the road, living on their wits."

"I should know better. I traveled with a poor scholar for a long while before I came here. And he was a thief and a scoundrel."

"Was he good to you?"

"Yes," said Yusuf, after giving the matter some thought. "As good as he could be. He never tried to sell me to the traders—or only once, when I first met him, and he was out of money—and if he had food, he shared it with me, always. He started to teach me to make letters in the Roman fashion. He said learning was important. Only then he was taken for thieving, and hanged," he added. "Is your master good to you?"

Hasan shrugged. "What is good? He feeds me, usually. He beats me when he's angry, sometimes. I would kill his partner if I could," he added thoughtfully. "He beats me and kicks me for pleasure. He keeps saying I'm growing too big, and my voice will change soon, and that they had better sell me before I grow a beard. And Marieta is a bitch, as well as a whore. But I must go and buy some fish.''

"Wait a moment," said Yusuf. "I came looking for you because I have a basket filled with things to eat, and I thought you might like to share them with me."

"What's in there?" asked Hasan, peering into the basket.

"A *tagine* of chicken, from last night, with almonds and fruit, stuffed into a huge loaf of bread. And cakes. With honey."

Hasan looked around at the narrow streets and tall houses. "Where can we eat it? With my luck, Marieta will come back and find me."

"Bring your things and come with me. You can buy your fish later."

"What do you do at the brothel?" asked Yusuf, once they were ensconced in a niche in the city wall behind the cathedral, well hidden from prying eyes. "Or are you there for the customers?" he added, with the matter-of-fact realism that four years on the road had given him.

"Sometimes," said Hasan, tearing off a chunk of chicken-stuffed bread, dripping with sauce, and taking an enormous bite. "Mostly, though, I dress up in a silly costume, as if I were a boy attendant to a *harim*—or what the customers think a boy attendant would look like—and I bring incense and things like that. For atmosphere."

"How long have you been there?"

"At Marieta's?" He thought. "Remember the time it was so hot that animals were dying on the road? And then there was a terrible storm?"

"This summer?"

"Yes. This summer. We came into town that day. My master and I and Lup. We were soaked to the skin, and so was everything we carried. Our donkey had died, and we were carrying her load. Lup said he knew someone who would give us shelter. That was Marieta, and we've been there ever since." He licked his fingers and pulled off another piece from the loaf.

"How long have you been with your master?" said Yusuf, grabbing a good portion before Hasan could eat it all.

"Oh," he said vaguely. "A long time. Traders found me—they stole me from my family, I mean," he emended hurriedly, "and sold me to my master. He was good to me then. We traveled all over. He talked to the crowds, and I went 'round in my costume with a collecting bag. We did well. We had the donkey to carry things, and when I was tired, he let me ride her."

"What happened?"

"I got older and not so pretty. People didn't give as much money. Then Lup joined us and we came here. But who knows what will happen?" he added, and finished off the last piece of bread and chicken.

"You had better go and buy your fish," said Yusuf, handing his friend a small cake dripping with honey. The basket full of food had been reduced to a few sad fragments. "Bartolomeo will be running out."

"Marieta will kill me," said Hasan, jumping up. He grabbed the big basket, heaved it up on his back, and headed back to the market, a small, lonely figure in the crowd.

EIGHT

"Raquel?" said Isaac. His voice rang out loudly from the middle of the courtyard.

"You have no need to shout, Isaac. Ibrahim will fetch her."

"I'm in the kitchen, Papa." The two responses floated out to him simultaneously, intermingling like the voices in a complicated round song.

"Then wait. I will be with you in an instant," said the physician, and ran lightly up the steps to the first floor. He stopped prudently in the doorway into the kitchen. "Good afternoon, Naomi," he said. "I must steal your helper from you for now."

"Don't worry about that, Master Isaac," said Naomi. "I've prepared the supper by myself before this, and I can do it now."

"I'm sorry, Papa. I was passing the time bothering Naomi," said Raquel, guiltily, "instead of attending to my own tasks. What has happened?"

"We have received a summons to the house of Master Pons Manet, my dear," he said. "Fetch Yusuf from his books and fill your basket."

"What's wrong with him this time, Papa?"

"He did not say. As before, it is most urgent, and as before, it is a mystery. A few more soporifics and digestives in the basket, along with the usual things, should be adequate to the occasion."

The autumn day was drawing to a close, but the warmth of the afternoon sun still lay on the earth. Raquel snatched up a light cloak, stirred up Yusuf, and darted down to her father's study to fill the basket. When she came out, Yusuf was standing in the middle of the courtyard, deep in conversation with his master. He glanced at her, and then standing on tiptoes, murmured something into the physician's ear.

"Veil yourself, Raquel," said Isaac abruptly. "Closely."

"Yes, Papa," she said, and somewhat puzzled, pulled her veil over her entire face. Why Yusuf had spoken to her father she could not guess, but without a doubt, it had resulted in this extraordinary request. And when they were alone, she had every intention of dragging the reason out of him. Veil herself from whom? she wondered with growing indignation. Poor old Ibrahim? He was not even a man, really. Nathan? Not only a child, but her brother. Yusuf himself?

"And let us hope that Naomi is preparing something hot and comforting for our suppers when we return," added Isaac cheerfully, and set out with his long, swift-moving stride. "We may be late."

Raquel and Yusuf were left once more to cool their heels in an antechamber, and Isaac was led away to the wool merchant's study.

The smell of wood, leather, and beeswax greeted him gently; Pons took him by the hands, murmured a welcome, and led him to a place to sit.

"Good afternoon, Master Pons," said Isaac. "How have you been since my last visit?"

"In body, I have been well, Master Isaac," said the merchant. "I have you to thank for that. Your prescription for sound sleep has been helpful."

"I am pleased," said the physician. "But all is not well otherwise?"

"No, all is even worse than it was."

"May I ask in what ways it is worse?" asked Isaac.

Pons replied with a harsh and bitter laugh. "Indeed, you may ask. I have been attacked—no, let us be honest—I am close to being destroyed—by sorcery," he said. "But not in a manner I would have imagined."

"Tell me what has happened," said Isaac gravely.

"A man came to my house yesterday," said Pons. "He was a poor wretch, dressed in rags, but he told the servant he had an important message that he must deliver to me in person. Well—I saw him, and he told me, most humbly, that he had been hired to deliver a message. He swore on the grave of his mother that the message came not from him, and that as much as he might like to, he could not describe the man who hired him, except to say that he had a low, hoarse voice, and wore rough clothing. And also that he gave him five pence to deliver it."

"A good sum for delivering a message within the town," said Isaac. "Why could he not describe him?"

"His face was masked."

"Can you tell me what the message was?"

"It was a simple enough message that the poor soul could carry it in his memory," said Pons. "It accused me of bringing about the death of the weaver's son, owing to a grudge I had against Master Ramon. It denounced me for a sorcerer, and averred that all the world knew of it, and warned me that the witch who assisted me had been seen entering my house by stealth."

"Is there any truth to it?"

"None."

"Is there any appearance of truth?"

"I do not take your meaning, Master Isaac. Appearance of truth?"

"Something that could arouse suspicion in the minds of your neighbors. Is it possible that from time to time women do enter your house by stealth, Master Pons? Or have you quarreled with the weaver? Publicly, that is, so that it might be common knowledge in the town?''

"Not even that. My wife comes and goes, to and from my house, but openly, and all the world knows who she is. The servants come in and out, but they do not creep about in a stealthy manner. I will ask if any of them have had secret visitors, but it seems most unlikely. And as for Ramon, I have nothing to do with him." His voice rose in exasperation. "I trade in fleeces, importing special wools, particularly fine English wools, and exporting our own sturdy fleece. I have no occasion to deal with a weaver who makes cheap cloth for the local market. And why would I wish to harm his son? It is preposterous."

"Have you traced the messenger?"

"I have. Not to harass him, but because, when he finished delivering his message, he opened his hand and dropped the five pence onto the table here, saying that I had been kind to his wife and that he could not take money for delivering such a message to me. Then he left. I sent two men after him, to discover who he was. They found him in the hovel where he lives, outside the walls, and learned that his wife had been in our service. I sent him the money again, with more besides, to thank him for his honesty and scruples."

"Do you know if he has any connection with the man who sent the message?"

"I do not know," said Pons, "but I doubt very much that his employment by the sender extended beyond that one commission. If he is in his pay, then his guile is remarkable. And the rewards for it appear to have been very scant."

"And why have you sent for me?" asked Isaac. "What can I do?"

"I do not know," said the merchant. "In all honesty, I do not know. The previous threats to me could be settled with money, even that last one, against my—" He stopped, as if he could not force the next word out.

"Your son, Master Pons? It sounded to me as if you had been speaking of a son."

"I was, Master Isaac. My younger son. And I was sure that the person behind it all was a business rival who was attacking my domestic peace in order to see me bled dry. Without a doubt, it is the easiest and cheapest way to eliminate a competitor. Lead him to ruin, and then buy his assets for a song. This time, however, there is no question of money."

"In fact, it is not a threat," said Isaac. "It is an attack."

"It is," said the merchant desperately. "And, alas, skilled as you are, you cannot cure a sorely wounded reputation, can you, Master Isaac?"

"No," said Isaac. "I cannot. But I can and will inquire here and there and let you know if I hear anything. I have powerful reasons of my own to be interested in these threats of sorcerers and sorcery." He paused, hands together, forming a tent, with the top touching his lower lip, and considered the situation. "May I speak to the Bishop about your case?" he said at last. "He is, I assure you, not likely to believe you a sorcerer."

"If you feel it will do any good," said Pons, his voice flat from weariness and despair.

"And I will leave further remedies for you, for it often happens that both sleep and digestion suffer badly from such events."

"Thank you, Master Isaac. I am most grateful."

"And I recommend that you bring that fellow here, the one who delivered the message, warm his body, feed his belly, and relieve his poverty in whatever way you can. It is possible that he knows more things about the man who commissioned him than he realizes himself."

"What do you mean? How can he know more than he realizes?"

"His answer, as you described it, sounded to me to have been most carefully thought out. He told you what he thought was important, and it is probable that he left out what seemed to him to be unimportant details. But those can often tell us much.''

''You may be right,'' said Pons doubtfully. ''I don't think the fellow has much to tell us, but I have no quarrel with giving him further assistance.''

The Bishop's summons the next morning was peremptory, almost to the point of rudeness.

''Isaac, my friend,'' said Berenguer, in a worried voice, ''thank you for coming so promptly. And before you sit down, I must warn you that we have another short journey on this chilly morning. Over to the seminary.''

''Someone is ill?''

''Yes, of course someone is ill,'' said the Bishop, irritably. His gouty foot was still not free of pain, and his temper was short. He stood up and seized his staff. ''Have you your basket of herbs and remedies? Or should I send someone—''

''Yusuf and Raquel wait patiently with my basket,'' said Isaac. ''I am afraid, however, it is largely taken up with gout remedies. And that is a good thing, since I hear in your voice that you are still in need of them. But there are other mixtures in it as well, and Yusuf can run for anything that is missing. What can you tell me of the illness?''

''Not very much. But the sufferer is a seminarian who has been in failing health for the past two or three weeks. Not that anyone thought to tell me of it,'' he added, savagely, ''even though we have been having problems with the seminarians for weeks now. But he has lost flesh, and has no appetite for his food. The devil of it is, Isaac, that this lad is the son of a wealthy, honest, God-fearing parishioner, and I don't want a second mysterious death. One is enough, with that fool Ramon tearing about the city, screaming to one and all of witchcraft and sorcery! Ouch!'' he added as he banged his sensitive toe against his staff.

''Not a second mysterious death,'' said Isaac. ''A third. There was one in the Quarter—of Aaron, son of Mossé the baker.''

"Of course," said Berenguer, softly. "I had been thinking selfishly only of my own flock."

"And, Your Excellency, the first dead man, Aaron, was friend and drinking companion to the second, young Marc, the weaver's son. And there was a third lad who drank with them. A seminarian. What is the name of your ailing young man? Lorens?"

"I wish you had said any other name," said Berenguer. "It is indeed Lorens."

They gathered up Raquel and Yusuf at the foot of the stairs, and headed silently across the plaza of the Apostles in the direction of the seminary.

The Bishop knocked once on the door and threw it open, revealing a tiny bedchamber, with scarcely enough room for a bed, a small table with a high stool, and a shelf above the head of the bed that held a few books. A plain wooden cross hung on the wall above the table, and beneath it sat a candlestick and a small brass bowl. On pegs near the foot of the bed hung a short cloak, a clean shirt, and a tunic. On the bed itself lay a white-faced, emaciated-looking young man, whose dark eyes were ringed with hollows almost as dark, silent witnesses to many troubled nights. Raquel had pulled back her veil to observe more closely, for the window was shuttered, and little light penetrated the room. She murmured her observations into her father's ear as she set out the contents of her basket on the table.

"What the devil—" said Lorens, thickly, realized who was in the chamber, and stopped. "Your Excellency," he murmured, and pulled himself up to a sitting position.

"This is young Lorens Manet, Master Isaac," said Berenguer. "We have brought the physician to attend to you, Lorens," he said.

"I am not in need of a physician," said Lorens, gasping slightly on every phrase. "I am most well."

"Then why are you in your bed at well past tierce?" asked the Bishop.

"I will get up at once, Your Excellency," said the boy, and put his feet on the floor. "I suffered a momentary weakness, that is all."

"Nonsense," said Berenguer. "You look like a ghost of yourself. Get back into bed."

"I am very well, Your Excellency," he said again. "Only I have been fasting these past few days, and watching all the night. And praying for my soul's sake, and for the souls of two friends—two acquaintances—who died recently, sorely in need of all our prayers."

"Aaron and Marc?" said Isaac.

"No—certainly not," he said, in a panic-stricken voice. "Two other acquaintances."

"This is nonsense," said Berenguer, his temper rising again. "A lad like you, not yet grown, I warrant, needs food and sleep. Your duty at the moment is to maintain a healthy body for your soul to inhabit, not to fast and pray yourself into an early grave."

"But, Your Excellency—" he repeated stubbornly.

"Quiet," he roared. "I have not given you permission to interrupt me. The most virtuous act you can perform right now is to do what is necessary so that your life may be spared. You have dedicated yourself to the work of God. This is why you are here in the seminary, young Master Lorens. Not to starve yourself to death. You will stop fasting, and you will get proper rest, or by all that's holy, I will lock you up to make sure that you do. Now, let the physician examine you, and do what he recommends. That is not a request, Lorens. It is an order from your bishop."

"But, Your Excellency, I am not ill." He pushed himself to his feet to prove his point, staggered for a moment in dizziness, and collapsed in a faint on the stone floor.

"What has happened to him?" said Isaac at once.

"He has fallen, Papa, in a faint. Not a convulsive one, just a faint."

"Get him onto his bed," said the physician. "Your Excellency, please, summon a pair of strong lads to carry him to his bed without hurting him.''

But Berenguer was already at the door to the chamber, bringing in the priest who had led them to the chamber. ''We two will perform this office for him,'' said the Bishop. ''He is no great weight. Even two clerics may lift him.'' They picked him up easily and set him gently on his bed. Isaac bent over the lad, running his hands lightly over his face and neck, probing his belly, and listening to his chest. Last of all, he poised his head over the boy's mouth, as if about to kiss him, sniffed, and then rose to his feet.

''Raquel, ten drops of the blue mixture in a small amount of water.''

''Yes, Papa.'' She measured and poured with a steady hand, and then moved to the head of the bed to administer them.

Raquel lifted his head and moistened his lips with the water in the cup. He stirred. She coaxed more into his mouth. He moaned, and swallowed. With the third tiny mouthful, he swallowed and began to babble.

''What is he saying?'' said Berenguer?

''Listen,'' said Isaac.

''*Ma-ta-ra,*'' he muttered, tossing his head. Each syllable was clear, and prolonged, and given equal weight. ''*Ma-ta-ra,*'' he repeated, his voice rising, ''*et discipulis tuis.*'' He tried to push himself up, and the young priest stepped forward to hold him firmly down. ''*Misericorde—*'' he murmured, and his voice dropped to a mumbling in which no definable sounds could be perceived.

Raquel raised his head once more and slipped more of the liquid onto his tongue. Isaac located Yusuf, who was by the door, trying to stay out of the way, and whispered to him. The boy began to move unobtrusively around the crowded room, as if looking for something.

''What is this talk of killing?'' said Berenguer. ''And whose disciples?''

"Your Excellency," said Isaac, "I confess I do not know. It makes no sense."

Then out of the mumbling came, loud and with startling clarity, *"Ma-ta-ra et Ma-ta-na,* save us!" And he began to murmur softly. Raquel had taken a clean cloth, and was now moistening his lips with the liquid, without seeming to disturb him.

"What is he saying now?" asked Berenguer.

"A paternoster," said the priest, who had moved up to listen more carefully to his words.

"That is more reassuring," replied the Bishop.

Then Lorens's body suddenly twisted in a powerfully convulsive movement. The cup flew from Raquel's hand and fell with a clatter on the floor. "Hold him, for God's sake," said the Bishop.

"I cannot hold him still," said the young priest. "I am trying, Your Excellency."

"Papa," said Raquel, "he is having a convulsive fit. No. It is not that. It looks more as if he is in great pain."

"Then treat it, child, treat it. It is the only thing to do now." Isaac stepped up to the bed, took hold of the boy's legs, and straightened them out. "Hold his arms, and I will control his lower body," he murmured to the young priest.

Raquel flew over to her basket and took out a small vial. She moistened a fresh cloth with a few drops of its contents and moved back to the head of the bed.

"Away from me!" Lorens screamed, his body now straightened out and rigid. "Help me! Father in heaven, help me!"

Isaac laid his hands on the boy's belly, and massaged it gently, shaking his head.

Raquel passed the moistened cloth over his lips. He shuddered, and tossed his head. She repeated the action, and then added more drops to the cloth. He swallowed and ran his tongue over his lips. She dabbed more liquid on them and waited for a reaction. One minute. Then two minutes. It felt like an hour. Then his voice rose to a thin wail. "Take them off me, I beg you! I never betrayed.

Never. I will ask my father. Papa, help me!"

This time Raquel squeezed the liquid onto his lips and tongue. He swallowed convulsively. "I won't speak! I swear it." He shivered, and fought helplessly against the restraining hands. "Take them off me!" he repeated, but in a low murmur.

Then Isaac felt his muscles soften, and the boy began murmuring his prayers once more. "The pain is easing for the moment, I hope," he said. "And with it, the terror."

Berenguer took the young priest by the arm and sent him from the room. He knelt by the foot of the bed and prayed, loud enough to reach the ears of the tormented boy if he was still capable of hearing. Isaac bent over Lorens, his hand on the pulse in his neck, and his ear to his chest.

"They're coming for me. I see them," said Lorens, wearily. "Father, have mercy—they are coming."

"There is nothing more we can do for him, Your Excellency," said Isaac. "And I regret it deeply. But the damage had been done long before any one of us heard of his condition."

"I have sent for his confessor to hear him and comfort him," said Berenguer. "I fear he will only be in time for the last rites."

"Then we will await you outside. A word will bring us back if there is a change in his condition."

And as the three passed out of the small chamber, they were replaced by a priest followed by an acolyte carrying a small, ornately carved, wooden casket.

"It is over," said Berenguer sadly. "I would that we could have done something for him. He was a promising lad, and his father is a good man. But what did you mean by saying that the damage had already been done?"

"Your Excellency, that boy was poisoned, as were Aaron and Marc, I fear. Something was administered to him that sorely disturbed the balance of his humors, causing him to see false and terrifying visions, and to feel pain in every part of his body. As you could see yourself, he was rigid with it. I hoped with those drops to restore some balance, enough so that he could live, and his body could right itself," he said, his voice filled with sorrow, "but we were too late. I set Yusuf to search the room for traces of the poison, and with your permission, I would like him to finish. Although it seems, no doubt, a ghoulish task with the lad's body not yet cold in there."

"I shall instruct them not to disturb anything," said Berenguer. "His body will be taken to the chapel as soon as it is washed and prepared. If you can wait until that is done, then Yusuf may search as long as he likes."

Berenguer poked his head back into the chamber and spoke briefly. "Well, that is done," he said when he returned. "Let us move down the hall where the students have a common room for recreation and study, and sit down. My gouty toe has not appreciated all this."

"Of course. Raquel, are you veiled?"

"Yes, Papa, I am veiled," she said, exasperated, and trying hard not to lose her temper. "Why do you keep accusing me of flaunting myself in public? Whatever people may have been telling you, I am not in the habit of going about uncovered."

"And I am pleased that you are not," he said mildly.

"Indeed, Isaac, my friend, your daughter is well wrapped up—like a cheese for curing," said the Bishop. "Rest assured."

Raquel smiled invisibly behind her veil.

"Now, Master Isaac, tell me, what do you think that poor young man was talking about? We are, by the way, alone, except for your daughter, and Yusuf, who is out of earshot."

"I am here, lord," said Yusuf, who was across the room, looking out the window.

"Out of earshot for Yusuf is very far away indeed," murmured Isaac. "But do not worry. He is almost frighteningly discreet."

"That is good," said Berenguer, settling on a padded bench, and putting his foot up on a stool.

"Indeed. I thought of that—what the lad was saying—and I confess I am undecided. My difficulty is that some of those words seem not to have been in any language familiar to me. It is possible that it was not *matar* that he said, that he did not speak of killing, but that he said something in another tongue. What do you think, Raquel? And you may unwrap yourself a little in order to breathe and speak. I do not think that His Excellency will suspect you of evil motives or immodest tendencies if you do."

"Thank you, Papa," she said, and pushed her veil back from her face a little. "I thought it was a name he spoke. Or two names. Like those of some strange pagan gods." She stopped, appalled at what she had said. "But I must be wrong, Your Excellency, for a young man like that, a seminarian, would never be speaking the names of pagan gods, not even in his delirium. Where would he have learned them? They were not names that I ever heard. But they sounded strange, like . . ." Her voice trailed off in an agony of embarrassment.

"Alas, my dear child," said Berenguer, "do not be distressed. I thought precisely the same thing, and I, too, rejected the thought as impossible. But, impossible or not, it sounded to me like fragments of a chant that sorcerers and followers of pagan gods might use to raise evil spirits, and call up demons."

"It did have that air to it," said Isaac. "Although I am sure there are other possible explanations of his words."

"Well," said Berenguer grimly, "if that is what he was doing, and that is certainly what it sounded like, what we may have in the seminary is not mere discontent, but paganism, or heresy, and possible attempts at sorcery."

"Which is very serious indeed," said Isaac. In the past there had been investigations—most of them in the time of the grandparents and great-grandparents of the current generation—that had begun with a search for heretics and sorcerers. Before these investigations ran their courses, the city was filled with hysterical accusations; the malicious settled old grievances by denouncing their neighbors; the greedy denounced their rivals and competitors. In the end, always, an inflamed populace vented its wrath on the Jews, with mobs storming the Quarter. And before the King could step in and restore order, many died or were ruined.

"It could be fatal," said Berenguer. "Unless I can contain it at once, things could become as black as they were in the days of the hunt for Cathars, when informers crept out of every corner, and the innocent suffered as much as the guilty. Isaac, I don't want to live through that in my diocese."

"Before we consign the city to flames," said Isaac calmly, though his heart pounded with anger and fear, "is it not possible that we are exaggerating the consequences of what we heard? Consider this possibility, Your Excellency. Instead of a new heresy spreading through the town, we have three lads, unhappy with their lives, who are friends because of their common discontent. They seek something to ease it. We know that wine was one of their remedies. But somewhere, they come across a book, and try to dabble in unseen forces." He paused to let the Bishop consider the possibility.

"Including the drinking of potent mixtures that ended in their deaths?" Berenguer's voice was heavy with doubt.

"Perhaps even that," said Isaac. "For certainly both Aaron and Marc were very solitary boys, with no friends that others ever knew about. Was Lorens also solitary? For you see, Your Excellency, if this is something endemic in the seminary, Lorens would have had friends here, or at the very least, partners in evil."

"I have no idea," said Berenguer. "He was a quiet lad, and very studious. He loved poetry, and borrowed many of my books, kept them for a time, and returned them. In the three years he was here, he was never part of the crowds hauled up before me for riotous or unseemly behavior. And that means he probably was a solitary boy." He stopped, and for the first time that day, something of his old energy returned to his voice. "Isaac, whatever those misguided lads were involved in, whatever it was that killed them, if we can discover that it had nothing to do with the seminary, and was not part of some huge wave of error and false doctrine in the city, you will have saved me again—once when you rescued me from the fever, and this time, when you save us all—the people of the city, the dean and chapter of the cathedral—from the Archbishop's wrath! And I will say many masses for the poor lads' souls.''

Heavier footfalls than usual echoed down the corridor from the student's chambers. ''They are moving his body away, lord,'' said Yusuf. ''Shall I go and finish searching his room?''

''Yes, indeed,'' said Berenguer. ''We will await you here.''

NINE

Yusuf stopped at the doorway to Lorens's chamber, reluctant to enter. Before, in the atmosphere of tension and bustle and crisis, surrounded by familiar faces and horrified young priests, he had been able to regard the body of Lorens Manet as a side issue, a medical device, something for his instruction. And his previous search of the room had been a game, a game at which he excelled. He had slipped about in the crowd, into tight spaces and around people without ever drawing attention to himself. But now three people were waiting for him to find something, and there was no one to tell him what he should find. There is nothing here, he thought despairingly. The room was more than empty, reduced to hard stone, a heap of tangled and unclean bedclothes, and a few scraps of personal possessions. Then the wind moaned in the shutters like the sighing ghosts of a hundred murdered men, butchered like his father, and lying unavenged. He shivered, feeling suddenly alone and panic-stricken. All through those empty corridors, in this deserted room, he could feel the dying breath of the tormented young man on his neck, the empty eyes watching his search, expecting, demanding. He did his utmost to thrust the thought aside and, with a powerful sense of futility, turned to the task at hand.

What would someone like Lorens Manet, son of a wealthy merchant, hide? Where would he hide it? Where would anyone—rich or poor, student or stable lad—hide something in here? It wasn't simple. The room had not been designed or furnished for the keeping of secrets—it had no dark corners or locked chests. He raised the humble straw mattress from its wooden platform and peered under it. Nothing. He got down on his knees and investigated under the bed. A chamber pot, a great deal of dust, and a wooden cup, resting on its side, shared the space.

He reached in and pulled out the chamber pot and the cup. Like all the previous inhabitants of the room, he left the dust where it was.

The chamber pot had a small amount of liquid sloshing around in the bottom. Urine, no doubt, he decided, and imitating his master, he sniffed it. It smelled like—well—urine. What was he supposed to be sniffing for? The cup was another matter. It had been filled with some liquid quite recently, and the wood was still wet. He sniffed at that, too, and decided that—whatever had been in there—he would not have touched it. Not if someone had dangled a gold *maravedí* in front of his nose. But no doubt his master would recognize some strange odor in the urine, and some exotic herb or other in the drops of liquid left in the cup. He set both containers on the table. He noted that the candle in the candlestick had burned down to nothing, and that the brass bowl beside it could use a thorough cleaning. He shook his head and moved on.

There were no pouches or purses or secret hiding places in the clothing on the pegs; nor was there anything caught in the tangled bedclothes, which Yusuf shook out and then folded neatly. Nothing remained but the books.

There were three. He reached up and took them down, carefully, one by one, and set them on the bed. The first was much higher than his fingers were long, and as deep and as thick as a man's hand. The other two were twice the size of the first in height and depth, but no thicker. One of the larger ones was bound in fine leather; the other two were bound in coarse, heavy leather, and all three were written on parchment. He picked up the book with the more expensive, beautifully crafted binding, and opened it cautiously. The wide margin of the first page was decorated with the elongated figure of a woman and, standing just beneath her, a man. They were both rather melancholy looking. The woman's golden hair spilled down from her head to form part of the first letter of the book. She was looking downward, and her fingers just barely touched the raised hand of her companion. She was clad in a gown of a blue so deep and brilliant that it made his heart ache for the colors of home; her knight, splendid in burnished armor emblazoned with scarlet, gazed up at her.

Yusuf sat down on the bed, enchanted. He closed the beautiful book and picked up the other two, opening each in turn. No magic letters, no elegant script this time, just dead black ink on cramped little pages, going on and on and on with never a break, and decorated only with ugly ink blots where the parchment was rough. He turned the pages carefully, looking for something—anything—out of the way, and finally held each one, spine up, over the bed and shook it. Nothing came out but more dust. He put them down again and returned to his first choice.

The script in it was ornate, but clear. He had no difficulty in sounding out the words, and recognizing the meaning of most of them, but the sense of the lines in front of him remained puzzling. They had been written in the old tongue of the Latins, about which he still had much to learn. He shrugged and ceased to worry about it. The words were unimportant at the moment. It was the painting and decoration that delighted his eye. He turned a leaf of the book and found a thin, lithe hunting hound, its head turned back toward its curling tail, lying at the foot of a page, as if on guard; then four pages farther, a section of work had been finished off with an intricate design in scarlet ink, just touched with gold. He stared at it for a long time, trying to commit the design to memory, and then turned the next page. A piece of paper fell out onto the floor.

He set the book on his lap, leaned over, and picked up the paper. It was folded into a small square, and addressed to Master Lorens Manet. "I must open it," he murmured apologetically to the ghosts, who had lost, at least partly, their power to terrify while he carried this book in his hand. "It could be important." Yet, as he undid the first fold, his heart pounded as if he were engaged in a dangerous and shameful criminal act, and he began to hurry. At the last fold, he half opened it to see what nature of missive it might be. He was no further ahead. The writing was cramped and spiky, and the letters poorly formed. He spread it out on top of the book on his lap and struggled to make out the first words. When their meaning finally jumped out at him, it startled him so that he dropped the paper on the floor again.

A voice boomed out in the corridor, "Where is that lad? He's had time to take the room apart stone by stone, and put it back together again by now."

Yusuf grabbed the paper, folded it roughly, and thrust it into his tunic without thinking. Guiltily he closed the beautiful book again just as the Bishop came striding into the room.

"Good lad," he said, looking down at the book. "You found my Ovid before someone could decide to add it to his private collection."

"It is a very beautiful book, Your Excellency," said Yusuf hastily, scrambling to his feet, and handing it to the Bishop.

"It is indeed, and very expensive, and much too amorous in nature for a lad of your age. Did you read any of it?"

"Only a few words. I wanted to look at the pictures."

"Well then, when you've told Master Isaac what you've found—just think, my friend, the clever lad has discovered a pisspot at least—you may sit quietly in the corner and look at the pictures."

"Do not scorn a container of humble urine," said Isaac, who had been listening to the scene with some amusement. "It can tell us a great deal concerning the lad who died."

"I found a cup under the bed as well," said Yusuf, who had escaped the Bishop's teasing by hiding behind His Excellency's book. "I put it on the table beside the chamber pot."

"What else has he set out for us?" asked Isaac.

"On the table, Papa?" asked Raquel.

"Start there. Give me everything."

"There is a candlestick. The candle in it is burned right down to the clay holder. And there is a brass bowl, in need of cleaning—"

"Is anything in it?"

"Just some fragments—of ash, I think."

"Give it to me," said Isaac. He took the small bowl, and dipped his finger into the residue at the bottom. He rubbed his two fingers together, and then smelled the substance in the bowl. "Incense," said Isaac, "mixed with other substances."

"Can you tell what?" asked the Bishop. "And what the devil was he doing burning incense in his chamber? No wonder we're having problems!"

A few possibilities formed in Isaac's mind, some rational, some beyond probability, but he was reluctant to say anything until he was more certain.

"I might be able to find out," he murmured. "But now I must check the urine."

"I strongly suspect," said Isaac as they walked away from the room, "from the manner of his death, and other signs, that he has taken some poisonous substance. His urine has a distinctly bitter taste and acrid smell. I would also guess that he took it quite willingly. It was in that wooden cup, not disguised in food or drink."

"You mean he killed himself?" said Berenguer.

"Only in a sense. I believe he drank the contents of that cup in the belief that it would heal whatever was wrong with him. Why else would he assure you in such a confident voice, Your Excellency, that he was getting better, unless he, too, believed it to be true? When a man has made a desperate attempt on his own life, he either regrets it, and cries out to you to save him, or he is determined in his wish, and begs you to allow him to die. Lorens cheerfully asserted that he was fine."

"What was in that cup, Master Isaac?"

"I am as yet unsure," said the physician. "I will set Raquel to search through the books for poisons of that nature."

The golden light of the October sun poured in the library window, and illuminated the heavy book that Raquel was perusing. A faint rustle behind her made her jump, startled, and look around.

Yusuf stood in the doorway, looking pale and haunted.

"What's wrong with you?" she asked, with far less compassion than she would have shown to a beggar at the gate. But then the beggar would not have interrupted her in mid-sentence, and frightened her out of her train of thought.

"Mistress Raquel," he whispered, "I have done a terrible thing. I think."

"Well, come over here if you're going to whisper," she said crossly. "What did you do? Steal something?" she added, lowering her own voice to a more discreet level.

"How did you know?" he asked, looking, if possible, even more terrified.

"I didn't," she said. "What did you steal?" She reached out and caught him by the hand, and dragged him closer. He followed, unresisting.

"This," he said, reaching into his tunic and pulling out a piece of paper, folded several times.

"A piece of paper?" said Raquel, raising a sardonic eyebrow. "Well—that's not a hanging offense in this household—not yet, at any rate—so you can take that look off your face. Where did you get it?''

"From the chamber of the student who died. It's a letter. I didn't mean to take it, Mistress Raquel. It fell out of the book I was searching, and then the Bishop came striding in, looking like a giant—"

"He does, rather," said Raquel.

"I was so startled, I hid it in my tunic and forgot I had it."

"That's it?" said Raquel, looking him straight in the face.

He colored. "Well, no. I had started to read it when I heard him," he confessed. "It is a terrible letter."

"You finished reading it." It was not a question. She, too, would have finished reading it before confessing to the crime.

"Yes," he said guiltily.

"Well—let's see what's in it, then," said Raquel. "After all, we're the only people in the house who can read it. Mama can't read, nor the twins, nor the servants, and Papa can't see it. Hand it over."

It was written in the common speech of the time, dressed up with phrases in the old Latin, and words that Raquel recognized as being in the Moorish tongue. She spread it out on the table so that they could both look at it, and read the spiky, scrawled hand slowly, one painful word at a time.

"I could wish," she said, "that Master Lorens's correspondent had hired a scribe, instead of using his own poor hand to write this with."

"What does it say, Mistress Raquel?" asked Yusuf, more humbly than was his wont. "I cannot make out all the words."

"I'm not surprised," she answered, and began reading, letting her finger travel lightly under the words as she read them. " 'My most esteemed Lord, Don Lorens,' " she started. "That seems rather an elevated title for a wool merchant's son, but never mind. I will read and not comment.''

> My most esteemed Lord, Don Lorens,
>   Heed these words if you wish to escape the foulest of deaths and certain damnation. I write to you out of charity, as a fellow seeker after truth and enlightenment, to warn you of the consequences of the path you are taking. Your companions, although worthy men and sincere, had not the strength to withstand the forces of evil that surround every seeker of the truth. They succumbed to temptation; they allowed foul and lustful thoughts to pollute their minds; they fought against the visions, finding them too powerful for their small souls to bear. Accursed be they by all the powers—

Here Raquel broke off. ''What are those words?'' she asked, pointing to the next line. ''They are in your language, are they not?''

''Yes,'' said Yusuf. ''But here they make no sense.''

''What do they say?''

Yusuf looked carefully at the Arabic and then burst into giggles. ''It means fish,'' he said, ''almonds, and figs. He is cursing them by the power of fish, almonds, and figs. Perhaps it is some secret language.''

''You mean, 'fish' means 'I'll meet you by the river'?'' said Raquel, with a snicker.

''And 'almonds' means 'at moonrise.' '' Yusuf snorted with laughter.

''And 'figs' means 'bring gold, wine, and dancing girls?' '' At that they both began to howl with mirth.

''You two do not appear to be busy,'' said Judith, sweeping in from the passageway. Then she glanced at the table, saw a large, important-looking book, a paper covered closely with writing, and nodded, reassured.

''I'm sorry, Mama,'' said Raquel soberly. ''We paused but for a moment. We will return to our work at once.''

Judith went back to her housewifely duties, and Raquel continued to read, in a softer voice:

> If there is no trust, there can be no movement upward on the path to enlightenment. You swore a most solemn vow, before all the spirits of the air who bring truth and knowledge to those brave enough to confront them. Your companions faltered on their way, and you have seen what happened to them. *Excelsior, discipule.* Do not follow their path, if you value your life and your soul.

"And that is all," Raquel said. "In his modesty, he does not append his name to the page."

"I would not like to receive that letter," said Yusuf.

"We must take it to Papa," said Raquel. "Because stripped of all its fancy talk, it is a threat. And he must know of it."

"So you see, my lord Bishop," said the physician, "I felt you should be acquainted with this at once." He took the letter, folded as it had been when Yusuf found it, and passed it to the Bishop. "I must beg indulgence for my wayward apprentice. He says most earnestly that the paper fell out of your book, and as he opened it, you came in the room. Feeling frightened and very guilty, he slipped it into his tunic, and forgot it until after we had returned home."

"I wish I could instill a similar sense of fear and guilt in some of my flock," said Berenguer, and turned to the letter.

He read it, tossed it down on the table, and then picked it up again. "What folly! What pernicious nonsense these charlatans spin out to make their webs! Vows! That foolish child. What business had he with taking vows? Except his religious vows, and he was not yet ready for them. Oh, Isaac, these children—they think they are men because their beards begin to show, but they are children yet, in many ways.''

"It was the threat that interested me," said Isaac.

"That is part of it. If he had not taken whatever strange vow is alluded to, then this monster would have had nothing to threaten him with, would he? Isaac, you would not believe the foolish vows that boys stuffed with ideals can take—vowing to fast until they have accomplished some impossible task, and we find them in their beds half-dead from starvation.''

"And girls, too, no doubt?" murmured Isaac.

"No doubt. But it is the Lady Elicsenda at the convent who must deal with them. And short and sharp she is with them, too, until they drop their nonsense." He picked up the letter again and read it more carefully. "And the Arabic? What do you make of that?"

"It appears to be someone's list for the market, copied out in a clumsy hand," said Isaac. "Or so says Yusuf. But Your Excellency reads the Moorish tongue, do you not?"

"I can make it out," said Berenguer. "But not with the skill you had while you had sight." He peered at the paper. "But by all that's holy," he said with delight, "I can read this. And the boy is right. Fish."

"Almonds, and figs. Yusuf suggested it might be a secret language—but I suspect he was amusing himself at our expense."

"There is one thing of comfort in this letter. And I suspect you noticed that as well.''

"It would suggest that the three boys were alone in their quest, guided by the writer of this letter."

"Who must have been stripping them of every penny they could raise from their families," added Berenguer. "But I will ask Francesc what he has discovered from the seminarians."

"I have brought Bertran, Your Excellency," said Francesc Monterranes, canon vicar when Berenguer was away visiting far-flung parishes, and most trusted aide to the

Bishop. "He can tell us something of what is happening at the seminary. I have no desire to raise doubts and speculation among the students by questioning everyone at once."

"As ever, wisely done, Francesc. Now, cousin Bertran, what have you heard in a fortnight of keeping your ear to the ground?"

"A great deal, my lord, but little of importance. As you suspected, much of the discontent arises from the replacement of Father Miquel, who was much beloved, with Father Garcia, who would need to be an angel straight from heaven to measure up to his predecessor. The new students, who did not know Father Miquel, admire Father Garcia. All the rest of the complaints are about terrible food, unreasonable hours for recreation, and the excessive amount of time you expect them to spend at their studies. I would ignore them," he said, with the wisdom of twenty for the complaints of fifteen-year-olds. "Whatever is done, they will still complain."

"You had spoken earlier of an inner group, a set of conspirators, so to speak."

"I had, and they exist. Six boys, although one has become doubtful about their cause. They are not, however, interested in religion—"

"You don't need to tell me that," said the Bishop.

"They are a political group, boys whose families had leaned toward the would-be usurper in the uprising, but not publicly enough to suffer from it, and who are worth watching for signs of disloyalty." This was the young soldier speaking, not the potential cleric.

"It is an age of rebellion," said the Bishop. "Fifteen, that is. But the group will be broken up, and they will be watched to make sure that they do not persist in disloyalty. But that brings us no closer to Lorens Manet."

"Lorens Manet? I was not told that he was to be investigated," said Bertran, stiffly, "or I would have spent much time on him." He was clearly annoyed that his report had fallen so far from the mark.

"You could not know, Bertran. It was only this morning that we realized the importance of the lad."

Bertran stopped and thought, and then began again, speaking slowly as he organized his knowledge. "Lorens, I think, had few friends—nay, few acquaintances—among the students, and no friends. He was unlike most other boys, seminarians or not, who jest rudely about women, and find great amusement in drinking wine enough to render them senseless."

"You surprise me," said Berenguer sardonically.

Bertran bowed slightly to acknowledge his effrontery in attempting to teach the Bishop anything about the basic nature of boys. "As you well know, my lord," he murmured by way of apology, and then returned to his subject. "By chance, I think I may have met his only friends. I took a cup of wine with them one day. Two grave youths, not at the seminary, who sat with him at Rodrigue's, and talked of writing, and philosophy, and the nature of beauty."

"And were these youths named Aaron and Marc?"

"They were, my lord. I was not there long, but you could ask them what else was talked about."

"Scarcely, cousin. They are both dead."

"Both?" said Bertran, in astonishment.

"Yes," said Berenguer. "As is Lorens Manet. This morning. And now all three of those boys are beyond questioning."

"Dead! All three? That is almost beyond belief," said Bertran. "I beg your indulgence, Your Excellency. This news has shaken me. They were pleasant lads," he added, and paused. "I first noticed them together," he said at last, "six weeks ago—in the meadow, listening with rapt attention to a preacher who claimed to know the wisdom and secrets of the Magi. I was curious, I admit, and followed them when they went up to the master—"

"His name?"

"He calls himself Guillem de Montpellier," said Bertran. "They asked if he gave private lessons. He seemed willing, and named a price. Later, at Rodrigue's, they were agreed that Master Guillem wanted more than they could raise. I had other business to attend to then, and left them there.''

"Then it does not seem likely that they became pupils of Master Guillem,'' said Francesc. "Which means he is unlikely to have been the writer of the letter.''

"Unless they managed to convince him to teach them at bargain rates,'' said the Bishop.

"From what I could gather,'' said Bertran, "their pocket money and his demands were very far apart. They had trouble scraping up enough for a cup of Rodrigue's worst.''

"But it indicates that they were looking for someone to teach them,'' murmured Isaac. "If not this Master Guillem, then some other charlatan. And for a little while they had an extra source of revenue.''

"What revenue?'' asked the Bishop.

"I'm afraid that Aaron was helping himself to his father's strongbox to pay for wine, and possibly lessons from Master Guillem. But Aaron died. What did they do then?''

"And what did Master Guillem teach them?'' said the Bishop. "I shall send an officer to ask this Guillem de Montpellier.''

The early morning mist off the river was still hovering over the city when Isaac rose from his bed. A rustle of clothing from the direction of the door made him turn. "I am so glad you are awake. You must hasten, Isaac.'' It was Judith's familiar voice. "But the morning air is cold. I will prepare you a cup of something hot to drink,'' she said, "and a morsel to eat, and then you must be off to the bakery, husband.''

"Why this haste for bread, my dear?''

"You know it is not for bread. Why would I ask you to go out and fetch bread? Esther is ill, and begs you to come to see her.''

"In what way ill, Judith?''

"A cough, the boy told me, and a fever, and no stomach for her food. Myself, I think she's grieving over Aaron," said Judith. "And is more in need of sympathy and proper nourishment than physicians. Mossé is no companion for a woman in sorrow." She turned to go so that he might say his morning prayers in peace. "But I am coming with you, husband. Naomi is warming some strong broth, and preparing hot spiced wine with beaten egg. I should have taken such things to Esther days ago. I have been most remiss in my duties as a neighbor and friend."

"And we will take medicines for her illness," said Isaac mildly. "Between us, I trust, she will become no sicker than she is now."

There was an air of grim desperation in the bakery. Mossé was scarlet in the face and dripping with sweat as he slid the last loaf of the batch into the giant oven. Sara was stacking cooled loaves into baskets, and struggling out to the front to set them out. "I don't know what my wife thinks she's doing," said the baker. "Taking to her bed like some great lady, and sending the lad off to fetch you just when I needed him to stoke the fires." He wiped his face with his apron. "Oh, good morning, Mistress Judith. I didn't know she'd sent for you as well."

"She didn't, Master Mossé," said Judith coldly. "I came to see how she was."

"Well, she's in the bedchamber. Sara will take you up there."

"Judith—why don't you and Raquel go up to her now?" said Isaac. "I am sure she would like some broth or spiced wine while it is still warm and at its best. I will be with you in a moment."

"Certainly," murmured the physician's wife, and grasping Raquel firmly by the elbow, propelled her out of the room.

"And how have you been, Master Mossé?" said Isaac. "It must be difficult for you to manage without Aaron."

"Not so difficult as managing with him," said Mossé.

"Out every night, and trying to make bread in the morning with a head as big as a melon." He held his hands out from his ears to indicate the massiveness of Aaron's hangover. "Oh—I knew about it all right. They all thought they could keep it from me, but I knew how drunk he was when he came home. And there's nothing gone from the money box these days either, except it's to Mordecai for taxes or His Majesty's rents. That's theft enough for one business to suffer. The apprentice is back and doing Aaron's work and I'm training the lad to work with dough now. He's not bad, for all he's so small."

"Feed him more and he'll grow faster and stronger," said Isaac, who had always suspected that the children who labored in Mossé's household were underfed. "That way you'll get more work out of him."

"He eats enough for two as it is," said Mossé sourly. "But you may be right."

"Sometimes a son is not well suited to his father's profession," said Isaac casually, pausing to note Mossé's reaction.

"There was nothing wrong with the boy, not when he was small," said Mossé defensively. "He loved helping me any way he could. Then he changed, and it was all from learning to read and such. I never learned more than I needed, to recite passages and prayers that I was taught. But Aaron!" The baker began moving loaves from the racks to the basket as he talked. "He couldn't be happy until he knew his letters, and could read, not just the law and the prophets, but Christian books, and heathen writings, and he was determined to learn to read books by the devilish Moors as well. I ask you, what good does that do a baker, to be able to read such evil stuff? Begging your pardon, young sir," he added hastily, remembering, rather too late, that Yusuf was standing beside the counter at the front of the shop.

Yusuf pulled himself to his full height and nodded stiffly. "It is of no importance, sir," he murmured.

The baker was silent for a moment. "It ruined him,"

he muttered. "All that learning. Ruined him."

"I must go up to your wife," said Isaac. "Yusuf?"

The boy walked quietly over and stood beside him. "Here, lord," he murmured.

Isaac placed his hand on Yusuf's shoulder and allowed himself to be led up the narrow staircase.

When Judith and Raquel entered the chamber, Esther lay in her bed looking like a much diminished sketch of herself, pale and unhappy looking. Daniel was sitting beside her, patting her forehead with a cold cloth, and trying to convince her to eat from a large bowl of stewed beef. He rose hastily when he saw them.

"Take that away, Daniel, please," said Esther in a faint, hoarse voice. "I cannot eat it."

"I'm sorry, Mama," he murmured. "I will bring you something else later." He picked up the bowl, bowed to Judith and Raquel, and left.

"Of course you can't eat that," said Judith, moving in on Esther like a well-dressed bird of prey bearing food to her hungry nestlings. "We have brought you little things to drink, warm and soothing, that Naomi made for you just this morning." She set the two bowls on the table, and uncovered the wine and egg. "This will slip past your sore throat so gently you won't even feel it," she said, "and you must eat or you won't get better." She held up a hand to forestall a reply. "And don't tell me you don't want to get better, because there's Daniel, sitting with you for hours, I'll warrant, so fond of his mother he is. What would he do if you let yourself just fade away? You should be ashamed of yourself." She stopped long enough to catch her breath.

"I'm not—"

"I know you're not. But you'll have some anyway, won't you?" And she held the bowl up to Esther's mouth. "Drink some," she urged.

"You might as well, Mistress Esther," said Raquel.

"Otherwise you'll never get rid of her. I know my mother."

The baker's wife gave her a feeble smile, and drank. After three or four mouthfuls Judith took the bowl away. "There," she said. "I hear Isaac's foot on the stair. He won't want me in here, filling up all the space. I'll just take these down to the kitchen, and keep them warm until he's through."

"She must rest and keep warm," said Isaac as he reentered the bakery. "I have left a soothing syrup for her throat, and embrocations for the chest, and herbal mixtures for her fever. She is to have very light and nourishing food, but I have spoken to your maid of that. Your son promises to stay and help nurse her."

"Well, I can't sit up all day and all night with a sick woman," said Mossé defensively. "I have work to do. And I have to be out of my bed to fire up the ovens well before dawn."

"Indeed," said Isaac. "My wife is encouraging her to eat a little broth. She will send over more dishes that are likely to tempt a sick woman's appetite as soon as they are prepared."

"Thank you, physician," muttered Mossé. "How much do—"

"My wife does not charge for her services," interrupted Isaac. "Good day. I will return to see how Mistress Esther does. Send for me if she becomes worse."

"Mossé grows more surly by the day," said Isaac.

"He does," agreed Judith. "If he were not such a good baker, it would be difficult to put up with him." She took her husband's arm affectionately, as in the old days, when they were newly wed, and gathered up her skirts with her other hand. "He was always a greedy man, in little ways," she observed. "And he was so pleased with himself, getting his brother-in-law to pay for that oven, big enough for the most lavish feasts, and a handsome sum he charges for it, too—every time there's a wedding, a bar mitzvah, anything, Mossé gets his share—and he got rid of a troublesome son in the bargain. Only then Daniel grew up to be clever and hardworking, and Aaron turned rebellious and died. Now he has an oven, but no heir, and no one to slave all day using it. It's a judgment on him, Isaac."

"You're probably right, my dear. He'll have to make do with a son-in-law."

"He should find a match for Sara, and get them betrothed now," observed Judith. "That way he'll have time to get the boy ready to take over the business."

"But, my dear," said Isaac. "She's only ten."

"Nonsense," said Judith. "My mother was betrothed at six, and had as happy a marriage as most women."

"But no one does that now to their children—or almost no one."

"And is the community happier? And more blessed with good families and dutiful children than it was in our parents' time?"

"I don't know, my dear. All I know is that I married you for love of your fiery temper and your strength and your beauty, and my parents might have chosen quite another for me. One who grew up to be cold and weak and helpless in adversity."

Judith was silent.

TEN

As they neared their gate, Isaac stopped suddenly and turned his head to listen. Quick footsteps behind them echoed between the houses. "Who is that, my dear?" he asked. "It sounds like—"

Judith looked back, and then, alarmed, put her hand on Isaac's arm. "It is Daniel, husband. I fear for Esther. She must be worse."

Raquel's pale cheeks reddened, and she raised her hand quickly to draw her veil close.

"Master Isaac," called the baker's elder son. "Master Isaac. A word with you, please."

"Is it your mother? Am I needed?" asked Isaac, turning, prepared to go back.

"No, Master Isaac. She drank some of the broth that Mistress Judith brought her, and has fallen into a peaceful sleep. I am very grateful for your kindness." Before either could reply, he rushed on. "I left the maid to watch over her and came to speak to you."

"Then we can talk more comfortably inside, by our own fire," said Isaac. "Come in."

"Thank you, Master Isaac," he said, following them into the courtyard and up the stairs to the common sitting room. Yusuf slipped away to the library, and the others sat down politely.

Judith rose again almost at once and whisked off to the kitchen to see about refreshment. Raquel turned pink, and with a murmured and incoherent apology, pursued Yusuf to offer him some unwanted help.

"And what is it that you would like to tell me?" said Isaac, once they were alone. "Is it about your mother?"

"No, Master Isaac. I am not worried about her at the moment."

"Your father? He has been in some distress, I believe."

"My father distresses me a great deal. He was never a patient, cheerful man, Master Isaac, but in these last few weeks his disposition grows worse by the day. At every visit I make, he falls into a rage. My mother cannot bear it and flees to her chamber. Sara and the apprentice bear the brunt of his anger, but even the boy and the poor little maid are becoming terrified of him. But I'm afraid that there is little that you—or indeed anyone—can do to moderate his fury."

"A curious reason to visit a physician, Daniel," said Isaac dryly. "To tell him that he cannot help you. But you may be wrong. Have you asked yourself why your father falls into such rages?"

"Out of sorrow for Aaron's death, no doubt," said Daniel.

"I don't believe so," said Isaac. "Or not altogether. I fear that your father has made the same error you did. He feels responsible for Aaron's death, because of—"

"Sending me away?"

"Yes. But depriving the elder son of his birthright does not ordinarily lead to the death of the younger son, Daniel. Aaron's death was odd, but it had little to do with you or your family. Two other young men, both friends of your brother, have died recently in similar ways."

"Friends of my brother? What friends? And they are both dead?"

"Yes. Your brother had friends, good friends, even

though he did his best to shield them from your notice. Young men whose family circumstances were very unlike yours. They were both Christian, one the son of a weaver, working at his father's trade, and the other a student at the seminary. They did not die because you are your uncle's heir. Tell me," said Isaac without a break in the line of his discourse, "did your brother receive a letter shortly before his death? A disturbing letter?"

"No. Or not that I knew of. My mother or the maid might know. If you like, I will ask them."

"If you do not know, Daniel, I doubt that either of them would." Isaac rose to his feet to bid farewell to the young man.

"Master Isaac, please," said Daniel, rising as well. "Just one more word. You asked me before why I came to see you, and it seems so unimportant now that I am almost ashamed to take up your time. But you asked what we talked of in the last few weeks or months, and he did tell me about a great Magus, a scholar from foreign parts, who impressed him very much with his wisdom and learning. He said that he went once or twice to Marieta's to hear him give a class in theology."

"To Marieta's? The brothel?"

"I believe so," said Daniel in a troubled voice.

"Are you sure he was not jesting with you? That he was not actually going to Marieta's in pursuit of pleasure?"

"No!" said Daniel firmly. "It's not possible. Not Aaron. Master, you must believe me. Aaron was an ascetic. He had renounced pleasure—"

"Not all pleasures, surely," said Isaac. "He spent much time at Rodrigue's tavern, drinking wine with his friends, and talking."

"Well—he was not interested in women," said Daniel. "I know that men lie about such things, especially to their families, but we talked much about it. He seemed able to ignore them, not just battle with temptation, sometimes winning, sometimes losing, like the rest of us. It irritated

him that Mama kept wanting to marry him to someone—
anyone—just to improve his temper, as though he were a
bull to be castrated so he would pull the plow without
complaint.''

"He must have been unhappy," said Isaac, thoughtfully.
"But it had nothing to do with being his father's heir,
rather than his uncle's."

"I don't understand you, Master Isaac," said Daniel.

"Perhaps it's just as well," said the physician. "I may
not even understand myself."

That evening, in Rodrigue's tavern, Ramon the weaver accepted a cup of wine graciously, if drunkenly, and prepared to tell his tale once more. As his fame grew in the
wake of the sensational stories circulating about the town,
so had his drinking habits changed. Instead of a small cup
of wine with his neighbors at the little tavern down the
street, he spent his evenings recounting elaborately embroidered versions of his son's death, seeking wider and
wider audiences for his tales of horror and tribulation.

"And I heard a knock on my door, I did," he said,
lubricating his throat with a hefty swallow of Rodrigue's
best. "It was late and I was about to go to my bed. A dark
night, too, and windy—a proper night for malice and
witchcraft."

"Who was it?" asked a stranger—the only person in
the room who had not heard the tale before, in some version or other. The rest of Rodrigue's customers had long
since stopped listening to him.

"A lady in black, tall, and veiled. I couldn't see her
face. But I could tell, from how she moved, and from her
voice, that she was a beauty, and wicked. There was something wicked in her voice."

"What do you mean?" asked the stranger.

"It was low, and hoarse, like. A voice of a temptress.
She walked right into the house and up the stairs to my
son's chamber, chanting. It was enough to freeze your
blood just to hear it. Then she burned incense and chanted

louder and louder, in a high, screechy voice." He leaned forward and whispered, "It was so powerful I was over-come. God himself knows how long I lay in a spell, and only He knows how long she stayed."

"You never told us that, Ramon," said the man across the table. "Last time you said she was small, and had a little, high voice."

"And before that," said another, "you said she looked like an angel, with—"

"I feared for my life," he said sulkily. "I didn't dare say the truth."

"And now you do?" said a skeptic.

"Yes, I do, because the Bishop himself sent one of his most important men to see me. He promised that the Church will protect me from sorcerers."

"And then what happened? You were under a spell, you said."

"And when I opened my eyes, I was standing at the foot of the stairs, and she was at the top. She floated down without a sound. Not one sound. Her feet never once touched the stairs."

"Like the physician. They say he can go down a stair without a footfall," murmured someone.

Ramon nodded. "That's how I knew it was the physi-cian's daughter. Let them deny it as much as they like. But I know what I know," he added, in tones heavy with significance, and drained his cup, looking hopefully around for another contributor to his general state of inebriation.

Isaac satisfied himself the next morning that Esther was, if not mending, at least more comfortable than she had been the day before. He left more syrup for her throat, checked that Judith had sent enough broth and other light dishes, and then sent Yusuf and Raquel to the herb seller's stall to replenish their supplies. "I shall walk home, and savor the experience of being alone for a while," he said abruptly. "There is much I wish to think about, and walk-ing stimulates the wits."

"But, lord," objected Yusuf.

"Until a few months ago, Yusuf, I went about the town alone a great deal. I wouldn't like to forget how it's done," he added, dryly. "And Raquel, are you covered?"

"Yes, Papa," said Raquel, in mutinous tones. "Of course I am covered."

And so the two of them were left to make their way out of the Quarter to where the herb seller had her stall set up. Raquel established herself in front of the display, and pushed aside her veil, the better to examine, sniff, compare, and bargain over the goods laid out before her.

"I can gather these on my own from any field," said Raquel, waving her hand at a collection of fresh and dried common herbs, and dismissing the pungent rosemary, the aromatic sage, along with great swatches of thyme and stiff branches of laurel. "And you want a farthing for one miserable bunch?" she said, pointing at the fat bundles filling broad, flat-bottomed baskets.

"You won't find any like these, Mistress Raquel," said the herb seller indignantly. "These are grown on our own hillside, and well watered and tended. They have more power and nourishment in them than the scraggly things you find by road, all trodden over by donkeys and oxen. But since it's for you, and your father, as a kindness . . ." She paused, as if preparing herself for a monumental sacrifice. "If you take four bunches—any four—I'll let you have them for an obol."

"Which is more than they're worth," said Raquel. "But it will save me another trip to the fields," she said, picking out eight prime bunches, some for her father, and some for Naomi, and giving her a penny. "Let's be off, Yusuf," she said.

There was no response.

She turned and looked around the crowded stalls. Yusuf was deep in conversation with a boy near his own age. She sighed, as if most of her life were spent waiting for the boy, and headed over to fetch him.

She was halted by a voice calling her name. It was

Dalia, with her mother, and their manservant. If Dalia had recognized her from across the square, she realized at once, then she must still be unveiled; she blushed, covered her face, waved, and hurried over to them, all in an instant.

"Raquel," cried her friend. "Come with us. Please. We are looking for silk, and we need your opinion."

"For a gown?" asked Raquel.

Dalia nodded.

"A special kind of gown?"

"Oh, Raquel," said her friend, clasping her hands, "Papa has been to Barcelona and seen that gentleman I told you of—"

"Dalia," said her mother. "You are indiscreet. Nothing is arranged as yet. What if you tell everyone and then—"

"Oh, Mama, Raquel isn't everyone. She never gossips. She knows everything about everyone, and never says a word. Do you, Raquel?"

"I certainly may not say anything about Papa's patients," said Raquel. "Even who they are, without his permission."

"There, you see. So I can tell her, and she won't talk. I need a beautiful gown because he's coming here on business, he says, but really it's because he wants to meet me, and look me over." At that she giggled, with the security of one who is sure that any man who looked her over must find her endearing. "And if we like each other well enough, we shall marry." This she said in a whisper, as if hordes of their neighbors were surrounding them, trying to catch every word. "Papa says he is handsome, as well as rich, and very sweet." She sped up to get somewhat out of her mother's hearing. "I have to admit that Jahuda is not sweet," she whispered. "He sulks when he doesn't get his way, and people say that sulkiness is very difficult to live with in a husband."

"Then he's going to be very sulky when he hears this," said Raquel.

"Yes, but I won't have to see it, will I? I'll be in Barcelona." She giggled again, and pulled Raquel by the hand toward the shop where piles of silk lay displayed for the delight of customers.

Dalia and her mother had narrowed down the choices to two heavy silks of excellent quality, one scarlet and the other a plummier red. "That would be splendid in a gown," said Dalia, pointing at the scarlet, "trimmed with—but what could I trim it with? There's the surcoat—it has to be a different color, and I want slashing for the sleeves that looks brilliant—but green or blue would be—" Doubt was edged across her face. "What do you think, Raquel?"

Raquel looked at her friend, and looked the silk, and thought it a disastrous pick. "Not green or blue, Dalia," she said. "But perhaps the other color would be easier to trim," she murmured.

"Mistress Dalia shouldn't wear either color," said a light voice from behind them. "Look at this, instead."

All of them turned. Yusuf was standing in the shop, with a bolt of warm yellow silk in his hands, the color of gold, or the sun in autumn, rich and glowing.

"But I don't like yellow," said Dalia.

At this the silk merchant intervened. "Ah, but, mistress, this is not yellow. It is gold, almost saffron in hue, and most becoming to the young lady's complexion. Look, madam, at how your daughter's beauty comes alive, even in my poor shop, when I place the cloth near her face." He whipped the bolt of material out of Yusuf's hand, and threw a length of cloth over Dalia's shoulder. "If Madam would like, I will send the material over, and with it silk to trim in various hues, so that you may choose."

They looked at Dalia. Yusuf and the merchant were right. Raquel thought that few men could resist her friend dressed in a gown of that cloth.

Dalia's mother looked at it, stood back, and contemplated it against her daughter's face and hair, and settled in for serious discussion on price. The two girls drifted out into the street, bringing Yusuf along.

"How did you come to pick that one out?" said Raquel.

"I never would have thought of that color."

"I like color," said Yusuf. But in his mind's eye he caught a glimpse of his beautiful mother, dressed in a glorious silk robe of just that hue. Her image disappeared, and he wondered if her complexion had been like that of the young woman standing beside him, now veiled from prying eyes.

"Well, you certainly impressed everyone," said Raquel. "Who were you talking to?"

"Hasan," said Yusuf. "His master is a scholar—but not a very kind one. He speaks my language, so I like to talk to him sometimes," he added, rather lamely.

"I'm sure you do," said Raquel.

Then Dalia's mother emerged triumphant from the shop, the transactions concluded.

"I must return home," said Raquel. "Or Mama will be worried. Yusuf will accompany me."

And Dalia and her mother and the servant went on in search of more bait to hook a goldsmith.

In spite of her professions of haste, Raquel was in no hurry to go back. The day was pleasant for the time of year, and she was enjoying herself. She stepped inside the shop of Ephraim the glover, who had some new gloves on display, a pretty shade of dove gray, embroidered with tiny beads. Yusuf idled along behind her. The shop appeared deserted for the moment, and she pushed aside her veil to be able to examine samples of Ephraim's work spread out for her delight.

A shriek, coming from the street, startled her; she walked to the door, saw nothing, and stepped outside again to look.

"There she is," said a woman across the way.

Raquel moved farther into the square to see who the object of attention was, and realized that the red-faced matron in the doorway opposite was pointing at her.

"I knew I saw her cross the square, bold as can be,

wearing that veil, just the way she was when she came to the weaver's house."

"It's the physician's daughter," said another woman, who had just erupted from her own house. "Ramon said it was the physician's daughter."

The street was filling up with interested spectators. Raquel, mortified, pulled her veil over her face. A hand grasped her arm. But it was only Yusuf, trying to move her back toward the shops.

"Is that your witch?" said a man, in the door of a wine shop. "She can bewitch me any time she likes," he added, with a shout of laughter.

"Over here, pretty witch," called out another, and began to lumber purposefully across the square.

More people drifted into the street, drawn by the noise. Someone jostled Raquel; she bumped into Yusuf and almost knocked him over. She grasped his shoulder and prepared to leave with as much dignity as she could muster. Then a hand gripped her arm firmly, and dragged her and the boy backward into sudden darkness. A door slammed.

"Who's that?" she sputtered.

The hand let go of her.

She turned, pulled her veil from her eyes, and realized she was back in the glover's shop. "Daniel," she said. "What are you doing?"

"I thought someone was going to attack you," he said defensively. "And you had only the boy to protect you."

"Really, Daniel. It was only a couple of silly women, and a drunken lout or two. I was not under attack."

"Daniel? What is going on?" said a grave voice from the doorway at the back of the shop.

"Master Ephraim," said Raquel, with a small curtsy. "Your nephew was rescuing me from a mob of three, for which I am very grateful, however unnecessary it may have been."

Ephraim laughed. "Well," he said, "I do not blame him. A mob of three can easily turn into a mob of thirty.

And we would not wish any harm to come to you, Mistress Raquel. Would we, Daniel?''

"No, Uncle," said Daniel. "And it was not far from here that the woman was hit by the stone," he added.

"No one was threatening me with stones," said Raquel, more bravely than she felt.

"Nonetheless, Daniel and the manservant will accompany you and your lad to your gate, and see you safely behind it, will you not, nephew?"

"Certainly, Uncle," said Daniel. "I will fetch Samuel."

And they made their way through the back of the shop to the physician's house peacefully enough. But Raquel, although she teased Daniel all the way there for his reaction, went up to her chamber when she entered the house, and brooded over the incident with more alarm than she had felt until now.

ELEVEN

Raquel came slowly down the stairs to the courtyard, rehearsing various ways in which she might describe this morning's ugly little incident. It would be best to make light of it, she decided. She would turn it into a comic moment in which hysteria and drunkenness were defeated by her imperturbable demeanor. She stopped briefly to consider how to begin her tale, and looked over at the dinner table, bathed in the warmth of the late October sun. The twins were arguing over trivialities as always, but for all their noisy ferocity, they looked unbearably small and vulnerable in their protected world. The birds in their cage sang and fluttered energetically from perch to perch. The wild birds in the trees and shrubs that grew against the wall rose in answer and wheeled about, chattering shrilly, and settled again. Raquel stifled sudden tears, hurried down the last few steps, and took her place. She could not bring this morning's hatred into this charmed place.

Dinner started out quietly. The twins were too hungry and their elders too immersed in their own preoccupations for conversation. Raquel looked at the simple meal of cold dishes in front of her—the kitchen was deep in preparations for the Sabbath—and nibbled at a dish of greens dressed with vinegar and egg. She scattered some crumbs of bread on the stones behind her. Not one pair of wings fluttered down to snatch them up. "I wonder what's got into the birds," she said, unable to stand the silence any longer. "They don't seem to be hungry. And it's such a beautiful day." Before the words were out of her mouth, a gust of wind rushed into the protected corner where the table had been set out. The birds whirled frantically in the disturbed air, were joined by more birds, windblown and ruffled, until a whole flock had settled into the comparative shelter of courtyard.

"That's your answer," said her father, wryly. "Feel that wind. It isn't such a beautiful day after all, I think."

"The weather's changing," said Judith shortly.

Raquel shivered. "It's cold," she complained. "I'm going to fetch a shawl, Mama, if you don't mind."

The sun disappeared abruptly. The thrushes in their cage stopped singing and ruffled their feathers.

"I'm cold, too," said Miriam.

"Come with me," said her mother. "Raquel, take the birds in with you. I think it might rain."

Raquel was scarcely halfway up the stone stairs when lightning arced across the sky and the storm broke. Rain pelted down, splashing up from the paving of the courtyard, drowning out speech. The servants rushed out and began carrying everything in out of the downpour.

"You see," said Judith, to no one in particular. "The weather has changed." She hurried the twins and headed for the stairs. "Winter's coming."

Having dealt with the birdcage, Raquel had hastened back to lend a hand. "Oh, Mama, not yet," she said, as if her mother had the power to make it so by saying it. "We'll have good weather yet. The fair hasn't even started."

"It's always cold for the fair," said her mother.

"That's not true," said Raquel, and they argued all the way up to the dining room, where a hastily kindled fire was burning, and Naomi, as if by magic, was bringing in a hot dish of spiced ground lamb, shaped into flattened rounds, in a sauce thick with chopped olives and long-simmered autumn vegetables.

"It was for tomorrow night," she said defensively, as if there had been a general outcry against it. "But you need something warm inside you."

The rain ceased later in the afternoon, as suddenly as it had begun, leaving in its wake skies of a brighter blue, cold air and a brisk wind. Isaac accepted his warm cloak from Judith, and set out for the episcopal palace.

"As regards the boys' deaths, I have not learned much, but I did hear a few sad and intriguing things, Your Excellency," said Isaac. "I thought I would come by, inquire after your gout, and perhaps tell you of them."

"I suffer more from outrage and curiosity than from gout at the moment, Master Isaac," said Berenguer. "My wretched toe troubles me no longer. I can pull on a pair of boots with the speed of a young knight once more. But I am not happy about what I am hearing from the town." He paused for a moment. "More of that later. First, tell me what you have discovered."

"I discovered that the boy, Aaron, was passionately interested in learning. Not a comfortable tendency for Mossé's son. The baker makes excellent bread, but has little use for books. Aaron's brother tells me that the boy visited Marieta's establishment for at least one lesson in theology, and other branches of science, and probably more."

"Marieta's? To learn theology? Ah, Isaac, they are amusing themselves at your expense."

"That was my first thought, my lord Bishop. I know what Marieta is, and the kind of establishment she runs. But my informant swears that his brother was not unduly troubled by desire for women—"

"Is that what he said? Because Marieta caters to other desires as well."

"Indeed. I am aware. As Daniel did not seem to be, although he is very discreet. But he swears, as I said, that Aaron's passions were of the mind. And that at Marieta's, he sought, not a pretty companion, but a great Magus, new to the city, who could teach him all those things he did not know."

"This Guillem de Montpellier," said the Bishop thoughtfully.

"I suspect so," said Isaac.

"It must be, unless Marieta is sheltering a whole house-ful of Magi. I sent two of my officers out to discover what they could, as discreetly as possible, about this Guillem. And the first thing they discovered was that he lodges out-side the jurisdiction of the council, at Marieta's. Not very reassuring. Of course, he is well within my jurisdiction."

"Fortunately," said Isaac thoughtfully. "He does not seem to have very respectable friends. Although, in miti-gation, we must remember that life is hard for even the most learned of men if they are without a position and have no powerful friends to help them."

"Indeed," said the Bishop, who had never been without either since the age of nine, when he exchanged his mother's gentle care for the more rigorous upbringing of Mother Church. "But hard life or not, that man is begin-ning to annoy me. He denied most vehemently ever speak-ing to someone called Lorens."

"Did he? And did he deny offering lessons to credulous young men?"

"Not precisely," said the Bishop. "He admitted to speaking of these things from time to time, to interested hearers, and even to accepting alms from the charitable. There is no law against either of those things. But you understand, Master Isaac, that what the officers heard him do could well be considered preaching, and he has no li-cense to preach, as he well knows. That is a serious enough offense to worry him considerably."

"But he claims not to have given lessons at Marieta's?"

"Not exactly. He said that people do seek him out, and

ask him questions that he is pleased to answer, but that he does not remember the name of every person who has done so.'' He stopped and tapped his fingers impatiently on the wood of table. "I had told them not to press him too hard at the moment. I don't want to frighten him off, and I am not ready to demand his arrest. But the officers' impression was that he was sweating guilt from every pore. We must do something about him.''

"Indeed, Your Excellency. He is not a healthy influence in the city.''

"I agree. Even if he is not directly responsible for the deaths of those three young men, he is a fraud, a conjurer, a player with the minds and beliefs of poor innocents. If I cannot have him tried for his offenses, I shall see to it that he is ejected from my diocese.'' He drew a deep breath. "I must not let anger make me discourteous. I interrupted you, my friend. What else has crossed your path in the way of news?'' he asked, probing gently.

"One other thing, which I have pondered bringing to your attention for these past three days, Your Excellency.''

"Three days?'' said Berenguer in surprise.

"Yes. A long time to consider a question, perhaps, but you will understand, I think, when I describe the circumstances. One of my patients has told me that a man unknown to him has accused him of causing the death of Marc, son of Ramon the weaver, through sorcery, with the assistance of an unnamed woman.''

"Who is your patient?''

Isaac paused. "You see my difficulty, Your Excellency. It is a serious charge, you will agree, which may well be brought against him formally in a court of law. He has not given me license to speak of it—''

"Did he forbid you to speak of it?''

"No, Your Excellency, he did not. But to infer from that permission to reveal his affairs to you . . .''

"Ah, Isaac, you are a wonderfully conscientious man.''

"I did have his permission to bring to your knowledge

earlier threats against him and his family, threats to attack them through sorcery."

"On my soul, my friend," said Berenguer, "I swear I will not use your words, or even the knowledge of this accusation, as a basis for action against the accused man, Isaac. Only against his accuser, if I am justified in doing so. Is your patient from the *Call*?"

"No, Your Excellency, he is one of your flock. A staunch member of your flock. His name is Pons Manet."

"I cannot believe it," said Berenguer. "I cannot believe that anyone could even suggest that Pons Manet killed the son of a worthless, drunken oaf of a weaver using sorcery. Or that anyone would take the accusation seriously. Although the unlikeliest charges are taken for truth often enough," he added grimly.

"Life has been difficult for Pons Manet," said Isaac, ignoring the interruption. "I suspect strongly that his son, Lorens, is the same Lorens whose life I just failed to save. And the same Lorens who drank and argued philosophy and hungered for learning along with Aaron, the baker's son, and Marc, the weaver's son."

"Lorens was his son," said the Bishop. "And Pons Manet is a good man, Isaac, none better. He is generous, an excellent father, and an exemplary husband. He has struggled to achieve his present position, and to overcome the scorn of those around him who were born to wealth. I like the man, Isaac, and so help me God, this goes too far! I wonder if it cannot also be the work of our friend Guillem de Montpellier?"

"You may be right, my lord Bishop. But since sorcery is on everyone's lips these days, any one of his rivals could have used the charge hoping to destroy Master Pons."

"That's the very devil of it, Isaac. If it gets abroad, it will be all the more readily believed. Before you leave, I think we should have a discreet word with the captain of the guard. He only needs to know that Master Pons is being threatened. I would like to know who enters or leaves that house, and whether any of the servants have been suborned." He went to the door of the study, and spoke to someone standing in the corridor.

"I would be glad to have this matter resolved. My patient has suffered much since the summer began."

"We will consider Pons Manet's problems again, but there is one other thing we must speak of, Master Isaac," said Berenguer. "You have not mentioned it, and I do not know whether your silence comes from ignorance or from discretion, but—no matter—I shall be discourteous again, and speak of your private affairs without your permission. Has your daughter told you of her encounter in the streets of the town this morning?"

"What encounter?" said Isaac. "I have heard of no encounter. Is this more wicked idle gossip?"

"Not at all," said the Bishop. "It was reported to me an hour ago. They said that she came out of the glover's shop, her veil slightly askew, and was recognized by a certain Miquela, who accused her in intemperate terms of being a witch, the witch who helped kill young Marc. Two drunken men came out from the tavern and egged the accuser on, but before anything could happen, someone from the glover's shop pulled her back inside and bolted the door. The incident ended there, but I did not like it, Isaac, my friend. I did not like it."

"She has not spoken of it."

"Perhaps she thought it of little importance."

"She knows better than that. It must have upset her greatly for her to conceal it from me." He ran his fingertips over his forehead as if his head ached, and then, forming them into a pyramid, leaned his chin against them. "One day she will tell me," he said at last, raising his head, "and I will be very surprised to hear of it, my friend, and will tell her she acted with great bravery—and foolishness, in concealing it."

"If you wish it so, then no one shall learn of it from me, unless that woman has to be brought before the courts. But I beg you to consider the offer from Lady Elicsenda to keep Raquel at Sant Daniel. The convent will receive her gladly. She will be safe there.''

''I shall. But for now she will stay within our gates.''

''Excellent. Let us speak to the captain. And on Sunday I shall preach against inciting to riot in such terms that no one present is likely to forget the lesson for many years.''

The Sabbath dawned cold and gray. Wreaths of white mist rose from the mouths and nostrils of men on their way to prayer. In Isaac's house, yesterday's well-banked kitchen fires warmed that room, and the dining and sitting rooms on either side, with a gentle heat that took the edge off the cold. Beyond their courtyard, the calm and quiet was broken only by the usual small domestic noises, muffled by shutters that had not yet been opened because of the chill in the air.

But outside the Quarter, the bustle of Saturday's markets had turned to pandemonium. Next week was the fair, and holiday preparations were at full intensity. Housewives bargained and quarreled and rushed; children raced about in high excitement, adding to the general bedlam. Between tomorrow and All Saints' Day, a week hence, little work would be done in the town, and there was much to accomplish before this day ended.

Master Pons Manet was in his study, poring over the figures for the past two months of trade with his chief clerk. They had started work by candlelight, an hour after the bells rang for prime. When this was finished, he would spend the rest of the day in the warehouse, tallying and classifying stock with his chief warehouseman. Heavy trading could be expected to take place during the fair, and all this preparation had to be done before it began. Master Pons, for all his wealth, was working, as always, as hard as any of his laborers.

The last figures were checked, frowned over, commented on, and then put aside. Before the wool merchant could dismiss his clerk, the boy whose usual tasks were limited to making up fires and running errands for the house put his head around the door.

"Excuse me, Master Pons," he said, "only the mistress is gone with Caterina to the market, and Pere is away and cook said I should answer the door. There's a lady there who says she must see you, and I didn't know . . ."

Whatever it was that he didn't know remained unsaid. A woman, not very tall, heavily veiled, and wrapped in a thick, warm cloak that disguised her body well, slipped past him and walked quickly to the table where the two men were working. "I have something very important that must be spoken of today, Master Pons," she said. She spoke in a whisper, as if she were hoarse from shouting, yet her voice was clear enough to be heard and understood. "I will not take much of your time, but what I have to say should be said in private, I think."

Pons dismissed clerk and boy with a gesture. He continued to sit, and did not invite her to do the same. They both waited until the door was closed.

"And what have you to say to me that must be spoken in private?" said Pons harshly. He examined her closely, trying to divine the features under the veil.

"It is very simple. First of all, I am only a messenger. Pursuing me will not profit you at all. I know nothing about this matter beyond what I have been taught to say, and I do not know the names or professions of those who hired me. Nor do I know their features."

"That is a curiously familiar message, woman."

She paid no attention, but continued her set speech. "My employers have the skill to weave protective spells around you and your household," she said. "If you do not accept their assistance, your remaining son will die. If you still refuse, your wife will die, and then you."

"And do your employers offer this service out of charity?"

"No. The sum required for their services is written on this paper." She pulled a folded document, sealed with wax, out of her glove and dropped it on the table in front of him.

He picked it up, broke the seal, and began to unfold it. It was a sheet of the finest paper made in the city, folded in quarters and then folded again, twice, lengthwise. All that paper had only one thing written on it, and that was an amount in gold *maravedís*. Pons Manet looked at it, pushed the paper aside, and raised his eyes to the figure in front of him.

"This amount of money would destroy my business," said Pons. "My family would be saved from death by sorcery only to die from starvation."

"I was told to say that the money was never yours, and therefore you will have lost nothing. And that you have until All Saints' to pay."

"To whom do I pay it?" asked Pons.

The woman shook her head. "I do not know. You will be told."

Before he could speak again, she turned and fled, out of the room and down the stairs.

TWELVE

Berenguer de Cruilles sent for Bernat sa Frigola, scribe, secretary, and administrative officer to the diocese, early on Saturday morning and presented him with the task of writing down and helping to order the Bishop's thoughts on the crisis in the city in two fiery sermons, one for Sunday, the second for Wednesday, Sant Narcis Day.

"I cannot do it, Bernat. When I think of the stupidity of it all, I can only shake my head and put down my pen. Between whoever is spreading this superstitious pagan nonsense, and all the credulous believers in it, it will be the end of the city. Rescuing it from outside attackers, as Sant Narcis did so handily, seems a simpler task," said the Bishop, "than trying to rescue it from certain ruin at the hands of its own citizens. If they were tearing it apart stone by stone, they couldn't do a better job of destroying it from within."

"Indeed, Your Excellency," said Bernat, a man who kept his private opinions to himself. "Do you wish that to form part of Wednesday's sermon?"

Berenguer thought for a moment. "Somehow, we must convince them that they are damaging more than supposed witches and sorcerers. We could begin with that," he said. "After a suitable text."

"Perhaps a tale, Your Excellency," said Bernat quietly. "Something that illustrates rot from within. That will be understood by all."

"Do what you can, and bring me something this afternoon."

"Yes, Your Excellency. Francesc Monterranes is waiting to see you."

"A sermon?" said Francesc, once their business had been transacted. "Do you think that a sermon will solve the problem?" The disbelief in his voice was just a trifle short of disrespect.

"You do not agree, then, do you, Francesc?"

"No, Your Excellency, I do not. But it can do no harm, and—"

"And it will relieve my anger. That is a bad reason for preaching, Francesc."

"I was not intending to suggest that, Your Excellency," said Francesc. "I was about to say that it will instill valuable lessons for the future in some minds, even if it does little to solve the current problem."

"Cold comfort, Francesc. But I accept it. Poor Bernat has had to put aside his other tasks and is struggling with the sermons now. I had thought of asking you to work on them with me, but—"

"I think not, Your Excellency. Bernat is skilled in casting difficult ideas into clear and simple words. I am not."

"You are oversubtle, Francesc, and too adept a logician to address the common man."

"And I cannot write with ease in the common speech. I am no storyteller, which is why I keep accounts, and hear disputes instead of preaching the fear of God into crowds of awestruck believers."

"This is your suggestion for the first sermon, Bernat?"

"Yes, Your Excellency. It is short, and I realize that the

tale is not quite what you were looking for. If you prefer, I can work on another."

"No. Not at all. This will do very well."

The Bishop took his place, his face grim, and looked out over his congregation. The people had crowded into the cathedral in a holiday mood, all ready to take on a little spiritual polish before celebrating a great deal of hard work with an equal amount of intense feasting and merrymaking. There was much rustling, and movement, and whispering together, but as the silence from the pulpit lengthened, an uneasy hush settled on the crowd. *"Consilia impiorum fraudulenta,"* said Berenguer. "The counsels of the wicked are deceitful. Wise words for those who have the wit to hear them. Today we begin our celebration of the feast of Sant Narcis. I will say more on his feast day about the saint, and how he saved the city, and what that means in terms of our spiritual life, but for today, I shall talk about the counsels of the wicked.

"You know the tale of the king, who on seeing that he was close to death, gathered his family together to divide his possessions. To his eldest son he gave the kingdom his own father had left him, and to his second son, he gave the lands he had won with his sword. To his third son he gave three treasures. These he left with his queen, trusting her to guard them until she judged the boy wise enough to receive them. When the king died, the queen gave the boy the first treasure, a ring that made its wearer so lovable that whatever he asked for, he would receive. She also warned him that a woman would try to steal it from him.

"He put on the ring, and went out into the plaza. There he met a woman of incomparable beauty and grace. She begged him prettily to let her put on his ring, promising to guard it well and return it at once. He confided its secret to her, and placed it on her finger. Within moments she was gone. The boy returned to his mother in tears.

"Next, his mother gave him a jeweled collar that granted the wearer anything that his heart wished for. He met the same woman passing through the city gate. She saw the beautiful collar and threw herself at his feet, confessing to the loss of his ring, and weeping bitterly. He raised her up, and showed her the collar he had to replace the ring. With sweet smiles, she took it off his neck, put it on her own, and ran off.

"When the boy went back to his mother, she warned him that his father had left him only one more gift. It was a richly embroidered cloth that would transport those who sat on it wherever they wished to go. He took it to his wayward beloved, spread out the cloth, and invited her to sit with him. He wished them to the farthest ends of the earth, and at once they were alone in a forest, their only company the wild beasts. 'How clever!' said his beloved. 'How did you do that?' He told her. She sat beside him on the cloth, putting her head in his lap, and waited until he was asleep. Then she pulled the cloth out from beneath him, and wished herself back to their native city, leaving the young prince to the wild beasts.

"The treacherous woman represents those who foment riot amongst you, who offer you the deceitful counsels of the wicked. Those who spread lies, and rob you of your innocence and good name. You, people of Girona, are the foolish prince, listening to the voices of evil seducers. I have heard the rumors being spread of evil coming to the city; let me assure you that the evil is here, now, and it does not come from outside. It is within your hearts. Who else but you injured those helpless innocent women? No outsider, but one of you, was responsible for the death of one of your neighbors. You have spread lies with diligence about honest citizens." He paused to clear his throat, shook his head, and continued. "You are beloved by your heavenly Father who has given you every treasure: stout walls, rivers teeming with fish, abundant forests, vines, and groves. Your beloved saint, like the wise queen in our tale, watches over the city, rescuing you from attackers outside the walls, and yet again and again you do your best to ignore wise counsel, and destroy that which you love from within. Be warned, that your slanders, and threats, and attacks on the innocent will bring down not only the wrath of our king, but the wrath of God. It would be fitting punishment if you were, like the young prince, left to the claws and fangs of the wild beasts.

"But his Father in heaven, who forgives and forgives again, gave the prince one last chance to return to his native city and regain the stolen gifts. This may be your last chance to cease your evil behavior and retain the bounty we have been given."

"In nomine Patris, et Filii, et Spiritus Sancti. Amen."

And the Bishop of Girona, his cheekbones splashed with red from anger, turned from his startled congregation toward the altar.

The population of the city took the Bishop's homily as much to heart as such populations always do. Those the least at fault searched their consciences painfully, remembering pieces of gossip they had listened to in the past year, and determining not to fall into that temptation again. Those most at fault nodded, and felt virtuous, and agreed with the Bishop that they were surrounded by vile and malicious neighbors. A few were troubled in their hearts, remembering things they had said. But fortunately for everyone's peace of mind, the festivities that started the next day blew away such troubling thoughts.

From almost every house came intoxicating scents from preparations for Wednesday's great holiday. Cauldrons simmered; the bakers' ovens burned hot and long, roasting meats. Everyone in the town prepared to call on friends and neighbors, bearing baskets of delicacies, as grand as they could afford. But in a few houses the mood was somber, and there was no laughter. Pons Manet and his wife and son grieved over the loss of child and brother, and had no heart for eating or drinking; the husband of the pretty woman struck by the stone sat by his unlit hearth, and puzzled over the enigma of her death. Why had his neighbors thought her a witch? What had she done? Would they

think him a sorcerer? And fear, more than the chill of his
little house, made him tremble, and wonder whether it
would be better to cast himself off the great tower now
than to wait for what might come.

Across the river, on the fairgrounds, the artisans and
entertainers and sellers of everything from bright ribbons
and cheap trinkets to horses and mules and cattle of all
kinds were pouring in, setting up stalls, grumbling, and
cursing at the weather and the state of fairground and the
well-known miserliness of the population, as they silently
reckoned up the astronomical profits they confidently expected this week to bring them.

In the Jewish Quarter, Isaac the physician's house was
relatively quiet. Ibrahim and Leah had taken the twins to
watch the excitement of the fair being set up; Judith and
Naomi were in the kitchen, wrestling with a dinner that
would satisfy them all when they returned home. Isaac was
examining the supplies of herbs and tinctures in his study.
In general, he was his own apothecary, distilling and grind-
ing and mixing what he needed for his patients. Some ingredients, however, coming from across the sea, had to be
sent for from Barcelona, and that was best done before
winter rains and bad weather slowed shipping and muddied
the roads.

Isaac picked up each item, judged its weight and state
of freshness, and Raquel replaced it where it belonged.
"We are only lacking some of the common herbs, lord,"
said Yusuf, who had been tallying. "We can gather them
this morning, before the sun grows too hot."

"Excellent, but you must go alone, Yusuf. Raquel will
stay here with me. When you return she will check what
you have gathered to make sure that you have made no
mistakes."

This time Raquel did not protest.

Some of the most fragrant and most powerful herbs grew
on the steep hillsides to the north of the city. According
to tradition, they must be gathered on a cool morning after

the dew has dried on the grass, but before the sun has sucked their juices out of them. The moon must also be on the wane. "Are these things true?" Yusuf had asked.

"I do not know," Isaac had said. "They may be. People have long believed them to be. And it does no harm to gather them at the most propitious moment if you can."

And so, it being a cool morning, with the dew off the grass and the moon where she should be, Yusuf was not alone on the hillside. Not all of the usual gatherers were there, since the holiday mood had already enveloped the town, but he recognized Hasan's basket, almost as tall as the boy himself, and behind it, Hasan stooping down to pluck something.

Yusuf looked around to see if the boy had been accompanied before he spoke. "Hasan," he called, in a carrying whisper. "It's Yusuf, over here."

"I can't stop and talk," said the other boy. "I must fill this basket."

"Does the quality matter?" asked Yusuf.

"Not at all," said Hasan with a grin. "We burn them to impress the customers. And Marieta takes some of them for the kitchen."

"Then I will help you. I will take the best plants, for that is what we need. The rest you can have."

And for an hour they roamed the hillsides, moving farther and farther east until they were almost at Sant Daniel. By then they had scoured the heights and the valley, and gathered plants that loved growing in the cool damp soil by the stream as well as those that preferred sun and air. Both baskets were filled, and Yusuf took out the loaf stuffed with boiled lamb and rich sauce that Naomi had prepared for him, to keep him going until dinnertime, and broke it in half.

"I tell you, Yusuf, that I cannot stand this life any longer," said Hasan, biting into his share of the loaf.

"What has happened?"

"My master's servant makes my life unbearable. I have bruises all over my back and legs from his stick. He beats me, and kicks me, and locks me in a small room sometimes for a day and a night with only a jug of water to drink, and nothing to eat.''

"What did you do to make him so angry?" said Yusuf, interested. It had been his experience that every action, no matter how unpleasant, had its cause.

"Nothing. One of the girls said that a customer told her I was getting old and ugly. And so he did that."

Yusuf turned and looked at him carefully. "How old are you?" he asked.

"I'm not sure," Hasan said. "No one ever told me. Perhaps fourteen. But I am growing."

"What does your master say?"

"He says it isn't important, and gives me a sweetmeat, and then turns his back the next time I am beaten."

"I would run away," said Yusuf.

"That's easy to say," said Hasan, "but how do I do it?"

"There's nothing to stop you from leaving," said Yusuf. "You are not in chains. You could go right now."

"But I would starve," he said, appalled.

"There are people seeking workers. Always. You wouldn't starve."

"I would be taken by another trader, and sold again. I know it. I can't leave just like that." He paused, and plucked a stalk of long grass, which he used to clean his front teeth. "There is a way, though," he said. "I've been thinking about it, and I know how I could do it."

"Oh," said Yusuf, stretching out on the grass in the sun, and preparing to listen to another fantasy. "How?"

"If you would take my place."

Yusuf sat up and stared at him. "Me? Slave for your master and his brute of a servant?"

"Just for the evening, during one of the ceremonies. You could take my place, and I could leave. That way I can bring my clothes and the few pennies I've saved that people have given me."

"And at the end of the evening? What do I do then?"

"You can go as soon as your part is over. No one will notice. Once the customers leave, everyone falls asleep from too much wine. They don't wake up until the sun is high the next day. That would give me almost a day to get away before they noticed I was gone."

"Hasan, they will take one look at me and know that you are gone."

"You don't understand, Yusuf," said the boy earnestly. "For the ceremonies I wear a costume and a mask. And no one looks at me—they're too busy with what they're doing. And the light in the hall is so dim, except where the girls are dancing, that they can't see much anyway. You'll understand when you see it. You can fit into the costume, and you're almost my height."

"You're taller than I am. A lot taller."

"We won't be standing together, Yusuf. I'm shorter than all but one of the girls. And so are you. That's all that matters."

"When does this take place?"

"Tomorrow. After sunset."

"I don't know if my master will let me leave for the evening," said Yusuf weakly.

"He won't know. You told me yourself you have no trouble getting out of the house or out of the *Call*."

"But if someone is ill, he will need me."

"You won't be gone long, I promise you," said Hasan. "Please. Do it for me. I can't stand this life, and if you don't, I swear, I'll kill myself."

Yusuf felt a huge lump settle in his belly. "Where do I meet you tomorrow night?"

THIRTEEN

By the time most of the inhabitants of Girona had finished their dinners on Monday, the fair had grown until it swallowed up the town. The riffraff of fairground life, the peddlers, the sellers of cheap trinkets who had no wagons or stands at the fairgrounds, set out their wares on the bridges and in the streets. The idle, the curious, and the gullible gathered wherever the jugglers and tumblers, the magicians and fortune-tellers showed off their skills. The air was filled with the noise of pipes, and tabors, and plucked strings, all playing at odds with one another, and all attracting their own admirers. Anyone living within a day's journey from the city was there, claiming a bed with an uncle, a distant cousin, a long-forgotten family friend. And everywhere, the taverns were filled.

In the noise and bustle and confusion, no one was quite sure where the report started. Some said afterward that it had been brought into the city by a certain Jaume, a trader from Barcelona, who had ridden in that very afternoon. When the said Jaume was found and questioned, he stoutly denied ever having heard such a thing, and certainly denied having said anything so foolish to anyone. Others claimed that it had been disclosed by a fortune-teller with magic powers; that theory was even more difficult to investigate because as soon as the fortune-teller heard a whisper of it, she packed up all her costumes and paraphernalia and disappeared. After much inquiry, it transpired that only one thing was certain. By the time the sun was low in the western sky on Monday, everyone in the city knew that the Infant Johan, their own Duke of Girona, and at three years old most cherished heir to the throne of Aragon, had been bewitched, and was failing fast. On his death, civil war would break out and destroy them all.

"And Joana, wife to Romeu Rains, the joiner, has miscarried," said a woman standing by the bridge. "I have just come from her. Miscarried and for no reason at all."

"Perhaps she was overlooked by a witch," said the person beside her.

"What else could have caused it?" said the first woman.

And in the time a man might walk from one bridge to the other, everyone also knew that three honest women had been overlooked by witches as they came from mass on Sunday. In the very shadow of the cathedral it had happened, and they had all miscarried. Then a farmer sitting over a cup of wine began to talk about his cow who had lost her calf, and another about a stout and healthy sow whose nine farrow had been born dead, not mentioning that this tragedy had happened four years previously.

"Hang the witches!" said a drunken stonemason, who lurched out of a tavern in the south end of the city, blinked in the sunlight, and looked around him for a witch to hang. "Hang them I say!"

Those words lit a flame that raced through the crowd like fire through straw. Answering shouts went up, and the crowds streamed out of the taverns in hopes of finding some exciting action.

The first victim was one Guillema, whose dark hair, glowing richly with henna, painted face, and half-unlaced gown spoke only too clearly of her profession. She had been strolling near the river, close to the south gate, when the crowd drew near her.

Out of it a male voice shrilled loudly, "There's one. She's a witch. A grasping evil woman, and I have proof she's a witch."

She turned, startled, caught the mood of the crowd, and headed in the opposite direction. "Catch her!" said someone farther back in the ranks.

At that, she caught up her skirts and began to run in earnest. Guillema moved quickly, but not quickly enough. A hand grasped at her skirt, caught her surcoat, and held her back a moment. She wriggled free of the captured garment and darted down an alleyway like a frightened doe. But for Guillema, the delay had been deadly. A lad from the country, with a quick eye and a strong arm, used the time to pick up a stone and hurl it after her. It caught her on the head, and she dropped like a dead bird. Whether she was dead or not, no one knew or cared. After the crowd had surged over her, she certainly was.

Some of the wives and daughters of the town, along with their country cousins, trailed along behind, impelled by morbid curiosity and sick with almost pleasurable fear; the rest, appalled and terrified by the roaring crowd, turned and ran for home, dragging their children with them. In minutes the public streets and plazas of the city and its surrounding suburbs were empty except for the rioters. Frustrated in its hunt, and with the smell of blood still in its nostrils, the mob surged northward, pouring up deserted side streets and back down again to the main, like a river that parts on either side of an island and then joins together again.

When the mob reached San Feliu, its leaders caught sight of new prey, a woman whose thick brown hair had tumbled out of its fastenings and whose veil had been lost in her panicked rush for asylum. She was dragging an exhausted child up the steep steps to the San Feliu plaza; the child stumbled, and stumbled again. She stooped and picked it up.

"There she is!" called out a voice. "There's the real witch! Whore! Murderess! Throw her down, and that witch's spawn with her!"

Voices around him argued, but could not be heard in the clamor. The drunken stonemason who had led them in the beginning had been left behind before they had overrun Guillema, and had returned in happy ignorance to his cups. Those now in the lead crowded up to the panting woman. She backed up, and tried to push them away, someone laughed, another pushed from behind to see what was going on. The crowd pressed closer, bearing her upwards until she tipped over the low, broad stone balustrade onto the cobbled plaza below.

Someone said, loudly enough to be heard by those next to the balustrade, "But that was Venguda, the wife of Tomas de Costa."

There was a scuffle in the middle of the steps, and a small dark-haired man broke through. He ran, not in the direction of his wife's broken body, or of the hysterical crying child, but back through the north gate into the depths of the city.

With that discovery, for Venguda had been accounted a pleasant, modest young woman, the energy began to dissipate from the group. Several people at the back of the crowd slunk away, ashamed, or afraid, and the rest wandered up through the streets of San Feliu. Someone whose voice carried better than most said what was in many hearts. "It's all very well, Pere my friend, to tell me to hang witches, but who can tell me who they are?"

"Indeed," said the man next to him. "And if Tomas's wife was a witch, then so could any of our wives be accounted such. I don't believe she was." And the two men fell out of the group, and made their way back toward the city.

In that moment of relative quiet, around the next corner, a door opened and a beautiful, black-haired woman, holding a blond child by the hand, stepped cautiously outside.

"They've gone, I think," she said to someone behind her. The door closed, and she headed quickly across the cobbled street.

A man turned the corner in front of her, and stopped, standing between her and her front door. "It's the physician's daughter," he said. "Yes, it is. I've found the physician's daughter," he cried out loudly, and suddenly what she had assumed to be distant murmur erupted into a very nearby roar and rush of heavy boots.

"Nicholau," screamed Rebecca, and turned to face the crowd.

The man placed his hands on the wall on either side of her, trapping her. "I've been looking for you," he said. "You and your kind."

She tried to back up. There was no room. "Let me pass," she said. The child whimpered, and buried his face in her skirts.

"Oh, no," said the leader. He towered over her. "Look how small she is," he said, raising his voice so that all could hear. "That's what Ramon said. He said it was the physician's daughter, for all she was too small. He forgot the physician had two daughters, didn't he?"

He was answered by a muttering from the diminished crowd behind, muttering that grew louder and louder. "That's what Ramon said," someone called out in relief. "He said it was her. We were right."

"Let me pass," she said again.

"We have business with you, mistress. You'll not go anywhere and kill anyone again."

"Marc de Puig," said Rebecca sharply. "I demand that you let me pass."

He backed up with a look of dismay at losing his sense of anonymity, and then thrust his face close to hers. "We'll have no witches in this town," he said. "We've dealt with two already, and we'll do the same with you." He changed stance, grasping her cloak just under her chin in one large hand, and pushing her against the wall. "Fetch me a rope," he called back triumphantly, "and we'll hang the witch."

But the people behind him, who should have obeyed, had heard what he had not, and that was the sound of hoofbeats from the direction of the city gate. Already the ones in back, those who were still left, were scattering as rapidly as they could. The horses pressed up against the ones who had made the mistake of entering the relatively narrow street, pinning them against the houses and effectively trapping them. A few burst past Rebecca and escaped to the north, scrambling down the steep bank and through the muddy bottom of the Galligans River.

The captain of the Bishop's guard dismounted quickly and bowed. "Mistress Rebecca," he said, with a flourish, for they had met before. "Are you injured?"

"No, not at all," she said. "Just out of breath, and angry, and very relieved to see you." At that, to her eternal annoyance, she burst into tears.

"I will escort you safely home, and then I must deal this drunken rabble here," he said. "They have done a great deal of mischief in no time at all."

By sundown, the city was unnaturally quiet. Those who had come out of their houses for news or gossip had been ordered back inside. The peddlers and entertainers, who had long experience in avoiding the law, had retired discreetly to their camps as soon as trouble started. The gates to the city were closed and barred. None could pass without permission.

At the first sign of rioting, the gates to the Quarter had been locked and barred, and Jacob the gatekeeper stood by the small postern gate with his eye to the peephole, ready to open and close it again for anyone caught outside. Those who had shops and houses with doors through the wall locked them up, and everyone waited.

The officers had collected almost thirty people, some witnesses, some rioters. City officials and the Bishop's guard were engaged in delicate but hostile competition for jurisdiction over the accused, who sat glumly on cold stone benches in the hall beneath the court. For Guillema had died in the city of Girona, but Venguda had fallen to her death in San Feliu, and Rebecca had been attacked there as well. All three at the hands, more or less, of the same now tawdry-looking crew.

"I knew that this would happen," said Berenguer to the captain of the guard.

"I accept the blame for those deaths," said the captain in a dispirited voice. "We expected this, but we were not fast enough, Your Excellency. As soon as we had word, we rode out to intercept the mob." He shook his head. "There was great confusion about the site of the trouble, and we were misdirected at first."

"I believe the mob kept changing direction," observed the Bishop.

"It did. Each time it saw a likely victim. We did not run it to ground until two women were dead."

"But, remember," said the Bishop, "that you took those most responsible, and that you prevented one certain death, and no doubt others with your swift reaction. That is not a meager achievement."

The captain shook his head. "You give me too much credit. They were beginning to sober up on their own by the time we reached them. That is why Mistress Rebecca is still alive. She spoke to them very sharply, and instead of killing her then and there, that wretch Marc de Puig stopped to talk back. She's a brave woman." He shook his head. "But then, she had her child with her, and that can make a woman as brave as a lion."

"Well—you shall have your way. Mistress Rebecca saved herself, and the riot ended of its own accord, and your men did nothing."

"We did round up the leaders. And you are right. For that, we deserve some praise, Your Excellency. What will happen to the fair?" he continued quickly, before the Bishop could respond.

"I have spoken already to the members of the council. We are in agreement, I believe. To shut down the fair would cause great hardship to the honest merchants and traders who journey here for it, and for those here who depend on this opportunity to trade with them. It would also cause profound discontent in the city and the diocese. We cannot allow it to open until those men are tried tomorrow morning, but if all is calm, they may begin an hour before noon. The council agrees," he added, leaving no doubt in the captain's mind who had won that particular jurisdictional squabble. "Closing it for this evening and tomorrow morning is sufficient to impress on everyone's mind that what happened was very wrong."

And shortly thereafter, the council that governed the Quarter was meeting at the house of Bonastruch Bonafet.

"A messenger has just arrived from the Bishop with news," said Mahir Ravaya, who walked into the room carrying a folded and sealed paper. Without delay, he broke the seal, smoothed out the paper and began to read. "The council of the city has met with the Bishop. The city is under curfew and the instigators of the riot have been apprehended."

"How can the councillors know that, unless they were there when it started?" said Vidal Bellshom wryly. "Surely they mean that they hope that the instigators have been apprehended."

"You are too pessimistic, Vidal," said Isaac. "Let us hope that they are correct in their confidence. Does the letter give the extent of the damage? So far, I have been told variously that no one, or perhaps ten people, or six women were killed."

"I will see," said Mahir, turning over the page in his hand. "Two women were killed. Guillema, a prostitute, was killed by a stone thrown by a young man named Bernat, who is being pursued. Venguda, wife of Tomas de Costa, was pushed off the steps of San Feliu by five men. Do you want their names?"

"We don't need them right now, do we?" asked Vidal.

"Certainly not. Anyone may see the letter. And then Maria Rebecca, wife of Nicholau Mallol, scribe"—Mahir stopped and then quickly read on—"was accosted and attacked by Marc de Puig, but resisted long enough for the guard to come to her rescue. She was not injured."

The room fell silent. Everyone glanced at Isaac. Bonastruch poured a glass of wine and pressed it into his hand. "It is good to know exactly what did happen," said Bonastruch. "Thank you. What else is in the letter, Mahir? We need to know what is going to happen in the next day or two. We have to decide what action we should take."

Mahir picked up the paper once more. "The decision of the council and the Bishop is that the fair not be opened until after the trial of the rioters, which will take place tomorrow morning. The city gates will open tomorrow morning as usual. And that is all that it contains except for the list of those killed that I read earlier."

"When do we open our gates?" asked Vidal.

Isaac pushed aside his untasted glass of wine. "My suggestion is that we keep the gates closed until the trial is over and people have time to hear of the verdict. If they are going to riot again, that is when they will do it. If they are quiet, they will probably stay quiet."

"And those houses that have access?" said Astruch des Mestre.

"I would advise them to keep those doors barred as well."

"I am a more cautious man, perhaps, than some," said Bonastruch. "I agree that we should stay tightly locked and barred until after the trial, but then open up gradually. If the city is quiet in the afternoon, the bakers may open their outer doors to sell bread outside, and anyone who has pressing business may go out and come in by the postern gate, where the porter would be standing by to bar it at the first sign of trouble. And I suggest that we stay that way until daybreak on Wednesday. Fortunately, this is not a week of great business."

"I agree," said Mahir Ravaya.

"And I," murmured the sixteen other men around the table.

The mist was still heavy on the river, and the morning air damp and cold, when the trial began. When all the witnesses had been questioned, and their depositions painstakingly recorded, five men had been charged. On that chilly, gray morning, after a night with no sleep and a miserable breakfast, they were hustled into the court to face a panel of three judges in all their splendor, headed up by the acute intelligence and terrifying countenance of Francesc Adrober. The remaining detainees had been stuffed into a small room where they were awaiting their turn as witnesses. Despite the earliness of the hour, the little courtroom was filled.

Five witnesses had been found who claimed to have had nothing to do with any rioting, but had heard the rumors that had started the drunken stonemason off.

"Yes, my lord," said a woman who had been screaming encouragement at the mob the afternoon before, but who now looked the model of domestic virtue, "everyone was very upset because of the Infant Johan—"

"Does the witness understand that there is no truth in that rumor?" interrupted Francesc Adrober in his severest tone. "And that such rumors are very damaging to civil peace?"

"Yes, my lord," she said, looking cowed at last. "And then the stonemason said witches should be hanged. He went outside, and everyone ran out looking for witches. He followed them for a while, but he was too drunk, and so he came back to the tavern."

"Where were you?" asked the examining judge.

"I came back, too. They were throwing stones and everything they could and I came back."

"And who suggested that Guillema was a witch?" asked the examining judge.

"Uh—" The woman looked around at all the people in panic. "I'm not sure."

"Mistress, you made a statement under oath last night giving a name," said Francesc Adrober. "I have that statement here. If you don't wish to go to prison for—"

"It was Pere Vives."

"Thank you. Who is our next witness?" he asked, turning to the examining judge.

"One Miquela, my lord," murmured a clerk. "She was a friend and coworker of the deceased woman."

Miquela lacked the bold look of her colleague, and in dress and demeanor looked more like an overworked housemaid than a woman of the streets. As, in fact, it turned out that she was.

"No, my lords," she said in a terrified voice. "I am only the maid. I sweep the rooms and cook sometimes for the—"

"Indeed," said Francesc, in gentle tones that astonished those who had not observed him at work before. "We understand. You had nothing to do with the customers."

"Only I let them in," she said.

And the chief of the justices continued on, in the same manner. "And were you a particular friend to Guillema?"

"Yes, Your Lordship," she said, staring at him like a bird at a snake. "We were from the same village. She was nice to me—nicer than the others."

"I see. And did any of the men standing there," he said, nodding at the prisoners, "visit Guillema?"

"Yes," she said. "That one. His name is Pere. He visited her many times. And last week he refused to pay her, and when she complained, he kicked her and punched her, and we had to call for Johan—he works there, too—and he threw him out. And then he came back two days later, and we wouldn't let him in, and he said he'd get even with Guillema, and she'd see she couldn't treat him like that." Then she took a deep breath and turned bright scarlet in the cheeks.

"You've done very well, child," said the august judge. "Were those his very words?"

"They were, my lord. I remembered because I was so

frightened. And others heard, too. You can ask them."

"Thank you. You may go. Who is next?"

And the rest of the morning was taken up with the sad tale of Venguda and Tomas. The court heard of her two great crimes in her husband's eyes, that she was barren, and that she had taken in her dead sister's child, causing her husband to incur great expense. And then of Tomas's claim in his defense that she flew about the house at night, and that she had cast a spell on him to render him impotent. The crowd stirred.

"I believe we have a witness who can clarify that statement," said Francesc Adrober. "Do we not?"

The woman who stood before the panel of judges looked as if she had had some experience in a courtroom. She gave her name boldly, in a clear voice, and looked the judges directly in the eye. But she answered their questions in a straightforward way, like someone with a clear conscience.

"Will you tell the court what you know of Tomas de Costa?"

"He visited me several times, Your Lordship," she said. "For the usual purposes of my trade. And I can attest that he was indeed impotent. As can the other girls he has gone with."

"And when was that?" asked the judge.

"He started to come to see me in the year of the famine, Your Lordship," she said. "And for some time after that."

"That was ten years ago," he said.

"Indeed, Your Lordship. It was all of that. And as everyone knows, he never married his poor wife until after the year of the Black Death. It's no wonder she never had a child."

A repressed explosion of titters and nervous giggles ran around the courtroom.

"She witched me way back, then. Before we were wed," shouted Tomas.

The clerk murmured something to the judges. "When

she was ten years old, living two days' ride away, in a convent?" asked one of them.   .

The judges withdrew briefly, and returned with their verdict. Marc de Puig was considered directly responsible for Venguda's death; Bernat, whose name and location were still being sought out, for Guillema's death. They were sentenced to hang. The stonemason was fined five sous for his part. Tomas de Costa and Pere Vives were fined fifteen sous apiece for inciting the crowd, and told that they were enormously lucky to escape hanging.

On the whole, except for the four accused present in court, everyone thought it a good verdict. Marc was not loved, no one knew Bernat, and the other three, it was felt, probably had more money than they had ever admitted to. What Bernat thought is still unknown, for he never came anywhere near the city of Girona again.

FOURTEEN

A brooding, restless quiet hung over the city on Tuesday morning. Even the caged birds were silent in the house of Isaac the physician, where only the murmur of Yusuf's soft voice reading his lesson could be heard. It filled every corner, like the maddening, persistent buzzing of insects on a hot day, jarring on ears that strained to detect signs of danger. Raquel wandered from room to room, seeking employment or amusement, anything to take her thoughts from the world outside. Since the first rumors of women dying in the riots had reached her, she had been silently resolved to accept her confinement to the *Call,* even to accept her father's concern over her behavior and dress, with quiet filial obedience. But the resolution did not make the day any easier to bear.

She picked up her needle and some long-neglected work, put in a long, badly placed stitch, and set the work down again. She was too distracted to sew, and stopped to consider what really needed to be done. With a pang of guilt, she thought of the reading her father had asked her to do. As soon as she heard Salomó the tutor depart, she hastened to the library, and took down two heavy medical books, a volume by Isaac Israeli and Arnau de Vilanova's

Speculum medicinae. She would devote the entire day to them, searching for maladies or substances that might have caused the odd group of symptoms suffered by the three young men who had just died.

And in the courtyard below, Isaac stopped his wife as she was hurrying from the storeroom to the stairs, intent on household tasks that could not be ignored, no matter what was happening outside their gates.

"Judith, my love," said Isaac, "I must speak to you for a moment. Somewhere where Raquel is not likely to be listening."

"She is by the fire in the library," said her mother, "When the sun warms the courtyard she will doubtless carry her books down here."

"We won't be that long. Come into the study."

Judith sat down near the table, and watched her husband as he moved to and fro, picking up objects and carefully setting them down again. "What is it, Isaac, that you hesitate to say to me?" she said, unable to bear the silence any longer.

"I do not hesitate," he said, turning to her and smiling. "I only collect my thoughts. Last night I spoke to you of two unfortunate women who died in the riot. What I did not say—what I could not speak about, even to you, at that moment—was that a third woman had been set upon by that terrible mob of fools and drunkards. Instead of fleeing, as the others had tried to do, she turned on them with great courage, demanding that they leave her alone. We must suppose that they were startled by her refusal to be afraid, since they backed away, and spent some time trying to justify themselves. It was most fortunate for the young woman, because in those few moments the guard arrived and rescued her. She was frightened but not injured." Isaac stopped, and resumed his pacing back and forth.

"Why are you telling me this?" Judith said in a whisper.

"She was with her child, a boy of two years of age. They came across her as she was trying to return home. She thought the mob had passed by. Some of this I learned at the meeting last night, and the rest in a message from the Bishop."

"Why did the Bishop send this message to you, Isaac?" asked Judith, her voice trembling with fear.

"Because the young mother was Rebecca, Judith. Do you understand? The woman who stood up so bravely to the rioters was Rebecca. Our daughter. Our firstborn. And she was with our grandson. They were looking for a rope to hang her with when the guard overpowered them."

And Judith burst into bitter, racking sobs.

A vague murmur from outside the walls of the Quarter was the first sign that the trial was over and normal life was beginning to resume in the city. Mossé opened his door cautiously, saw a few peaceful-looking people going about their business, and set out his baskets. Soon trade was almost as brisk as usual, for man must have bread to eat, even in times of riots and hangings, and he expects to find it at the baker's.

Taverns opened with equal caution, one by one. The jugglers and musicians and even the fortune-tellers edged carefully out of their camps and into the town, and very slowly, the holiday mood returned. By late afternoon, the fair was back in full swing.

Yusuf had spent the day in a torment of indecision. Somewhere, deep in his belly, he was convinced that going to Marieta's tonight could be the most disastrous mistake of his young life. But Hasan would be expecting him, confident that he would come and allow him to make his final dash for freedom. At last, Yusuf crept into the library, and taking out pen and paper, wrote, in his best, somewhat wobbly hand, a brief note to Raquel, explaining where he was, and why. He considered what to do with it, and finally set it down on the middle of his bed.

Then, without much zeal for the task, he sought out his master, and asked permission to eat his supper early and leave the Quarter for an hour or two. To help a friend.

"You sound loath to do it, Yusuf. Is this your friend Hasan?"

"It is, lord. He has a heavy task to complete tonight, and before asking your permission, I foolishly promised I would help him with it."

"Then you must go. A promise made must be fulfilled."

"Yes, lord."

"But be careful out on the streets tonight. The mood of the revelers could turn ugly again."

"Yes, lord. I will be as careful as I know how."

"That is all I ask."

When Yusuf slipped through the postern gate into the town, he entered another world. The streets were filled with torches and the cries of vendors carrying baskets of grilled meats, and roasted nuts, and other sweet and savory foods. Musicians on each side of the river seemed to be engaged in a life-and-death competition to drown each other out. Young unmarried women slipped into the crowds and away from the watchful guard of mother or aunt to join in the impromptu dancing along the cobbled streets. In all that cheerful confusion, he glided unnoticed into San Feliu, along the road by the river, and then up to the back gate of Marieta's establishment. It was unlocked, and off the latch. He pushed it open very gingerly. The hinges were as silent as water on a windless day; someone had had the foresight to oil them very recently.

Across the yard, a black silhouette was framed in the dim light of a doorway. "Where have you been?" it whispered, in Hasan's voice. "I thought you weren't coming."

"My master needed me," murmured Yusuf. "And the crowds in the street are very great. Where is the costume that I must put on?"

"It's on me, you fool!" snapped his friend. "Can't you see?"

"Not well, with all the light behind you. Can we go inside?"

"We must be quiet." He grasped Yusuf by the hand and pulled him through the door. He drew it almost shut behind them, and then pulled aside a curtain on their left. Behind it was a collection of baskets, wine jars, cushions, and incense burners. "Stand there," he said, pushing Yusuf into the farthest corner and then disappeared through the opening in the curtain.

He seemed to be gone for hours. In the distance, Yusuf could hear the murmur of voices, with occasional bursts of loud male laughter, answered by high-pitched little laughing shrieks. Then a set of footsteps, quick and hard, clattered across the tiles. "Where is that wretched boy?" said a woman's voice, not two paces away from where he stood. Yusuf shrank down into his corner, trying to melt into the shadows.

A hand flicked the curtain back for an instant and then let it go again. The footsteps clattered off again, and Yusuf drew in a breath of relief.

Through the curtain he saw a flickering light approach, and he shrank back again. The curtain moved once more, and Hasan came back into the little storeroom, carrying a tallow candle clutched in his hand. Yusuf clutched his mouth to stifle a burst of laughter. "What have you got on?" he asked at last.

"This is the costume," said Hasan. "Put it on, and carefully, because it cost a great deal of money, and if you tear it, they will notice at once." He stuffed the candle into a dirty candlestick and set it down on a wooden chest. He raised his hands and carefully removed his turban. "When I grew too big for all this, my master was going to sell me anyway, because it's cheaper to buy a smaller boy than to make a bigger costume," he said. "That's what happened to the boy before me. So I have to leave now, do you understand?"

Yusuf murmured something intended to be understanding, and returned to his examination of the costume he was to wear. The headdress was more a hat than a turban, he decided. It was large, and padded, and glittered with gold, or some like substance. Below it was a half mask of scarlet and yellow. Otherwise, the boy was dressed in a red tunic, with a whole shopful of brass ornaments stitched onto it. His hose were a saffron yellow in color, and were embroidered with scarlet patterns that snaked up the sides of his legs. The effect was unfortunate, making him look as if he were in the clutches of the monstrous tentacles of some fabulous beast. His feet were crammed into scarlet slippers, adorned with more brass.

It was the work of a moment, however, for Hasan to shed this particular false skin and put on his everyday tunic. He handed the elaborate hose to Yusuf, as if to prod him into action. "Hurry," he said. "Take off your tunic and hose and leave them in the corner. Put these on."

And working with feverish haste, Yusuf clad himself in the bizarre costume. "You will do well enough," said Hasan, picking up the candle and examining Yusuf. He set it down again and retied the yellow cord around his waist. "There. That's better."

"What do I have to do?"

"All the supplies are kept in here. I've moved most of them out to be ready for the ceremonies. I lit the braziers for you, but you'll have to do the rest as it goes along. This is what happens."

And speaking in a whisper, at top speed, he ran through a list of instructions.

The voice that had almost discovered Yusuf earlier called out again. "Ali!" she said. "Hurry! We must begin."

"We have to go," he said. "She's looking for me."

"Why does she call you Ali?"

"They all do. They call all Muslim boys Ali. They say it's easier than remembering my name when they're in a hurry. I hate them." Hasan left the candle burning on the chest, snatched up a bundle that lay hidden behind a wine jar, and pulled Yusuf out into the passageway. "Come with me," he said.

"Why not go up those stairs?" asked Yusuf, pointing to a circular staircase across from the storage alcove.

"We'd be caught," said Hasan shortly. He pulled Yusuf into a considerable passage that ran the length of the house. Hasan's scarlet slippers were too large for Yusuf's feet, and they slapped on the stone floor; the two boys pattered noisily along to the end of the passage, where there was another set of stairs. "Up there," murmured Hasan. "When you get to the top you'll see a doorway with a curtain over it. It leads to the ceremonies room. The things you'll need are up there. Stay in the shadows, and keep your head down. They don't like to be stared at."

And who are they? wondered Yusuf as he hurtled up the stairs and stopped outside the arched doorway covered with rough brown cloth.

Facing him was a much wider curtain that formed a fourth wall to the area at the top of the stairs, turning the space into a small room. The first thing he had to find out was how to leave quickly in case of trouble. He moved silently over and pulled the wide curtain back far enough to look out. The hall in front of him was empty. He was on street level now, as far as the front of the house was concerned, for, like most houses in the city and suburbs, this one was built into a hill. A long passage, decorated with sundry benches, chairs, and small tables, and lit by candles in wall sconces, stretched from the front door on his left, to the top of the other staircase, on his right. While he was observing it all with interest, the door across the hall was suddenly pulled open, and he ducked back rapidly. He took a deep breath and slipped through the curtained archway into the room where the ceremonies were to be held.

Whatever he might have expected, it was not what he saw in the scene in front of him. His first impression was of space and darkness. The entrance he had used was in the back wall of the room. The only light came from four candles on the wall, all near the front, where the participants were gathering. The room was long, with an arched ceiling, supported by two large pillars that divided it roughly in half. Six large, well-stuffed cushions, arranged in a semicircle between the pillars, were sitting on a rug of some dark stuff. In front of each was a brazier filled with glowing coals. Another brazier sat on the far side of a curious circle drawn on the tiles of the floor. He moved as quietly as he could up the far wall to see what it was. A cloying, choking smoke rose from the braziers, filling his nostrils as he drew closer.

The circle, about three paces in diameter, had been drawn in black. Inside it was a large triangle, and inside that a five-pointed star. Around the edges there was a motley collection of symbols, some drawn from astrology, some from more arcane sources, and some perhaps from no source at all but Hasan's fertile imagination. Two large seven-branched candelabra, holding massive candles, only a little burned down, stood on the far side of the circle, about three paces apart from each other.

Four of the cushions were occupied at the moment by men of various ages, all of whom appeared to Yusuf to be in various stages of the more cheerful sort of intoxication. They had clearly come in from the fair, where they had been having a raucous time, and were determined to continue until they could no longer stand. One turned to his neighbor and whispered something in his ear. The neighbor laughed and jabbed the other in the ribs in merry camaraderie, and then lurched to his feet.

"By all the saints, you're right, friend. We didn't come here to sit on a cushion," he called loudly. "Let's begin."

And the other three added their voices to the cry. "And more wine," called one of them. "We're perished with thirst."

"And lonesome," said another, throwing his arm around the man next to him and grasping him in a great bear hug.

At that moment two more men came through the door near the front, and looked around the room in some confusion. Yusuf took a deep breath, and decided it was time to act. He bowed, almost lost his headdress, and escorted them to the remaining two cushions.

"Are those things for us?" asked one of them.

"And we thought we'd get a nice soft lap to sit in," said the other. The rest guffawed with laughter.

Yusuf had no intention of speaking, no matter what happened. His voice was not at all like Hasan's. One word and he would be discovered at once. He put his hands together and bowed again, as deeply as he could, deftly retrieving his shifting headdress once more.

"We can wait five minutes," said one of them, laughing, and the two newcomers sat down. The man on his feet tried to do the same, tripped, and sprawled over his cushion, much to the delight of the rest.

"What's that thing?" asked one of the newcomers, pointing at the circle on the floor. Yusuf placed his hands together, raised them to his lips in a gesture of silence, and fled to the back of the room.

Hasan had told him that his first task was to light the candles. Then as soon as the Magus arrived, he was to add a spoonful of the mixture in the clay jar to each of the braziers in front of the cushions.

He could see no clay jar. Perhaps it was still in the storeroom, and he was supposed to run back to get it. He moved back and forth, searching, in a quiet and desperate panic, until finally, in the darkest corner of the back of the room, where he had looked twice already, he saw a squat, dull brown jar. Beside it were a tin spoon and a taper for lighting the candles. He picked the taper up hurriedly, lit it from the flame of the wall sconce nearest him, and walked with as much dignity as he could manage up to the front of the room.

He touched the taper to the first candle, and a great cheer went up from the men on the cushions, followed by a great many loud remarks that Yusuf did not find amusing. He

could feel his cheeks growing scarlet under his mask, and
his hands trembled so much that he could scarcely light
the last few candles.

When he finished, and returned to his position in the
rear, he could see the effect that was intended. The space
within the circle formed a brilliantly lit stage; the rest of
the room retreated into darkness.

The lighting of the candles must have been a signal. A
tall, thin figure strode into the room, dressed in a long,
narrow tunic. It was black, embroidered around the hem
with many of the symbols that had been drawn on the
floor. With it, he wore a black pointed hat and a gold sash.
He stood at the outside edge of the circle and, directing
all his attention to the empty space within it, began to
chant in a low voice.

"What's that thing?" called one of the audience.

"I'm not paying for him," grumbled another. "I
thought they had girls."

"They do," said a third. "There's one out there who's
worth waiting for, friend."

The Magus glanced at his unruly group and spread his
hands wide in a beseeching gesture. "Protect us, Almighty," he called in a loud voice, "from the spirits that
hover about us."

Then he reached into the stitched-together point of his
sleeve and brought out some substance that he sprinkled
into the brazier in front of him. "And from the spirits
above us." He sprinkled more into the brazier. "And
around us and below us," he cried, his voice rising to a
shriek. Thin, acrid smoke wafted up from the brazier.

He reached into his sleeve again and cast a handful of
something on the coals. "Vile root of mandrake of great
power, and magic hellebore, and all the food of demons I
give you. Spirits, come!" he cried, and raised his hands in
the air. That was Yusuf's signal. He picked up the jar and
carried it up to the front. He dipped the spoon into the
mixture and cast generous amounts onto the glowing coal
of each brazier. The smoke thickened considerably, and

the men coughed with watering eyes and muttered curses. Yusuf dumped the last heaping spoonful onto the sixth brazier, and fled to the back before he began to sneeze.

From the hall behind the room, a drum began to beat, with a soft, persistent rhythm. Yusuf's head began to swim, and something Hasan had said popped out of his memory. "Do it fast, don't breathe in the smoke, and don't give them too much." He had ignored all three instructions. Fresh air, he thought. That was what he needed. He pushed back the curtain covering the rear door, and jumped back in fear. He was face-to-face with a man whose twisted body and scarred face would have engendered terror in almost anyone.

He grabbed Yusuf by the arm and pushed him back into the room. "Where's Romea?" he hissed.

Yusuf shrugged his shoulders.

"Idiot," he said. He raised his hand to box his ear, but dropped it again. "No time," he muttered. "Get to work." And he slipped out again.

The Magus had raised his arms one more time. The drum, which had paused for a while, began again. Yusuf grabbed the jar, and hastened on somewhat unsteady feet up to the braziers in front of the participants. This time he flung a scant half spoonful of the mixture in each as rapidly as possible without taking a breath. Even so, when he came to the sixth person, he realized to his horror that he had used it all.

The next item was the wine. He'd give them wine instead. No—everyone would notice if, instead of more herbs they got a cup of wine thrust into their hands. And so, when the drum stopped, and the Magus raised those skinny hands again, Yusuf rushed up, dipped his spoon into the empty jar, and sprinkled nothing onto each pile of glowing embers.

"What's wrong with you?" snapped the scar-faced man, who had come back in. He grabbed him tightly by the arm and gave him a shake. "You're running around like a nervous cat. You know where Romea is, don't you?

If you've helped her get away," he said, with another painful shake, "I'll strip your Moorish hide right off your back.
Don't just stand there, you fool, get the wine. The girls
are ready to come on."

And with a very unsteady hand, Yusuf poured spiced
wine into six cups that were stacked beside the jar. He
carried them up, two at a time, struggling not to spill too
much as he went. As soon as he handed the last cup to
the last customer, he turned and made a dash for the door.

"Oh no, you don't." The scar-faced man was standing
at the door, and caught him by the arm again. "You'll stay
and pick up those cups. You're not sneaking out of here
to warn her. Or to save your back. I'll be right behind this
curtain," he said, and left. The drum began again. At that,
the droning voice of the Magus rose to a crescendo of
shrieking entreaty or threat, he waved his hands above the
brazier at his feet, and Yusuf, forewarned, shut his eyes
tightly.

Even so, the flash lit up the world on the other side of
his eyelids. When he opened them again, the curtain over
the door in the front of the room was pushed aside. Three
girls, dressed in gauzy material that scarcely covered their
nakedness, ran with bare feet into the circle; three more
scampered in and knelt behind them. They all raised their
arms as if beseeching the Magus, holding them there until
the dazzled eyes of the customers were capable of seeing
them. Between the shock of the flash, and the almost naked
dancers, the audience subsided into an awed silence.

The three in the center began to sway to the rhythm of
the drum, and broke into a complex, but seductive round
dance. Then one tripped, a shout of laughter arose from
the watching men, and the illusion was momentarily destroyed. The dancers looked at each other in panic, and
one of the kneeling girls began to sing, in a thin melancholy treble voice.

"The lovely spirits I have conjured up cannot be lured
out of their circle without gold—or silver, or other coins,"
said the Magus in a loud voice. And somewhat awkwardly,

and drunkenly, but with a good-natured laugh, the men reached into their tunics for their purses and placed some coins on the floor in front of them.

The scar-faced man slipped back in and grasped Yusuf painfully by the arm. "Collect the money," he whispered, "and hurry." He shoved him forward. Yusuf saw his chance, perhaps his only chance. Instead of picking up the money, he skidded rapidly over the tiles to the front of the room and dashed out of the door in front, hoping to get to the stairs.

His way was blocked by a girl of twelve or thirteen, also in a gauzy costume. "Where are you going?" she asked, in Arabic.

"Outside," he replied automatically in the same tongue.

She turned and stared directly into his eyes. "You're not Hasan," she said. "Who are you?"

He looked around wildly. "No one," he said. "Just a friend. He asked me to take his place for tonight. But if I stay any longer—"

"Come here," she said in a whisper, pulling him around the corner and behind another curtain. They were in small room, filled with clothing. "This is where we change. Lup was just in here—he won't come back for a while. Where's Hasan?"

"Gone," said Yusuf, lowering his voice as well. "Out, I mean. He wanted—"

"Good for him," she murmured, holding up her hand to stop him. "I hope he gets there."

"Who are you?"

"Romea. I'm supposed to be playing the flute, but one of them," she said with venom, "tried to grab me and stepped on it, and it's ruined. There's another one in here somewhere."

"Your name can't be Romea," he said. "That's a Christian name."

"I've no time to argue about it now. Lup will back in a minute. Here, give me that hat and the mask—where are your clothes?"

"Downstairs in the little room with the wine jars and things," said Yusuf as he stripped off the offending items.

"Marieta is down there. You'll never make it. Go out the front."

"But my clothes," said Yusuf, appalled.

"I'll bring them to you tomorrow at ten. On the San Feliu steps. Wait for me. Now hurry." And she dragged him out of the little change room, back toward the doorway he had come from. As they approached it, a hand from inside grabbed the curtain and pulled it aside. Romea shoved Yusuf through an arch across the hall and followed him in. Ahead was a set of narrow curving stairs going up to the next floor. "Wait until it's clear," she said, "and then go!" She turned and walked out into the passage, moving with insolent grace.

Yusuf ran up until he was around the first curve and waited.

"Where've you been?" snapped a harsh voice.

"Where do you think? One of that lot tried to get a free sample, and broke my flute. Ali went up to see if there was an extra in my bedroom. I was just going to look in the change room. Tell Maria to sing another chorus."

And then the mournful notes of a wooden flute filled the passageway and drifted up the stairs. Yusuf crept down and looked around the corner. The passage was empty except for Romea, who was standing behind the curtained doorway that led to the front of the room. She lifted one hand from her instrument and gestured imperiously at him to go. He waved and fled, all in scarlet and gold, into the night.

FIFTEEN

Yusuf reached his master's gates out of breath, dizzy, and squirming with embarrassment. His way through the streets had been blocked by drunken louts and rude, outspoken women, hailing him with loud shouts of laughter and obscene suggestions. Now he wanted nothing more than to crawl into bed, and late or not, he would drag Ibrahim from his chamber to let him in. He clenched his teeth and knocked, and then pulled on the bell. He had scarcely settled himself down on his heels to wait when he saw Ibrahim heading across the courtyard.

He scrambled to his feet in astonishment. "I'm sorry to be late," he muttered, staring fixedly at the ground.

"Late?" said Ibrahim, bewildered. He opened the gate sufficiently to let the boy in, and relegated the comment to that vast realm of unanswerable questions that popped into his life every day.

Yusuf bid him good night and fled across the courtyard toward his chamber, fully occupied in wondering what to do about his clothing. He could not walk around in scarlet and brass until Romea brought him his own tunic and hose. If she did. Nor could he go to San Feliu dressed only in his shirt. Perhaps the kitchen boy had something—but Yusuf knew that the clothes on the lad's back were all he owned. Ibrahim might have an old tunic he could borrow. He stopped outside his door, wondering if he should disturb the houseman once more.

Then it occurred to him that something was wrong. A light burned in his master's study. It was not unusual for his master to be awake late at night, but he had never known him to light a candle or a lamp unless other people were in the room with him.

The door opened, and Raquel came out, a candlestick in her hand. "You're back," she said, holding up the candle, and then burst into laughter. "Whatever are you wearing? Helping a friend, indeed! You went to the fair in disguise, didn't you? You shouldn't lie like that, Yusuf."

"Did you find it, Raquel?"

His master's voice from the stairs was the last thing Yusuf wanted to hear at this particular moment.

"Yes, Papa," she called. "I'll bring it. And Yusuf. In fancy dress. I wish you could see him." She dragged him by the arm—the same arm that was bruised and sore from being squeezed and dragged already—across the courtyard and up the stairs, like a huntress bringing back some exotic trophy. She pushed him into the warm and pleasant sitting room, well lit by a fire and an abundance of candles. "Here he is. All in scarlet and gold for the festival!"

"I'm sorry to be so late," said Yusuf in a small voice.

"Late?" said Isaac. "You can't have been gone much more than an hour, can he, my dear?"

"No," said Judith, looking at him in a sort of rigid horror. "He can't."

"An hour," said Yusuf, staring at them. "I thought I had been there half the night."

"You've been gone long enough to lose your clothes," said Judith. "Where are they? And where did you get that costume?"

Yusuf shifted uneasily from one foot to another, aware suddenly of a heaviness in all his limbs and an aching desire for sleep. "It's difficult to explain," he began.

"Try," said Judith.

"Yes, mistress," he said, in a subdued voice. "I was helping a friend. The costume is his. I took his part this evening, and I will get my clothes back tomorrow at ten on the San Feliu steps. But, lord, I saw the Magus and his servant, and the ceremonies that they hold there."

"Guillem de Montpellier?" asked Isaac at once.

"I didn't hear his name. Hasan called him the Magus. Or Master."

"Where were these ceremonies? No." He held up his hand. "I want to hear all about this, but not right now. Are you warmly enough clad?"

"No, he is not," said Judith. "He is wearing a thin, foolish tunic, and is shaking with cold. Sit by the fire, and I shall see what I can find for you to put on. Raquel, come and help. Bring a candle." And mother and daughter swept out of the room, leaving Isaac and his apprentice together.

"Were you at Marieta's in San Feliu?" asked Isaac. "The brothel?"

"Yes, lord," he said miserably. "But not—"

"I didn't ask that. Does your friend Hasan belong to Marieta?"

"No, lord. His master lives there. Marieta uses him to run errands and help in the kitchen. When his master holds the ceremonies, Hasan takes part in them, fetching things, and keeping the braziers alight."

"Tell me about these ceremonies. Quickly, before your mistress returns."

And haltingly, weary and stumbling over his words in the excess of his embarrassment, Yusuf began to describe the events of the evening. As he went on, and Isaac neither exclaimed in shock nor reproached him, he picked up the pace of his narrative.

"You say he sprinkled mandrake root and hellebore on the fire?" said Isaac incredulously.

"No, lord," said Yusuf. "That is what he said he was doing. I think he threw kitchen herbs on the fire. Hasan gathered them to burn to impress the clients. I do not know what those things—mandrake and hellebore—smell like, but there was an odor of sage coming from that brazier.''

Isaac interrupted several more times, making him go back and describe certain things and events more specifically, particularly the circle and the figures drawn on and around it. "That will do for now," he said. "These were not serious ceremonies. Clearly, they were but extra trappings for the raising of prices in the brothel. Still, it is interesting. Tomorrow I shall come with you to pick up your clothes. I would like to speak to this Romea. She sounds like a courageous child." He stopped. "But I think we should bring Raquel as well, to reassure her." Lively footsteps sounded on the stairs to the floor above. "Here comes your mistress, no doubt with armfuls of clothing. Put on something warm, and then go to your rest."

"He shall have some hot soup first," said Judith.

Marieta's household in Sant Feliu was not the first to be stirring on the morning of the feast day of Sant Narcis, but some of its members were up and on their feet much earlier than Hasan had confidently expected. Master Guillem de Montpellier lay groaning on his bed, suffering from a powerful hangover, but his servant was as clearheaded and sharp-eyed as ever. Lup set a cup of black, noxious-looking liquid down beside the Magus. "Drink that," he said. "We have a problem. Your intellect, feeble as it is, might be needed." He left the room, and thrust open the door of his hostess's chamber without knocking. "The boy is gone," he said.

"What boy?" said Marieta, who was not at her best in the morning. "Gone where?" She blinked the world into focus and sat up. "Ali? When?"

"The very same," said Lup. "The kitchen girl hasn't seen him since last night."

"The maids are useless," said Marieta with contempt. "They wouldn't notice if a goat walked into the house. Ask Romea. She'll know where he is."

"I asked her," he said, gently rubbing the scar on his

face. "She said she knew nothing, rolled over, and went back to sleep."

"What do you want me to do?" asked Marieta fretfully. "He was your slave. I have control over mine."

"That girl—that Romea—helped him get away. I know it. And she's lying on her bed up there laughing at us." He shook the bedpost in a spasm of fury. "Something very strange was going on last night. I've never seen Ali behave like that. Running back and forth, nervous as a cat. Usually you have to kick him to get him to cross a room." He stopped to consider the situation, gave the bedpost another, more deliberate shake, and came to a decision. "And she was mixed up in it. It's time to get rid of her."

"Get rid of her? The little bitch cost me a fortune. Besides, the customers like her, and when I can get her working I intend to get my money back from her."

"She can destroy us, Marieta, and if we fall, you come with us."

As full consciousness finally restored her to her normal combative self, Marieta leaned forward, glaring at the scarred face in front of her. "You have no business talking to me like this. Your master and I have a clear understanding—"

"One of my master's flaws is his politeness. He can't tell hard truths to a lady. That's my job." He stepped closer to the head of the bed and leaned over her, his scar livid in his leathery, distorted face.

Marieta gave an involuntary jump backward.

"Get rid of her," he said quietly, "or I'll do it for you. You can sell her today—Sancho is still at the fair, but he's leaving tomorrow for the south—or I'll strangle her and toss her in the river. One way you get some of your money back, and the other you get nothing."

"But she'll fetch twice what that thief Sancho will pay for her," said Marieta, appalled.

"You sell her to Sancho today and get her out of Catalunya, or you'll regret it for what little time remains of your miserable life."

• • •

A short time later the physician climbed the steps leading
to the square of San Feliu, and stopped in the shadow of
the church. "Let us wait here," he said.

"Why, Papa?" asked Raquel.

"We do not wish to be too close to the church on the
saint's day," he said. "Especially if it is filled with people.
It was not a good place to choose for a meeting, Yusuf.
Did you not think of that?"

"Romea set the time and place, and then she fled," said
Yusuf, with a worried frown. "But there is no one
around."

"I cannot hear sounds coming from the church," said
Isaac. "There may be no service now. Do you see the
girl?"

"No, lord," said Yusuf. "Perhaps she is sheltering
around the corner."

"It was foolish of me to bring you this morning, Raquel," said her father. "I worried that the girl would be
too frightened to speak, and hoped your presence might
reassure her. You must promise me that if there is the
slightest possibility of trouble—if more than two or three
people approach us—that you will slip away as unobtrusively as you can."

"Yes, Papa," she said.

"My reason for wanting you here was insufficient considering the possible danger to you."

Considerably subdued, Raquel waited by the balustrade,
looking down on the shabby little houses clustering along
the river and wondering how the people in them lived. Her
father touched her lightly on the arm. "I hear them coming, I think," he said. Raquel turned and saw the apprentice leading a waiflike creature dressed in a gown much
too big for her. In her arms she clutched a large bundle
wrapped in a shawl.

"Lord," said Yusuf, "Romea is here. She has my clothing. Romea, this is my master, Isaac the physician, and his

daughter, Mistress Raquel. They wish to speak to you. You do not need to fear them.''

Romea fell abruptly to her knees in front of the three newcomers. "Master Isaac," she said, "I implore you to help me.''

"Do not kneel," said Raquel in a shocked voice. "Not here, and to us, on the hard cobbles." She reached out a hand to raise her to her feet.

"How, my child?" said Isaac. "And my daughter is right. You must not kneel before me," he added gently. "What can I possibly do to help you?''

The girl rose to her feet with the practiced elegance of a dancer. "I must have my freedom," she said firmly. "I am not trying to run away. My mistress is not a good woman, but she bought me in good faith, and I will repay her. I have my price with me. And my clothes and possessions, as well as Yusuf's.''

"If you have the means to buy your freedom, my child," said Isaac, "why do you need my help?''

"She will not let me go," said Romea. "I know it.''

"How can you be so sure?''

"It has happened before. If I give her the money, she will take it, and then put me in chains and sell me to a trader as a malcontent. She did that last winter to another girl, younger even than I, who had also saved up her price out of gifts from the customers.''

"I see your difficulty. But must it be done today?''

"Yes, Master Isaac. I fear tomorrow will be too late. Today she is in a fury. Hasan has gone, and everyone is as upset as if he were worth a whole chestful of gold. She suspects me of having helped Hasan to run away, and I know she plans to sell me while the fair is on. If that happens, I will never be free. Never," she said, in a voice heavy with despair.

"What do you want us to do?" asked the physician.

"Give me time to get away from this place, which is close to my mistress's establishment, and then take her my price, and tell her that I have gone.''

"And what good will that do?" asked Isaac.

"I do not understand you, Master Isaac," said Romea.

"Your mistress will tell me that the money I am offering her is not even close to your price, and she will accuse me of stealing you. Then, I suspect, she will call the officers, and denounce you as a runaway slave. Did you not realize that it would not be that simple?"

"I cannot go back there," said Romea doggedly, "to be beaten and then sold. I will run away."

"And be dragged back in chains?"

Romea stared bleakly at the ground. "I cannot bear the shame. I will throw myself from the wall rather than go back," she said in a low voice.

Raquel could not keep herself from glancing toward the south, where the city wall towered dizzyingly above them, and then back at the fragile-looking child. She shuddered and pulled her cloak tighter around her shoulders.

"What will you do if you leave your mistress? What can you do?"

"I can sing, and dance, and play the flute," said Romea. "I know that I can earn an honest living."

"Truly?" said Isaac. "I would not like to be instrumental in achieving your freedom for you, only to hear that you have starved to death or worse for lack of honest employment."

Romea looked around nervously, but the four of them were still alone. "There is one, a gentleman, not a wise and learned man like you, master, but kind and generous. He is with a troupe of players. He heard me in the spring at Marieta's, and he told me then that they have need of a girl who can play and sing. They are back now for the fair. He sought me out, and repeated his offer. I believe him to be honest. Or more honest than my mistress. He gave me the extra money I needed for my price," she whispered.

"That may be," said Isaac. He turned away from her until the sun fell on his face, and was silent for some time. The town was hushed, and in the distance they could hear music and laughter, and cattle lowing and the braying of mules from the fairground. At last he turned back in her direction. "There is perhaps one way, Romea—but your name cannot be Romea," he added suddenly.

"No, Master Isaac," she said. "When Marieta bought me, she changed my name to Romea, and told me to say that I was Christian. For there are laws against having Muslim girls in an establishment that is frequented by Christian men. But I am glad that she took my name from me, for my mother named me after a woman of great virtue, and it would shame me to be called by my own name in that place."

"What is your name?" asked Yusuf suddenly.

"Zeynab," she murmured.

"Zeynab," said Yusuf in astonishment. "It is my sister's name. I had not thought that I would ever hear it again. When you are free you will be able to call yourself by it once more."

"Well," said Isaac, "it is possible that she might. But we ought not to stand here all the day. Romea must return to Marieta before she is missed. And she should take your borrowed raiment back with her."

"Return?" said Romea. "To that place?"

"Yes," he said firmly. "Return. If you have the courage to return, then I promise you that by the setting of the sun, you will be free. I must make some inquiries, but if all goes well, you will join your troupe of players. In return, you must take me aside, and tell me all that you know about Marieta. And quickly."

Leaving Yusuf and Raquel to stand at the top of the steps, Isaac and Romea moved away into the shadow of the steep church steps and conferred in low voices for a considerable length of time. At last Romea emerged and handed a bundle of clothing to Yusuf. She reached into her own bundle and took out a small square of cloth that had been tied up around some coins.

"Here is the money that I have saved, Master Isaac,"

she said. "It is exactly what Marieta said would buy my freedom."

Isaac took it from her, and felt the coins through the cloth protecting them. "Good," he said.

"Do you think that is enough?" she asked anxiously. "For I do not have a penny more to add to it."

Isaac tossed the slender bundle in his hand and smiled at her. "I'm sure it is. It may be more than she wants, and if it is, I will return the rest to you later today. Now go back to your mistress, and say nothing of any of this to anyone. That is imperative."

"Yes, Master Isaac," she murmured, and fled down the steps.

"Do you think you can arrange her freedom?" asked Raquel. "From that woman?"

"I am very sure I can," said Isaac. "I understand the language of greed as well as most men. Now come. Since we are in San Feliu, let us stop and visit your sister and her husband, and see how they fare."

"Rebecca? Oh, Papa, that's wonderful," said Raquel. "But Mama . . ." Her voice died away.

"I think your mama may be changing her opinion on the question of your sister," murmured Isaac.

"Mama? Surely not," said Raquel. "But if you will take me there, I promise not to say a word of it to her." She took her father by the arm and pulled him toward the steps. "Oh, Papa, let us hurry. I would so like to see her again, and to see the little boy."

When the moment came to knock at Rebecca's door, Raquel hung back. For three years she had been dreaming of this meeting. Sometimes she fancied herself escaping to the warmth of her elder sister's arms for comfort when she felt alone and misunderstood, and sometimes she imagined herself berating Rebecca in anger for abandoning a young sister who needed her. But now that the meeting was about to happen, there was nothing but confusion in her mind.

She heard the door open, and a familiar voice say, "Papa! I'm so happy to see you. And Yusuf. How are you? Carles has drawn a new horse he wants to show you."

Tears sprang into Raquel's eyes, and she stepped out from behind her father. "Hola, Rebecca," she said tentatively, and then threw herself onto her sister's neck, clutching her like a drowning man.

"Now, now," said Isaac. "If you two are going to cry, let us go into the house. Your neighbors will think some terrible tragedy has struck us, and will spend all day trying to discover what it is."

Keeping one arm firmly around the shoulders of her younger sister, Rebecca pulled her into the narrow hallway of her modest house, followed by Isaac and Yusuf. At the sound of the door closing behind them, she spoke again. "Carles," she called. "Come and see who is here."

A blond-haired boy of almost two and a half years of age, with dark, lively eyes, raced out of the room beside them, and flung himself at his grandfather. Then he turned to Yusuf, dragging him imperiously by the hand back toward the common sitting room, where he had been engaged in some complicated play. At that point his eyes fell on the strange, tall lady standing beside his mother, and he became instantly tongue-tied.

"Oh, Rebecca," said Raquel in an awed voice, "is he yours? Is this my nephew? He is so beautiful."

Rebecca took her son by the hand and led him over to Raquel. "Carles," she said, "this is your aunt, Raquel."

And nephew and aunt looked gravely at each other with eyes that, in shape and expression, were exact mirrors of one another.

"Papa," said Rebecca. "It is amazing."

"What is, my dear?"

"People say that Carles looks very like me, but it is not true. He is the very image of Raquel. But come and sit down. I am so happy to see you. All of you."

And once they were settled, Isaac turned to his eldest

daughter. "I am delighted that I did this—bringing Raquel to see you, my dear—but I am almost ashamed to admit that it was not the reason for my visit. And perhaps that is better. These events are too difficult if they are coldly thought out beforehand."

"Papa, whatever are you talking about?" said Rebecca. "What is your reason for coming that could possibly be more important than seeing Raquel again? Is Mama ill? Has something gone wrong?"

"Not at all," said Raquel. "Mama is as strong and ferocious as ever."

"Oh, dear," said Rebecca. "And I can guess that after what I did, she must suspect you of the worst of motives every time you are out of her sight. I am sorry, Raquel."

"I do wear rather more veils than you ever had to," said her sister, with a laugh, "but the twins are old enough and strong-minded enough to occupy her thoughts for at least part of the time."

"They were just babies when I last saw them," said Rebecca wistfully. "Not much older than Carles."

"Two full years older," said Isaac firmly. "And you asked me why we came. Let me tell you, before you start on an endless stream of family reminiscences. I came to ask when you expected Nicholau home."

"Nicholau?" said Rebecca, and stared at her father in astonishment. Had he come to see her, bringing Raquel, only to inquire after Nicholau? Then her surprise changed to amusement. No other man in the city would have arranged a meeting between the two sisters after such a time—three years—and then dismissed his action so casually. Her father's endless capacity to amaze had always baffled and delighted her. "Very soon, Papa," she said. "That is his braised mutton on the stove in the kitchen, almost ready."

"Excellent, for there is a very delicate task at hand. I need his assistance. If he is free."

"I believe so," said his wife. "He is visiting neighbors

this morning, but you may ask him yourself, for that is his footstep on the street outside.''

"You have Papa's ears," said Raquel. "You know everyone from their footfall.''

The door opened and slammed shut again. "I always did," said Rebecca. "I thought everyone did. Nicholau, Papa is here, and my sister, Raquel, and they have need of you after dinner.''

Shortly after the dinner hour, a tall man in a black tunic walked along the street above the river, accompanied by a solemn-looking boy. Raquel had been prised away from her sister and nephew, and delivered safely behind the firmly locked gates of home. Her father had paused to eat a mouthful or two of dinner, gathered up Yusuf without any explanation, and left the Quarter. And now the boy was heading purposefully along the street with his master's son-in-law. They halted at a brightly painted doorway. Nicholau bent over to murmur something in Yusuf's ear.

It was the door through which the boy had made his hasty exit the night before. It cost Yusuf all he had in self-respect and strength of will to walk up and knock upon it, even though both Isaac and Nicholau had assured him that no one would recognize him as the masked and costumed Moorish slave of the night before. That slender reassurance had little force against his own knowledge—painfully acquired on his travels—that the law provided heavy penalties for helping a slave to escape. As soon as he heard footsteps inside, he stepped back behind his companion.

The tired-eyed kitchen maid who answered the door gave them a quick look. "The mistress isn't receiving any gentlemen right now," she said. "Because of the holiday. Come back at five." A loud crash and a distinctly masculine roar echoed through the hallway behind her. She winced and started to shut the door.

"I am not here for amusement," said Nicholau coldly, leaning on the door with one hand to prevent her from slamming it in his face. "I have a business matter to discuss with your mistress. I would like to see her at once.''

''She never said she was expecting a gentleman on business,'' said the kitchen maid quickly. A volley of oaths and obscenities came tumbling out the door as an afterword to the crash. She pushed as hard as she could on the door, but it was an unequal contest.

''Perhaps not,'' said Nicholau. ''That does not change the fact that I am here to talk business, business involving considerable profit for her, and she will be very angry if you do not show me in.''

This was a more serious argument than the stranger's brute strength. Marieta's capacity for anger was legendary. The kitchen maid released her pressure on the door and stared at the tall gentleman. He did look more like a clerk or a lawyer than a customer, and it was customers she'd been told to send away. She shifted uneasily on her feet. Caught between the twin evils of depriving her mistress of her rest, and depriving her of possible profit, she made the safer choice. She opened the door wider, and gestured for Nicholau and Yusuf to enter.

The kitchen maid ushered them into a sitting room, comfortably furnished, with a modest fire burning on the hearth. It was a room that resembled the private apartments of an honest merchant more than a reception room in a brothel, and it was as far from the exotic fantasies of last night as one could get.

It took a considerable time—time in which there appeared to be considerable activity in the other rooms of the establishment—to pry Mistress Marieta from whatever occupied her when they arrived. At last she entered, dressed as befits a businesswoman, and with a shrewd glint to her eye. Nicholau and Yusuf rose to their feet. ''And what manner of business do you have that you interrupt my afternoon rest?'' she asked. ''I work late into the night, and must rise early in the morning to set my affairs in order for the day. I don't expect to be disturbed during the dinner hour. Especially on the day of the blessed Sant Narcis." A shriek and a crash on the other side of the door caused her to frown, disturbing her look of gentle piety.

"A profitable manner of business, Mistress Marieta," said Nicholau curtly.

"And what would that be?"

"You have a slave girl on the premises, I believe. A thin little creature, no more than a child, who possesses a small talent in singing and playing the flute."

"I have several girls on the premises. Most of them are free, working here of their own volition."

"I am not interested in them. This one is called Romea. A malcontent, they tell me," he added, with a casual wave of the hand. "Unmanageable and unprofitable for you."

"Romea," said Marieta thoughtfully. "She is not to be so lightly prized as that. She is a girl of spirit, true enough, but a dash of spirit enhances her value in this establishment."

"But, madam, as you well realize, there is spirit, and there is rebellion. Of course, I only repeat what I am told, but I believe my sources to be accurate." Nicholau walked over to the window and glanced out, as if he were anxious to be off to another engagement.

Marieta seated herself in a small carved chair, as if prepared to spend the day in fruitless negotiation. "And what would your interest be in Romea? Why would you want a girl who is, according to you, only to be managed with the whip?" There was a look of anticipation on her face that was not pleasant to see. Yusuf shivered.

"My interest in her? None," said Nicholau, turning back from the window. He caught the look on her face and noted it. "I am an intermediary, only that. I care not at all what happens to her. But the person whom I represent thinks he can make something of her and is considering buying her. He leaves the town before sunset, and therefore the deal must be concluded this very hour."

"I am not interested. I expect to earn a great deal of money from her. Why should I sell her?"

"Why indeed? But you were offering her to Sancho the

trader this morning. I am told that he refused to meet your price for a girl who is too wild to tame, and therefore of no use to anyone.''

"Nonsense. You were misinformed. I have not spoken to Sancho since the summer, when he was last in the city.''

"Come now, Mistress Marieta. Your modesty astonishes me. Do you think you are so little known in town? Several people saw you at the fairgrounds this morning, bargaining with Sancho.''

"And what if I were considering, for one moment, what she might fetch on the market? One likes to know the value of one's possessions. How much, for example, would your principal offer for a girl such as Romea? One of great beauty, very young and trainable, and skilled in the flute and the dance, with an excellent voice?''

"For a wild and unbroken filly like that, even if she sang like an angel, he will give you two silver groats,'' said Nicholau, naming the amount that Marieta had told Romea was her price.

"Ridiculous,'' said Marieta. "And what does he want with her if he thinks her so useless?''

"He buys horses that no one has managed to school, one at a time, and breaks them. He does the same with slaves, one at a time. He is patient and relentless. It amuses him, and brings him great profit when the time comes to sell.''

Marieta's cheeks grew pink, and for a moment Nicholau felt sick. He himself was a gentle person, raised by a sweet and loving mother. That a woman, even one like Marieta, could derive pleasure at the thought of Romea in the hands of such an owner—even though he was mythical—filled him with horror. "I would not part with such a jewel for less than ten gold *maravedís*,'' she said at last. "She is very dear to me.''

"We are talking about a skinny child who has never been trained,'' said Nicholau, coldly, "not about the Emir's favorite courtesan.''

And so it went, back and forth, until at last Nicholau

counted out a store of coins considerably heavier than had been tied in Romea's handkerchief, and set them on the table. Marieta reached out to sweep them into her hands.

Nicholau's hand landed on the money just ahead of hers. "We will see the girl first," he said, and left his hand where it was.

His father-in-law had been very specific. "That woman might well try to palm some sickly kitchen maid off on us," he had said. "That is why Yusuf must go with you. Only he and Raquel have seen her. And I cannot allow Raquel to go into that house."

"You are not a very trusting man," said Marieta.

"Perhaps not. We will see the girl."

Marieta gave him a black look and left the room.

"Yusuf," said Nicholau, "when this slave girl comes in, if she is the one that my father-in-law wants me to buy, keep silent. If she is not, then say something, anything you like."

Before he could answer, the door opened again, and Marieta entered, pushing a veiled woman in front of her.

"Unveil her," said Nicholau.

Marieta snatched off her head covering, revealing a sulky-faced young creature, the clumsy dancer who had tripped during the ceremony. "It grows chilly," Yusuf remarked casually, and turned toward the fire.

"This girl may be for sale," said Nicholau, picking up the coins from the table, "but she is not Romea. My principal is interested only in Romea." He began to jingle the money in his hand. "My principal has heard some curious things about your establishment, things that would be of great interest to the guardians of the law. Acts have taken place here that could result in heavy fines for you and your clients. I would think that being pursued by the law would be very bad for business. Do you wish me to give you a list of the things he has heard?"

"I am not a child to be frightened by threats," said Marieta. "Go, Caterina, and help in the kitchen. You might do that better than you dance." Caterina shot them a venomous glance and flung open the door. All the noise and tumult that had reverberated through the house was now gone, and an uncomfortable silence replaced it.

Nicholau waited until the door had closed. "My principal is not a forgiving sort of man," he observed. "And for some reason that I cannot comprehend, he seems determined to have this Romea. When I explain to him how you attempted to defraud him, and then to cheat him, I expect he will be very angry. And he has some powerful friends in the diocese." He paused to give her a chance to reply. "I suggest that you bring us Romea, and take the overgenerous sum he is willing to pay before I am forced to go back and tell him why I do not have the girl."

Marieta walked over to the window and looked out on the street. She shrugged her shoulders and left the room again, returning almost at once with Romea stumbling behind her. Her hands had been tied together, her face was bruised, and her gown was torn; her hair hung, half-dressed, over her shoulder. "If he wants her that much, he is welcome to her."

Romea looked up and saw a total stranger, with a stern face and a cold eye. He glanced at her and paused. After a moment's silence he handed Marieta the coins and grasped the girl by the arm as if he expected her to run. "My principal demands a proper bill of sale, lest you decide to play the fool once more. I have prepared it. You have only to sign or to make your mark. Here, boy, take hold of the girl, and if you value your hide, don't let her escape." He pushed Romea at Yusuf.

She almost fell, then righted herself, and for the first time saw the boy, standing in the shadows beside the hearth. She caught her breath and then burst into tears of relief.

"Well might you cry, you useless cow. I told you if you didn't behave I'd sell you to one who'd make sure you did," said Marieta venomously. She walked over to a small table with an ink pot and a quill pen on it. "And I can sign my name," she added. "I have no need to make a mark."

"First I must fill in the sum that changed hands," said Nicholau, setting out the paper, and gravely entering the figure in his best scribal hand.

"I'm sorry that I cried. I thought you were from Sancho the trader," said Romea, as soon as they were safely out of the house, and Yusuf had untied her hands. "I was very frightened, until I saw Yusuf with you."

"You have been beaten," said Nicholau.

"Yes," she said simply. "Marieta caught me while I was still carrying the costume and my bundle of clothes. Then she knew I had helped Hasan, and was planning to leave. She beat me and locked me up. She told me I was to be sold today. To Sancho."

"That's likely true," said Nicholau. "She was reluctant to sell you to us."

"But she took my money?"

"Yes, she did," said Nicholau, and a great deal more of my father-in-law's money as well, he added silently to himself. "There are a few coins left. My father-in-law instructed me to place them in your hands."

"He is very kind," said Romea, "to take this trouble for a slave."

"Technically, of course," said Nicholau, "you are his slave right now. It is his name that is on the document."

She stopped. "You mean I am not free?" she said in a despairing voice. She sat down on a rough stone by the side of the street and covered her battered face with her hands.

"Oh, please," said Nicholau, sitting down beside her and taking her hand. "Don't cry. That is not what I meant. You are indeed free. He had me prepare your manumission at the same time; it is at my house."

She lifted her tear-drenched face to look at him. "Is that true?"

"It is. And you must remember always to keep the paper

very safe, for it is your only proof that you are a freed woman. If you lose it, you will have to come back to Girona and get another from me. Do you understand?''

"Yes, sir," she murmured.

"And now you are to come home with us. My wife will find you something to wear, and she will dress your bruises. She is very skilled at healing.''

SIXTEEN

"And now I must return to my master," said Yusuf in his own tongue, when they had reached the Mallol household. "Believe me, Zeynab, little sister, my master's daughter has great skill in healing," he said. "As her husband says. And she is very kind, as kind as her father."

Nicholau walked across the street to exchange a word with a curious neighbor, leaving the two to their conversation.

"Thank you, Yusuf," said Zeynab, in somber tones, "for making me mistress of my own fate. I do not know why you and your master have done it, except that I had the temerity to ask. You have saved my life."

"When I first saw you, I thought of my own sister, and how I would give all I had to the man who rescued her, should she be taken into slavery."

"She is in Granada?"

"Yes. And she is very like you, Zeynab. My other little sister."

"Your sister could never be like me, Yusuf."

"Why not? Except that she may be somewhat taller than you are. She was near my height when I last saw her, and she is a year younger than I. Perhaps now you can return to your family—''

"Oh, Yusuf," she said in exasperation, "you understand nothing about girls like me. I can hear in your speech what kind of family you come from. I am not like your sister. My father was neither rich, nor learned, nor powerful—or if he was, no one knew. He could just as easily have been a shepherd, or a sailor, as someone like your father. Don't you understand?''

Yusuf looked blankly at her.

"My mother didn't even know who he was," she said. "I have no family to return to.''

"But I have met many women of the streets, Zeynab, and you are not at all like them.''

"My mother was not born to disgrace," said Zeynab. "But she lived in a border village and her family was killed in a raid. She was taken and sold. It happened to many girls. When I was born, she smuggled me away, and gave me to a family of good people she had met. Well," she added judiciously, "fairly good people. Honest and respectable as far as they could be. She sent them what money she could for my keep, and they brought me up. My foster brother taught me to play the flute, and I learned to dance. But she must have died, for the money stopped coming. For a long while they kept me, but then times were very hard, and they said they couldn't afford an extra mouth to feed. They sold me.''

"How could they?" said Yusuf in sympathy, but knowing quite well how easy it must have been for them.

She shrugged her shoulders, and winced at the pain. "My first master only wanted a girl to help in the kitchen, and that was not too bad, but then I began to grow, and my mistress grew jealous, I think, and sold me to Sancho the trader who sold me to Marieta.''

"Come, Yusuf," said Nicholau. "Let Zeynab go inside and be made more comfortable. She is pale with her hurts.''

•   •   •

It had been a sad dinner at the house of Pons Manet, the wool merchant. His admirable and usually gentle-tempered wife had tried her best to overcome her sorrow and place a tempting meal on the board, of the best of spicy cured meats, with olives and autumn fruits and pickled vegetables, followed by leg of mutton and braised hare, but each course came to the table, and left it again, almost untouched. Manet's firstborn son, Jaume, and Jaume's wife, Francesca, were in no more cheerful humor than the parents.

"It is a hard thing," said the son, pushing his plate away, "to be kept from mourning a dear brother because your mind is taken up with fear."

"Fear?" said his father, glancing at his ashen-faced wife, who had also abandoned the pretense of eating.

"Oh, Jaume," said Francesca. "Don't speak of it. Please."

"Yes," he said, with a gentle nod at his wife. "Fear. I saw Romeu, the cabinetmaker, in the south porch of the cathedral this morning, and he asked if the rumors he had heard about us were true. And this was not the first time I had heard of these rumors."

"What rumors?" asked his mother sharply.

"That I will be the next to die like Lorens. And that you—we, all of us—are close to ruin, Papa. He offered to help us. What is going on? If any of this is true, you must not keep me in ignorance."

"It is malicious nonsense," said Pons bitterly, "fit only for the idle gossipmongers of the town."

"I am as brave as the next man, I think," said Jaume, his face pinched and white. "But it is not easy to think of dying so young, and as terribly as my poor brother. And of leaving my parents destitute, and Francesca alone with a child I will never see, and nothing to live on."

"Poverty is nothing." Pons seized on the lesser issue, eager to avoid the greater. "When I was a boy, our larder was empty more often than not. Father worked hard, but times were difficult, and I fear he had not the shrewdness one needs to run a business. One survives occasional hunger. Then my brother tried to raise our fortunes, but he lacked the patience for hard work and cautious investment. It was only when I married—"

"Your brother," said Joana Manet, cutting off her husband's discourse, "was a shiftless and dishonest man, who thought he could make money by cheating his customers and his suppliers." She was the youngest daughter of an honest and prosperous fishmonger. The modest dowry she had brought her husband on their marriage—thrift and business skills learned from her father—had been one of the chief causes of their prosperity.

"That may be true, my love," said Pons sadly, "but he died young."

"How did he die?" asked Francesca, her voice tremulous with fear.

"From the fever. After he had left the kingdom. It was a cruel death, they said. Very cruel. He paid the price for his mistakes."

"We were the ones who paid the price for his mistakes," said Joana. "And his poor widow and babies that he abandoned when the law was hot on his track. He left the business in a shambles and his family penniless, as you well know, husband. Whatever tomorrow may bring, the good Lord and all his saints have been very kind to us, Jaume. Your papa was able to pay off your uncle's debts, and lure back his customers and turn a hole-in-corner business into the prosperous concern it is today. I pray daily that the evil man who is trying to destroy us now will himself be destroyed, and burn in hell forever," she added bitterly.

"Joana!" said her husband. "You must not—"

"I must speak, or I will choke," she said. "I have lost a son, as beloved to me, Jaume, as you are, or your father is. I cannot understand why—in this world where so many good people have died—such a man is allowed to live and prosper."

"We do not know that he is prospering, Mama," said

Jaume. "He may be a powerless man, uttering empty threats."

"He threatened Lorens with death. Was that an empty threat?"

"Well," said Jaume, helplessly, "if Papa will tell us exactly what is going on, we can help him to fight back."

"Perhaps you and Francesca should go, my love," said Pons, "and Jaume and I will talk about what must be done."

"No," said Joana. "It is our lives, and the lives of our husbands that are at stake. We will stay, will we not, Francesca?"

Francesca looked as if she wanted nothing more than to flee, but she nodded, her eyes wide with fear.

At that moment a maidservant slipped into the room. "Excuse me, mistress," she whispered, "but someone brought a message for the master."

"Thank you, Clara," said her mistress calmly. "Give it to him, and wait to see if it requires a reply."

"Yes, mistress," she said, nervously. For every servant in the house had heard some version of the threat that hung over their master's head, and expected disaster at any moment.

Pons broke open the seal and read the letter. He folded it and passed it to his son. "Who brought this letter, Clara?"

"A beggar man, master," she said. "He came to the kitchen door. Cook told him to wait until you had seen it."

"Good. Tell cook to bring him into the kitchen and give him something to eat. There should be plenty. We ate little enough of the magnificent meal she prepared. Now go."

As soon as the maid had left, Joana said, "Read me that letter. Every word."

Jaume looked at his father, who nodded. "Certainly, Mama. 'My most esteemed—' "

"Just the letter, not all that," she said impatiently.

"Yes, Mama. 'All Saints' Day is not soon enough. If

you and your family are to survive, the spells must be
wound up tonight. An hour before compline, bring one
thousand gold *maravedís* to the house of Marieta in San
Feliu. Come to the river door. It will be open. If you speak
one word of this to anyone, it will be known, and it will
be the worse for you.' It is not signed.''

Father and son stared at each other, saying nothing.
Francesca had shrunk into her chair, and was dabbing at
the tears in her eyes, trying to conceal them from the others. Joana looked around the table and took charge. "Do
you have a thousand *maravedís* in gold in the strongbox?''

"It is a vast sum," said her son.

"I know that. What I do not know is whether the strongbox contains a thousand *maravedís*."

"No," said Pons. "Two shipments of best-quality English wool have arrived in the last three weeks, and we
have also bought all the highest-quality fleece on sale at
the market. It is all paid for. We certainly have enough in
the strongbox to carry on comfortably until the new wool
is sold, but we do not have anything like a thousand gold
maravedís on hand.''

"Then the person who wrote this letter is not familiar
with the contents of the strongbox, or he would know that
you could not produce the sum right away.''

"That is true," said Pons, nodding. "He is probably not
one of our trusted employees.''

"Nor is it Jaume," said Pons's wife.

"Jaume!" squeaked Francesca. "How can you, his
mother, say—''

"It would not be the first time in this family that one
of its members defrauded those who trusted him most. I
didn't believe it was Jaume, but I am still relieved to have
my trust in my son confirmed. And since we do not have
the gold, there is no question of obeying the writer of the
letter," she added. "That is one choice we do not have to
make.''

"Could we not borrow such a sum, Papa?" asked
Jaume.

"Yes, but we would not survive the winter. The interest would cripple us, and every sou we earned between now and twelvemonth hence would be required to pay off such a debt."

"Indeed," said Joana. "We worked like slaves to pay off your uncle's debts. We are not now going to run ourselves into more debt. What then can we do?"

"We could go away," said Francesca wildly. "To somewhere where this evil person cannot find us. I want my child to be born, and I want him to have a father. Is there not some money we could take, and then flee the city tonight?"

Everyone spoke at once, but Joana's steady tones cut through them all. "A sensible suggestion," she said, "but let us see if we can discover a better one." There was silence. "If you have no others, then I suggest we seek help."

"From whom?" asked her despairing husband. "The Bishop himself could not protect Lorens."

"Did you ask him to? Did you say to him outright that our son, dwelling in his seminary, had been threatened with death? Or did you believe that he would be safe in the shadow of the cathedral, and let the Bishop discover what danger he was in too late to help?"

"You know me too well, my dear. I was greatly to blame."

"You did what you felt was best," she said, "but don't blame the Bishop. He is a powerful man. I would ask him—not for his prayers—but for his officers."

"The other person in whom I confided was the physician, although I did not tell him where Lorens was. I thought that while he remained in the seminary he was safe."

"Then send for the physician again. And if he cannot help, we will go to the Bishop, even if it is a holiday. We are not going to sit behind locked doors, weeping, and waiting for someone to destroy us."

• • •

Under her father's guidance once more, Rebecca worked
diligently on the cut and bruised body of the slave girl,
until strengthened with healing broths, and soothed with
compresses of arnica and willow bark, she could put on
borrowed clothing, and talk about her experience.

"I seems that while I was talking to you, master, Marieta was arranging to sell me. She told me that."

"I had not realized what she had in store for you when
you returned. For that, I am very sorry," said Isaac. "But
your bruises will fade quickly, and your cuts are not deep.
They will heal, child. And if you had not returned, she
would have pursued you as a runaway, and your position
would then have been hopeless. This was painful, but it
was the only way I could see to rescue you."

"It was worth the pain, Master Isaac, to have my freedom."

"Now tell me about this Guillem and his servant,
child."

"One thing I can tell you, Papa Isaac," said Nicholau,
who had been standing at the back of the crowded bedchamber. "They have left Marieta's house. Or so I believe."

"Why do you say that?"

"When we first arrived, I heard men shouting orders,
doors slamming, and great bustle and movement. The
voices sounded angry. Then there was silence so complete
that I would swear the entire house was empty."

"What do you think, child?" asked Isaac. "You know
the house."

"The loudest voice, the angry one, was Lup's," she
said. "And there was indeed much disturbance. It is possible that they have gone, but the servants and the girls
will have fled to their chambers in fear. When Lup is angry, he strikes anyone in his way, except for Marieta. And
his master," she added.

"And his master permits it?"

"Yes. He seems to fear him as much as we do. Only
Marieta is not afraid of him."

"How many people live in the house, besides Marieta, and the two men?"

"Six girls," she said, "and two servants. And me and Hasan—or Ali, as they called him. Two of the other girls were slaves as well. We were expected to help the servants when we weren't busy."

"Now tell me about the three boys who died," said Isaac, and Zeynab's creamy white skin turned gray with fear.

While Rebecca was dressing Zeynab's wounds, and most of the honest inhabitants of the city and its suburbs were still seated at table, enjoying the last remnants of their holiday dinners, Sancho the trader knocked on Marieta's door. Marieta tossed back her undisciplined hair and stalked toward the front door. The maid had crept out of her cubbyhole to answer the summons, but her mistress shooed her away as if she were a bothersome hen, and she fled again. Marieta opened the door just enough to indicate that she had no fear of the man, but not enough to constitute an invitation to enter. "You're too late," she said. "I got a much better price elsewhere."

"Now, that was a very bad idea, Marieta," said the trader, with a grin wide enough to reveal a mouthful of broken teeth. "This time you were too clever for your own good. The gentleman will be upset."

"What gentleman?"

"The one who asked me to take the girl away—far away—and get rid of her. I've known him a long time. Done a lot of business of one kind or another with him. He has a nasty temper, he does, and he wanted me to have that girl."

"Guillem, or Lup?"

"Who knows? All I know is that—whatever you're calling him—it's not his name." He chuckled and turned away. "I hope he isn't too close a friend, Marieta. Goodbye."

• • •

The evening shadows had already crept across the cathedral plaza when Isaac strode up the hill toward the Bishop's palace with Yusuf and Zeynab. In Rebecca's old gown, the Muslim girl looked like any other citizen of the city. But under her veil, her pallor accentuated the bruise that made a purple splash across her cheek. She had not been happy when this visit was proposed, but she toiled up the hill even so.

Berenguer was seated in the small reception room in the palace, at a table with Pons Manet and the rest of his family. The letter lay on the board on front of him, the focus of everyone's attention. Just as the Bishop leaned forward to speak, Francesc Monterranes opened the door. "Your Excellency's presence is required in the antechamber," he murmured.

The Bishop left, and the Manet family started, once again, the thankless task of trying to decide among themselves what to do.

"You have sent me a very unhappy man, Isaac, my friend," said the Bishop. "And all of his family. It might have been easier to work something out with Pons Manet alone."

"My apologies, Your Excellency. But Pons Manet has a habit of telling people only what he considers important. His wife is much franker, and she is goaded on by grief, and the presence of her son and daughter-in-law. I thought it would be faster this way."

"And who have you brought with you? That is surely not the good Raquel under all those veils? If so, she is sadly diminished in size."

Isaac laughed. "No, my lord Bishop. It is a very frightened and hurt Moorish girl, a freed slave, who seems to know much about what was happening at Marieta's, and about Guillem de Montpellier, and perhaps something about how the deaths of the unfortunate boys were encompassed. We must guard her very well."

"How did you come to know all these things?" asked Berenguer, turning to the girl.

"I was bought by Marieta last year," she said. "And she made me help with some of the things that happened. But after I had obeyed her, she told me that what I had done was very evil, and that I would be hanged if I told anyone about it." Even under her loosely fitted clothing and heavy veil, Berenguer could see that she was trembling.

"May we look at her?" asked Berenguer. "If she has such things to tell, I would like to see her face as she speaks them."

"Must I?" she whispered.

"Yes, child," said the Bishop. "How else can I help you? Unveil yourself, tell me your name, and then tell me what it is you know."

"Do as His Excellency says," said Isaac. "And then tell him about the ceremonies, and how they were used to deceive the boys."

"Must I tell him about the other—"

"He may be a bishop, my child," said Isaac, with a warning frown, "but I think he can understand what else Marieta forced you to do."

"Indeed," said Berenguer. "A slave has little choice, and I comprehend that. When did you achieve your freedom? She isn't a runaway, is she, Isaac? That will complicate things if we need her testimony."

"No, I am freed, and I have my paper," said Zeynab. "Since this afternoon I have been freed."

"This is your doing, I suspect," said the Bishop.

Isaac shook his head. "She had saved up her price from little presents people had given her. I merely arranged the payment, since she was frightened of her erstwhile mistress. Come, Zeynab, let His Excellency see your honest face, and tell him about the special ceremonies."

Reluctantly, she pushed aside her veil.

Berenguer looked at the heavy bruise and turned away.

"Not a kind woman, that Marieta," he said. "Let us hear your tale."

Berenguer, accompanied by his secretary, Bernat, and Francesc, came back into the reception room, where Pons Manet and his family were sitting in unhappy silence.

"You must forgive my absence," said the Bishop, "but it was on business intimately connected with your problem."

"In what sense, Your Excellency?" asked Pons.

"I have a witness to your son's activities, and to the crimes perpetrated against him and his two companions. I would like you to hear her. My secretary will take down her deposition, since it may be needed for the trial of those responsible for Lorens's death. Francesc?"

Francesc de Monterranes left the room, returning with Zeynab, once more heavily veiled, and Isaac. "Your Excellency," he murmured, "I have brought the girl, and the physician. Shall I bring the boy as well?"

Berenguer nodded, and Francesc beckoned to Yusuf, who was standing outside the door.

"It is not important," said the Bishop, "who this child is. She was a slave when she participated in the acts which she will describe, and she had to obey her mistress or be beaten, or sold, or worse. Any other slave would have done the same. In addition, her actions were not in themselves wrong. Tell us, my child, about this Guillem de Montpellier."

"Your Excellency," she said, "Master Guillem and his servant, Lup, and their slave came to the house of my mistress in the week when the summer's heat was at its greatest, just after the great storm."

"Who was your mistress?"

"Marieta, of San Feliu. Master Guillem is a magician, and a learned man, he says, and he gives performances to draw in customers."

"What kind of performances?"

"The master would tell the audience that he was going

to call forth demons, and then he would chant, and throw something on the brazier to make a great flash of light and dazzle the eyes. While their eyes were dazzled, we came in. The other girls danced in immodest dress," she said, "and I played the flute and sang."

"The lad Yusuf can tell us about these shows, I believe," said the Bishop. "As a favor to Guillem's slave, who wished to slip out that night on some errand of his own, he took his place, wearing his costume and mask. Tell us what you had to do, Yusuf."

And Yusuf went over the details of his tasks that uncomfortable evening.

"There was a substance in the incense," said Zeynab. "We were told to stay away from the smoke and to try not to breathe it in. But usually it only made them a little drunk, except for the last time. Yusuf put too much in the braziers."

"Did anyone believe you were demons?" asked Pons.

"Oh, no, master, no one. Not after the first moment or two. I mean, even the country boys realized when they saw us up close that we were just girls. But they seemed to like the dancing anyway."

"I don't suppose Mistress Marieta wanted to bring trouble onto her house for trafficking with demons," observed Francesc.

"And were these the ceremonies that involved my son?" said Joana, wife of Pons Manet, in a terrible voice. "Did he die because of some flummery with incense and dancing?"

"Oh, no, mistress, not at all. Master Guillem used to go out and preach to people, and collect money—that was what he did before he came to San Feliu—and your son and his friends became interested in learning from him. He brought them once to the ceremonies, but they were disgusted by them. They were interested in learning, not in Marieta's girls."

"Really?" said Jaume, in tones of disbelief.

"Your brother was a very serious young man," said

Berenguer. "I do not doubt that he was as troubled by the temptations of the flesh as any young person, but his heart was in things of the mind and the soul."

"The three boys were willing to pay a great sum for lessons from Master Guillem," said Zeynab, "and so he arranged something special for them."

"What was it?" asked Pons.

"I don't know all of it. Only the parts I had something to do with."

"Come now, child, describe what you did and saw," said Berenguer impatiently. "We have much left to do before this evening is over."

She made an apologetic bow and turned to the Manet family again. "In those ceremonies, there were only the three boys, Master Guillem, and Lup, his servant. I was hidden behind a thin curtain, playing my flute. I think they had spent time in study with Master Guillem before that, but I do not know. He put a very strange intoxicating incense in the braziers, and sometimes the boys began to see things that weren't there. I had a passage of sayings, sayings of the wise men of old, Master Guillem said, that I had to learn and chant from behind the curtain. And then I was told that I must recite a short passage from the Koran."

"And did you?" asked Berenguer.

"Oh, no. I wouldn't have known what to say, and it would have been a great sin to recite holy verses in that place, for evil purposes. Instead I chanted a recipe for cooking sheep's head and tripes the way my foster mother taught me. I was very frightened the first time, because I thought they would know what I was saying, but they didn't. Then Master Guillem invoked some protective spirits, and called upon the angel of knowledge and enlightenment. He threw some powder on the fire, and made a great deal of smoke. In that time Lup lit the lamp behind me, and I raised my hands and pretended to be the angel. I chanted more things in Arabic—"

"What?" asked Berenguer, intrigued.

"How to cook rice, and bake bread, Your Excellency. Then I was to say in a very loud voice, 'Dig deep within yourselves for truth, and keep solemn faith with those who lead you to me. A thousand demons bearing a thousand deaths in each hand, with scourges to flay, and flesh hooks to rip, and burning pincers to pull out the lying tongue, await the false one, and the betrayer. The path to enlightenment is treacherous; for those who succeed in reaching it, the rewards are a thousandfold.' Lup put out the lamp, and I was free to go. I never had to stay with any of them," she added shyly.

"Say that again," said the Bishop. "The adjurations you made to the lads."

"Yes, Your Excellency," she said, and repeated the sentences.

"Is that exact?" he asked.

"Yes, Your Excellency. I have a good memory."

"It is clear that he wanted them to feel threatened, so that they would remain under his power," said Berenguer. "But how did they die?"

"Some poisonous substance was given to them," said Isaac. "Either after the girl left the room, or on other occasions that she knows nothing of."

"By the woman who visited Marc, for example," said Francesc. "Who is she? Do you know, child?" he said abruptly, turning to Zeynab.

"I am afraid she knows nothing of that," said Isaac. "I questioned her closely, and it would seem that she was not trusted to leave the house unless accompanied. Perhaps we may discover the truth from Marieta."

"Marieta?" said the Bishop. "Truth and Marieta are but slight acquaintances, I would guess. But one of the other girls might know something. There will be time to question them later. You may wait outside in the antechamber, child. Yusuf will go with you." He waited until they were gone. "And now. About this meeting tonight."

SEVENTEEN

The late October afternoon was coming to an end, bringing chill and gloom to the otherwise comfortable sitting room in Isaac's house. At last Judith could no longer see where to place her needle, and called for the fire to be lit, and candles brought in. To everyone's relief, the twins were crouched on the floor, out of sight of their mother, playing an elaborate game of make-believe, involving a doll, a wooden box, and a carved horse. Within the limits of their power, they had spent the afternoon destroying domestic peace. Like hounds that scent far-off prey, and cannot slip their collars to pursue it, they had scented the fair in full swing over the wall and across the river, and felt that fate and their mother had combined to deprive them of all happiness. Judith drew her chair near the fire, and Raquel, working her way doggedly through the book in front of her, pulled her table and chair close by. A pair of bright candles burned between them.

The hand in which it was written was not of the best, but she was used to it now, and made quick progress through pages and pages of information which was interesting in itself, but of no use to her father in his quest for the herbs or substances that had caused the deaths of the three unfortunate boys.

Judith put down her work and stared off into space. Raquel glanced up and was appalled to see her mother, her fearless lioness of a mother, looking tired and frightened. She was about to ask her what was wrong, when a phrase on the opposite page jumped out at her. She read the sentence it was in, and the one before it, and the one before that until she reached the beginning of the topic. She shook her head with a frown, and forced herself to read it all again, slowly and carefully, to make sure that she had understood each statement. She pushed away the book in disappointment. Like everything else she had found, this passage explained some, but not all of what they were looking for.

"Mama?" she said. "Where is Papa?"

"If you do not know, Raquel," said her mother sharply, "then I'm sure that none of the rest of us do. He ate scarcely a mouthful of his dinner before he snatched up Yusuf and was out of the gate. Without a word." She picked up her work again. "Why?" she asked.

"I have found something that I wanted to ask him about, Mama, that is all. A description of a very potent herbal compound. And I have no idea where he is, except—" And she suddenly realized that she could not explain the complication introduced by the Muslim girl without mentioning Rebecca. She fell silent.

"Except for what?"

"Except that he seemed very hurried, Mama, as if he had many things to do," she said, truthfully enough. "Do you think he would mind if I went to his study to look at another book? I believe it has more about this compound, but the book is too big and heavy to bring up here."

"Take that with you," said her mother, pointing to a three-branched candlestick. "You will strain your eyes with all this reading."

"Yes, Mama."

"I must go and see to supper," she added, putting her work down again.

"Mama, Naomi will have done all there is to be done. Rest. You look tired."

Judith looked at her daughter in astonishment. "What a strange thing to say. I am not sick, my dear. Why should I rest?" And she hurried out to the kitchen.

Pons Manet walked with a deliberate stride along the narrow street by the river. A lantern hung by a ring from his right hand, and on his broad left shoulder he carried a small wooden chest. At a curve in the road he came to a gate and stopped; the last time he had walked through that familiar back gate to Marieta's house in San Feliu he had been a scrawny, ignorant youth without a penny to his name. The house had belonged to one Ana, Marieta had been but a girl, and he had been taunted into the embarrassing and ill-fated adventure by his elder brother. Even now, his cheeks burned at the remembrance of it, and he tried hard to push it from his mind. He gave the gate a gentle nudge. It opened without a sound. A horse or a mule moved restlessly in the darkness.

Some distance behind him two people, one tall and the other short, walked in companionable silence, their soft leather boots making little sound on the cobbled street. They paid no heed to the burly gentleman who had pushed open the gate to Marieta's house, and entered the kitchen yard with the confidence of one who belonged there, but carried on until they had passed from sight around another bend in the road. At that point they halted, and waited, listening. After a few moments they turned and, walking as close to the walls as they could, retraced their steps until they reached Marieta's gate, pushed it open, and entered. Hooves moved on the hard surface, and a horse whinnied in soft inquiry. It settled itself back to sleep, and the yard was silent once more.

Yusuf, for the short man was in reality only a boy, led the way to the door, pushed it open wide enough to allow

him to squeeze in, and entered. At the far end of the hallway, he could see the black shape of the merchant. The
light from his lantern formed a pool around him. Isaac
followed his apprentice, pulling the door shut behind him
with great delicacy. The latch caught with the slightest of
clicks, but the sound was lost in Pons Manet's quiet footsteps. Yusuf stepped to the left, pulled aside the curtain to
the storage chamber, and drew Isaac in after him. The footsteps stopped, and the only noise they could hear was their
softly drawn breaths. "Why did you shut the door, lord?"
he murmured.

"They might have felt the wind come through it. And
now do not speak."

They waited in silence, without moving, for three or
four long minutes, before they heard any further sound.
Then a distant voice called, "Up here, Master Pons. We
are preparing the room now."

Yusuf peered around the curtain. At the end of the long
hallway, he saw the edge of a cloak in the faint glow from
a lantern on the stairs to the main floor. Standing on tiptoes, he murmured into his master's ear. "The voice is
Guillem's, lord. And Pons is going up the stairs at the far
end. I can see the glow from his lantern."

"Then let us go up as well. Is there not another staircase
to the next floor?"

"Yes, lord. Directly opposite us. How were you able to
tell?"

"Even Marieta has occasional need of a physician, Yusuf," whispered Isaac. "Can you see the way?"

"No, lord. It is too dark."

"Then follow me." Isaac held up the curtain and traced
his path with his fingertips along the rough stone walls,
until his foot touched the bottom stair of the circular staircase. The light from Pons's lantern was still visible at the
far end of the corridor; otherwise all was inky black.

Halfway up the stairs they were stopped by a noise that
made Yusuf's skin crawl. It was a dull thud, the distinct
sound of a heavy object striking hard against human flesh,

followed by a loud crash. Something wood or metal had landed on a tiled floor. Such light as there had been wavered and went out. Isaac stopped, and laid his hand on his apprentice's shoulder. "Is there light?" he murmured.

"No, lord. None."

"Then let us wait here, close to the door. We are less likely to be trapped. Shall we make ourselves comfortable on the stairs?"

At about the time that Pons Manet left his premises in the south end of the city to make his way north to San Feliu, a man dressed in a black cloak and cap that flopped over his face walked up to the officer of the watch outside the north gate to the city.

"Officer," he said, in a harsh and confident voice. "Follow me."

"And why should I leave my post to go with you, my man?"

"Listen, you—" He paused and changed tactics somewhat. "I'm after a runaway slave," he said impatiently. "A Moorish girl, and a devil of a price that son of a whore screwed out of me for her at the fair yesterday. Five groats. And the first chance she had, she ran. I have the bill of sale here," he said, pulling a paper from his sleeve and holding it front of the officer.

The officer nodded wisely. The fact that it was too dark where they were standing to see the words on the paper mattered very little. Reading was not one of his accomplishments.

"I think I know where she is," said the man. "And I want her back. I'll soon teach her not to do it again."

"What would you have me do?" asked the watch. "At this hour?"

"She's in a house in San Feliu. I want you to go get her for me."

"Harboring a runaway is a serious offense—"

"Don't worry about that. I don't know what tale she told to the people who live there, but I hear they have

taken her in as a serving girl. Their neighbors say they are
honest enough. I have no quarrel with them. In fact, there's
something in it for them if they'll turn her over to me
without giving me any trouble. And for your help, sir. Five
sous. I want that slave back before the morning. I have to
leave then for Figueres. A Moorish girl,'' he repeated.
"She calls herself Romea.''

"Show me the house, then, and we'll see what can be
done.''

The officer knocked, and the man in the cloak stood back
to allow the officer to deal with his complaint.

It took a minute for the door to open a crack. "Who is
it?'' said a small voice, sounding youthful and nervous.

"We wish to speak to your master.''

"He is away from the house.''

"Your mistress, then.''

"She is away, too. It is the holiday, and they are out.''

"We would like to come in,'' said the officer, pushing
on the door.

"You can't,'' shrieked the maid, doing her best to close
it. "I'm not allowed to let anyone in when the master and
mistress are not at home. You can't come in!''

"What's wrong?'' said a new voice from the kitchen.
And Zeynab hurried in to help the young serving maid.

As soon as the man in the cloak heard the voice, he
said, "I knew it. That's her.'' He pushed past the officer
and gave the door an enormous shove. He hurtled in,
grabbed Zeynab by the wrist, and said to the officer, "I
demand my rights. She's my slave.'' Without losing his
grip on her, he flung a purse of coins at the maid. "Give
those to your master to pay him for his trouble.''

"I am free,'' said Zeynab, struggling wildly. "I have
my paper. Let me get it.''

"Lying little bitch,'' said Lup. "She's clever, all right.
She'll be useful once she settles in. Thank you, Officer.
This is for your pains,'' and a second purse fell lightly into
the officer's palm.

• • •

"God protect me. I've killed him." The words hung in the empty house, reaching to where Isaac and Yusuf were perched on the stone steps awaiting developments.

No one replied.

Out in the kitchen yard, a horse neighed and stamped impatiently. It was answered by a soft nickering, and then the sound of a confusion of footsteps. Isaac touched the boy's shoulder and rose to his feet.

The door opened, and a voice hissed, "Get in there." There were two sets of footfalls, stumbling and bumping against the walls, and the door slammed shut. Whoever they were, they took no care for any noise they might make.

"Do they have a light?" whispered Isaac.

"A small lantern, lord."

"Then quickly. Follow me up."

Master and boy slipped quietly up to the main floor. "Where shall we go?" whispered Yusuf.

"Is there still a bench behind the staircase where we can wait?"

"I don't know, lord."

"Is it dark up here?"

"It is."

And Isaac drew Yusuf after him to the niche behind the open circular staircase, found a wooden bench, and sat down, keeping a hand lightly on the boy's shoulder.

From the ground floor, they heard the man call out in a normal voice, "Guillem? Where have you got to? Are you there?" Isaac's hand tightened, and relaxed again.

"Thank God, it's you," answered Guillem, his voice shaking. "I thought it was the officers. I think I've killed him."

"Where are you?"

"In front. Up the stairs."

"Just a minute," he called.

Isaac pressed down on Yusuf's shoulder, and the two

scarcely breathed until they could hear footsteps retreating
along the corridor.

"The devil take this wretched thing," said the newcomer. "My lantern has gone out. Why have you not lit
the candles?"

"I didn't want to draw attention to the house," said
Guillem.

"Darkness is much more likely to do that. Has anyone
come by?"

"Besides Manet? Yes. Some men yelled and pounded
on the door. I hid, and pretended there was no one here."

"Where is he?"

"Down here. Near the entrance to the big room. Dead."

"Alive or dead. No matter. The world is well off without him, although I had a use for him alive. How did you
manage to kill him?"

"I hit him, exactly as you told me, and he just fell and
died."

"Did he bring the gold?"

"I think so. He was carrying something heavy on his
shoulder."

"Good. Now take her. And don't let her go." There
was a prolonged moment of silence before the man spoke
again. "It will need more than one of your feeble blows
to finish off this thing," he said contemptuously. "Listen
to that."

"Is that him breathing?"

"What else would it be? He's stunned, that is all, and
will wake after a while. Get me some light."

Footsteps rang on the hard floor. The crash of something
falling over reverberated through the house. Guillem cried
out in pain and then cursed loudly.

"Where are the officers?" murmured Isaac. "They
should be here by now."

"I found a candle," said Guillem.

"Thank the Lord for that," said his companion. "Light
it, man. I'm sick of groping my way around in the dark."

"I don't have flint and steel."

"Find them, you fool."

The sound of searching began again.

"Why do we not move closer, lord?" whispered Yusuf.

"We can hear perfectly well where we are," said his master, "and will be more comfortable sitting here than being struck on the head by Master Ferran."

"Who is Master Ferran?"

"An old friend, Yusuf. A very old friend," said Isaac.

Light sprang up from the other end of the passage and Yusuf laid a warning hand on his master's arm.

"What's in the box?" asked Master Guillem. "Is it the gold?"

"Of course it is. What else? He's a coward and always has been. A frightened little wretch. After what has happened, he would never dare to come here without the gold."

"But as soon as he wakes up, he will tell everyone what happened, and then what do we do?"

"No, he won't," said Lup. "I've left him a little present. Something he will have trouble explaining to the officers. I don't think he'll be in any position to cause trouble for us. We're safe, Guillem, my friend. Our horses are waiting. We have only to pack up the gold and leave."

"But what about the girl? Why did you bring her back here?"

"Don't worry about her. I had to ask the watch to help me get her back. I could hardly have thanked him and then tossed her in the river, could I? She's tied up quite neatly. We'll take her with us. No one will notice."

"Are you sure?"

"Of course I'm not sure," he lashed out suddenly. "Who do you think I am? God Almighty? Hold your tongue and light the candles in the wall sconce. I need light to collect the gold."

"Look," said Guillem, breathless with excitement. "There's a piece that fell through the break in the chest. Gold!" They heard a long scramble and then a roar of rage, echoed by a scream of pain, both cut suddenly short.

"Quiet! Do you want to rouse the neighborhood?"

"But it's—"

"I know what it is. A handful of sous and some rocks. I'm going to kill that bastard with my bare hands. Where is he?"

"In the hall. I left him there."

"Get me a lantern."

"Fetch the officers, Yusuf," said Isaac. "Quickly!"

"Where are they?"

"They should be standing by the horses. They're out there. Quickly!"

Yusuf scrambled up off the bench and ran for the staircase. He slipped, caught himself, and kicked over a small table.

"What's that?" said Guillem.

"Someone on the back stairs," said Lup. "Get him."

And Guillem, with the lantern, ran down the stairs at the front of the house in hopes of catching up to the intruder. Lup plucked a candle from the wall sconce and headed at a quieter pace toward the back of the house. When he reached the stairs, he held up his candle and smiled. "Well, well," he said, "look what we have here. An old friend."

"An old friend, indeed," said Isaac, rising to his feet.

The closed door betrayed Yusuf. As he struggled to get it open, Guillem grabbed him around the torso and carried him up the stairs to where his servant, Lup, was surveying the physician with some satisfaction.

"This is an old friend, Guillem," said Lup. "You look well, physician. But I forgot! How rude of me. They tell me you are blind. And so you cannot know who I am. Not that perfect sight would help you very much. I am not as beautiful as I once was."

"I know very well who you are, Master Ferran. As soon as you opened your mouth to speak, I knew who you were. You have a very distinctive voice."

"What a clever man you are, physician. But then you always were. Clever and rich and arrogant. No matter what you did, it always brought you profit and friends and more power. How I hated you, even when you saved my miserable life.''

"I had not expected to meet you again, Ferran. They said that you had perished of the fever.''

"Not quite. I have been on intimate terms with death many times in the past ten years, but we continue in our friendly truce. I almost died of fever in prison in Montpellier. I came close to dying in the rebellion in Mallorca. You cannot see it, but a sword laid bare my flesh to the bone, somewhat rearranging my countenance. And the leg that I broke escaping from imprisonment left my body somewhat shorter and not as straight, but I am still alive,'' he said bitterly. "In a manner of speaking.''

"And does Master Pons know who his tormentor is?''

"I have had to forgo that pleasure. He has not as yet heard my lovely voice, and when he awakes—if I decide to let him live after the scurvy trick he has played on me— he will be in such trouble that he won't have time to think who his attacker was. I was surprised he had the courage to try to deceive me.''

Zeynab had been tossed to one side like an inconvenient bundle, and was lying with her head up against the door to Marieta's private parlor. The proximity of one of her enemies kept her still, until it occurred to her that if Marieta had been in that room, she would have emerged long since to find out what was going on. Zeynab wriggled uncomfortably. Her hands had been lashed together behind her back, and her mouth was gagged to keep her silent. She was enveloped in the hooded cloak that Lup had worn when he came to seize her and felt completely helpless.

But she was capable of movement. It had not been practical for Lup to tie her feet together, since she had had to walk through the streets with him in a normal fashion. Therefore, she was not helpless. She moved her hands as far down her back as she could and grasped her skirt in the back; then wriggling and pulling, and twisting, she managed to get her feet onto the floor unencumbered by Rebecca's heavy gown, conscious all the while that any sudden movement might draw her captor's attention. She pulled her torso forward, and rose to her feet. Very gently she backed up to Marieta's door, caught the latch through the cloak in her imprisoned hands, and raised it. The door swung inward, and she followed it.

As soon as she was in, she closed it as quietly as she could, and set her mind to getting free. First, she had to bring her hands 'round to the front of her body. She moved farther into the room in order to lie down on the floor again without hitting the walls or the furnishings, and kicked something soft and immovable on the floor. She peered down at it, trying to make out what it could be, but the windows were shuttered, and the night dark, and no light made its way into the room. Whatever it was, it was a good size, and felt to her foot like a rolled carpet of large dimensions. She dropped to her knees, bumping against it. She wriggled away to give herself room, and brought her hands down behind her narrow hips. She rolled over, and wriggling like a snake brought them past her thighs. She rolled onto her back, and slipped them easily under her calves and feet.

Then with quick, sharp teeth, she pulled at the knots holding her hands together until they loosened, and she was free. She unbound the gag from her mouth and took a deep breath. She knew Marieta's parlor as well as she knew her own room, for she had often enough cleaned it, laid the fires, and lit the candles. Unbarring the shutters was difficult enough to do if one had light, she decided. It would be safer to light a candle than to risk making a great deal of noise. Flint, steel, and candles were on the shelf by the door, and with the ease of practice, she laid her hands on them and had light in an instant.

She held up the candle, and looked down at the body of her erstwhile mistress.

EIGHTEEN

The night of Sant Narcis was a time for visiting neighbors and friends, and like everyone else Nicholau and Rebecca had had their calls to pay. When Carles had fallen abruptly asleep, exhausted by the excitement of the day, and Zeynab had settled herself in the warm kitchen with the housemaid, they had left for an abbreviated list of visits. Their last was to the house of Nicholau's cousin, Pau, and his wife, a cheerful, hospitable couple, who had acted not only as Rebecca's sponsors on her conversion, but also as little Carles's godparents. They had laid out an elaborate supper for their many friends, with excellent wines and platters covered with sliced ham and sausages, cold meats, olives, cheeses, and fruits, as well as great earthenware pots filled with braised and stewed meats. Fires blazed in every hearth, an extravagance of wax candles chased away the darkness, and the company soon grew merry indeed. But as pleasant as the evening was, Rebecca could make no more than a weak pretense at enjoying herself. The image of Zeynab's bloodied back, and bruised and swollen face came between her and the merrymaking. How could anyone celebrate when such things were commonplace in the world? Even her father, as concerned as he was, dis-

missed it as having happened, and being done with. She
searched the laughing faces of her fellow guests and wondered.

Nicholau raised his cup in a pledge to his hosts, caught
sight of his wife's face, and set it down again. Rebecca
was not going to be happy until she was home. As soon
as politeness would allow, they made their excuses,
fetched their cloaks, lit their lantern, and headed for home.

The trembling housemaid was waiting in the hall; she
greeted them with a flood of tears, a rush of incoherent
and unconnected words, and, eventually, a purse containing five sous.

"A man came and took her away?" said Rebecca.

She shook her head vehemently. "Two men," she
gasped at last.

"Two men came and took her away."

She nodded, dropping her head in abject misery.

"And because they gave you five sous you let them take
her?" said Rebecca. The look in her eye boded ill for the
maid's long residence in Nicholau Mallol's household.

"Oh, no, mistress. But one said he was the watch, and
he was. I know him. And the other just pushed the door
wide open and took her. She came from the kitchen to
help me and he took her. He threw me the purse and then
they were gone. It happened so quickly—"

"Too quickly to call for help? Too quickly to come for
us?"

"Now, Rebecca," said her husband, laying a gentle
hand on her shoulder. "She was frightened. And if it was
the watch who knocked on the door, what else could she
have done?" He shook his head. "How that man convinced the watch to help him, I do not know, but what she
says is likely true. I can believe it."

"I can't," said Rebecca.

"I have heard such things many times in court," said
Nicholau. "The watch was deceived. They are not always
the cleverest of men. But now we must get her back," he
added, as if nothing were easier.

"Oh, Nicholau, how are we to get her back? Whatever will Papa say? For either she is dead, or halfway to Barcelona by now."

"Now, my love, think a moment. Why would anyone want to kill a valuable slave?" he asked. "And I will fetch help before he can get too far away."

"Where?" said his wife bitterly.

"Where?" said Nicholau, considering for a moment. "I will speak to the watch first, and find out what he knows about this man."

The timid knock on Isaac's gate was hardly a sound at all. Raquel stopped work, listened, and decided it was an animal or a tree branch scraping against the wall. She sighed, closed the heavy volume she had been reading, and set it back on its shelf. She had worked on it long enough; it was difficult to read, of no use, and it made her head ache.

Then the bell rang, clear and demanding. She put her head out of the door of father's study, saw no sign of life from the direction of Ibrahim's room, and plucking a candle from its holder, walked quickly across the courtyard to answer the summons.

Standing on the other side of the gate, shivering with cold, and her face wet with tears, was Zeynab.

"Please forgive me, Mistress Raquel," she said, the words pouring out between her chattering teeth. "Your sister and her husband are gone, and Lup came and forced me to go with him, and the watch wouldn't let me get my paper. I climbed out the window and didn't know where to go, and so I came here."

While she was speaking, Judith, drawn by the sounds from the courtyard, came out of the sitting room and leaned over the balustrade.

Zeynab clutched the grillwork of the gate. "Oh, mistress," she said, "they've killed Marieta, and caught Yusuf," and broke into a storm of tears.

"Who is it, Raquel?" called her mother. Her skirts flew

out behind her as she hastened down the stairs, a lantern in her hand.

"And Papa?" said Raquel as she struggled with the gate. "Was he with Yusuf? Where is Papa?" She threw down the candle in exasperation; it flared and went out. She pulled the gate open. "Come in, quickly."

Judith hastened across the courtyard. "What did you say about my husband, young woman?" she demanded.

"Her name is Zeynab, Mama," said Raquel.

Her mother held up the light and shone it on the girl's face. "Come in by the fire," she said, shaking her head. "And tell us what happened."

Zeynab's story was wrested from her in incoherent little snatches. When she finished, Judith remained silent and thoughtful for a few moments. "We will go to the Bishop," she said.

"I will go, Mama," said Raquel.

"Certainly not," said her mother. "We will both go, but not alone." Having made up her mind, she hurried to the door of the sitting room. "Ibrahim," she called, in her most piercing tones.

A low mutter from the direction of the kitchen answered her.

"Go to Master Ephraim's. Ask young Master Daniel if he will come to help us. And quickly," she said. "There is no time to lose."

"Daniel, Mama?"

"And why not?" said her mother. "Ibrahim must stay at home and keep the gate. Daniel will be pleased to help. Now fetch Naomi. She will look after this poor child while we are gone."

"Lup," said Master Guillem in his most urgent tones, "we have to leave. Now. Pack up our things at once."

"I am not Lup," said the servant. "The Lup who cringes before his master no longer exists. That useless blind creature over there knows who I am. Ferran, merchant, soldier, trader. If it were not for ill luck—"

"It was not ill luck that destroyed you, Master Ferran," said Isaac. "It was greed, and disloyalty, and selfishness."

"You lie, Jew," he said wearily. "If we had won in Mallorca—if we hadn't been betrayed—I could have had great estates, and wealth and power that far outstripped yours, Master Isaac. Or my feeble brother's."

"You're mad, Lup," said Guillem. "This is no time for disputations."

"But I can have them yet," he said, ignoring his partner. "I still have the girl. I can sell her to a man I know in Valencia who likes her sort. He will pay enough to buy me a share in a ship to Constantinople. Do you know how much profit there is in one voyage to Constantinople?"

"Lup—"

"Ferran!"

"By all the saints, you waste time we do not have in these foolish dreams!" said Guillem in a frantic voice. "Lup, Ferran, whoever you are—let us go, or we will not get out with our lives, much less with the girl or a fortune that does not exist."

"Go fetch the girl. I must kill these two first. And the other."

"We have not the time!" shrieked Guillem.

"It does not take long." He turned to Yusuf, who was struggling in Guillem's grasp like an energetic trout. From one of the nearby small tables, Lup snatched up a polished wood carving of a horse. "Hold him still, Guillem. Away from you," he said calmly.

Isaac rose to his feet in a futile gesture of protest; Guillem thrust the boy out at arm's length; Lup raised up the wooden statue and brought it crashing down.

But Yusuf ducked and sprang sideways. The statue glanced off his skull, spending its force on his left shoulder. Pain raced down his arm and up to his head with an intensity that was as powerful as it was brief. Before he could even gasp, blackness rolled over him.

"That will hold him while I deal with his master," said Lup. "Now go get the girl."

The sound of Yusuf's fall and of Lup's cold words placed the two accurately enough for Isaac's purposes. He turned and picked up the small, heavy bench behind him. Holding the bench by one end in both powerful hands he stepped forward a pace and swung it hard in the direction of the voice. It hit his enemy, and he wrenched it back at once. He heard Lup curse and stumble, and swung the bench again.

"What are you trying to do, you blind beggar?" said Lup, ducking the bench easily on its second swing and raising the statue once more.

Yusuf emerged from a swimming state of blackness, his mouth thick with the taste of unconsciousness. He opened an eye. His shoulder throbbed with bright, hot pain, and his left arm lay useless and unresponding. The two men had moved a certain distance from the staircase by now, and Lup had stepped back onto a small, intricately worked carpet.

The carpet had been given to Marieta the year before by a wandering trader with more goods than money. Even though it looked very out of place in the long hall, and was a constant danger to the unwary of foot, she had prized it highly. It lent the house a touch of elegance, she felt, much needed given the sordidness of her trade.

Yusuf wriggled closer. He reached out and grasped a corner of Marieta's little piece of vanity. Just as Isaac swung the bench again, and Lup raised the wooden horse to strike the physician, the boy jerked the carpet as hard as he could along the smooth tiles of the floor.

It moved just enough to render his opponent off balance.

Lup staggered, took an unwise step to right himself, and like many before him, sent the carpet sliding. He grabbed at the wall sconce, caught the candle, and fell with a crash. The candle went out, plunging them into darkness once more. At the same time Guillem screamed from the front of the house, "She's gone. I can't find her anywhere. What shall I do?"

The Bishop's porter considered the two women and one young man who were standing on the steps to the palace and shook his head. "It's the feast of Sant Narcis," he said resentfully. "His Excellency is dining, and can't see anyone tonight."

"Listen to me, my good man," began Daniel, in his most assertive tones, "we—"

"Nonsense," said Judith, cutting in with the force of an ax blow, "he will see us. Go tell His Excellency that you have barred his door to his physician's wife, and daughter, and their escort. See then what happens. You will be very sorry."

"What is it, Matteu?" asked a voice from behind him.

"It is a woman who says she is the physician's wife, with his daughter and someone," said Matteu.

"Well, bring them in, man," said Francesc Monterranes. "His Excellency will want to see them. Quickly."

The porter stood aside, defeated, and ushered them into the palace.

"Your mother could breach the walls of Jericho," said Daniel as they followed Judith into the hall.

"Without a trumpet," murmured Raquel, amused in spite of the lump of pure terror in the pit of her stomach.

The captain of the Bishop's guard looked hard at his junior officer. "Tell me again," he said, in a voice that reverberated with controlled rage, "and quickly this time, what it is that you have done."

"Yes, Captain," he said. "Certainly, Captain, sir. I received your message that Master Pons Manet would remain at home this night, and that we were to call off our surveillance of Marieta's premises in San Feliu. We went as instructed to his house, and posted the guard there. When it was in place, I returned to report orders received and carried out. Sir."

"What message, Pere? There was no message," said the captain coldly. "Only a fool like you could be taken in by such an elementary trick. Arnau," he roared. "Put together a squad and ride at once to Marieta's in San Feliu. I shall follow in an instant. We'll deal with you in the morning, Pere."

A messenger poked his head into the room. "Message from the Bishop, sir," he said. "You are to come at once."

"I am on my way," he said. But outside the door, Berenguer was already striding toward him, followed by a breathless Nicholau Mallol, a young man, and two cloaked and veiled women.

In the space that lay between the top of the stairs and the service entrance to the grand room in Marieta's house, Master Pons Manet groaned once and rolled over. His head ached as if it were about to explode, and he had no idea where he was, or how he came to be there. He blinked and tried without success to focus on his surroundings. Then a few assorted pictures leaped out of his memory and presented themselves; he saw himself walking along the river road, and standing in a dark yard warm with the smell of horses. The last thing that came to him was a gate that opened too easily, into a darkened house that he knew, but could not identify. He swore under his breath with impassioned sincerity.

He sat up. Someone had lit a candle while he was unconscious, and he could see the staircase and the doorway, and in front of him, a curtain hiding him from the rest of the house. He ran his fingers tentatively over his head. He located a painful spot behind his ear, but his hair felt clean, and his fingers were not sticky. Somehow, he had hit his head, and fallen to the floor. Or perhaps fallen, and struck his head, but his scalp had not bled. Somewhat encouraged by that, he grasped the frame of the doorway and struggled to his feet.

The noise in the background had made no impression on him at first, but now words and sounds began to filter through his pain. An unfamiliar voice, quite close by, screamed something that made no sense to him, and caused the throbbing in his head to worsen. Then a crash resounded a little farther away, and echoed unpleasantly inside his skull.

"Yusuf," cried an urgent voice, "where are you? Can you hear me?"

The familiar voice was like a lamp in a dark room; when he heard it, his confusion cleared, and memory returned. That was his physician, they were at Marieta's, and something had struck him on the head. Without thinking further, he stepped past the curtain separating him from the main corridor and looked around. A candle burned brightly in the room across from him, and in it someone was fumbling with the shutters. The other end of the hall was in darkness. He plucked the candle from the wall and walked fearlessly toward the sound of Isaac's voice.

A man lay on the ground. As Pons approached, he groaned, rolled over, and began to raise himself onto his knees, swaying from side to side, as if groggy with some injury. Near him lay the boy, Yusuf, clutching his arm. Isaac stood between them, holding a squat, heavy bench in his hands, turning his head from side to side, like one who listens intently. Pons set the candle into a sconce. "Master Isaac," he said. "It is Pons. Why don't you put down the bench?"

"I cannot tell if I will hurt Yusuf in doing so," said Isaac. "Where is he? Can you see?"

"Yes. I have brought light. But give the bench to me, Master Isaac, and I will set it down," he said, taking it from the physician's hands. "What happened to that fellow?" asked Pons.

"He tripped and fell, I think. You do not know him?" asked Isaac.

"No," said Pons, "I think not. No, I have never seen him before." And he stooped over the injured boy. "Yusuf, can you hear me?"

"Yes, Master Pons," said Yusuf, trying to rise. He fell back dizzily.

"Yusuf seems to be in great pain," said Pons. "I think his arm is hurt. Who did that to him? This man?"

"Yes," said Isaac, in a curious voice, "he did. But you, Master Pons, are you injured?"

"My unfortunate head received a shrewd blow," he said, "but I shall survive it, I think."

Lup continued the painful task of pulling himself upright. He grasped the bench, and used it to raise himself to his feet. "It is an old wound," he said, cupping his scarred temple in one hand. "I have been injured in an old wound that never healed. I cannot bear the pain."

"My God in heaven," said Pons Manet in horror, and caught the swaying form. "That is my brother's voice." He lowered him onto a bench. "Ferran?" he said, and stared intently at the distorted features in front of him.

"Hola, brother," whispered Ferran Manet, and closed his eyes.

"Mistress Judith," said Daniel. "Allow me to escort you to your gate. It grows late, and there may be trouble this evening."

Judith looked around the cathedral plaza. "Where did all those officers ride off to?"

"To the house of that woman," said Daniel.

"Do you know where it is?" she asked, turning to him, and grasping him by the arm.

"I, mistress? I believe I could find it," said Daniel uneasily. "It is well-known. Do you wish me to take a message there?"

"No," said Judith. "You must take us there. That is where my husband is. I should be by his side." She let go of Daniel's arm, distracted by the sound of hoofbeats on the cobbles.

"Mama!" said Raquel in a hushed but vehement voice. "You must not go. Not to that place."

"No, Mistress Judith," said Daniel. "You must not go."

Three men on horseback pulled up beside them. "Mistress Judith," said the Bishop. "Was no one sent to escort you to your house? Arnau," he said. "I am astonished—"

"We tried, Your Excellency," said the captain.

"Your Excellency," said Judith, moving up to Bishop's stirrup, "I have a favor to ask—" Berenguer bent low to listen.

The murmur of their voices continued without a pause, and Daniel suddenly grasped Raquel by the shoulder of her cloak and drew her a little distance away from the group.

"Under attack again, Master Daniel?" said Raquel.

"I apologize," he said. "I cannot keep myself from dragging you here and there against your will, Mistress Raquel," he said. "But is it possible to convince your mother to return home?"

"You should ask whether it is possible to convince my mother to do anything," said Raquel, suppressing a burst of laughter with difficulty.

"It is not safe to be out tonight," he said. "Nor is it suitable for her, for either of you, to go to Marieta's. I cannot imagine even the most malicious of gossips assigning an evil motive to Mistress Judith, but still—"

"They'd be too frightened," said Raquel. "But if Mama decides to go there, neither you nor I nor the Bishop, nor even Reb Samuel will stop her. Oh, poor Daniel, I fear she will carry you along after her into the lions' den. But the Bishop's guard will be there to protect her."

"I am happy for that, at least," said Daniel. "The thought of trying to protect your mother against her will is a terrifying one. I don't mind going into the lions' den myself. It is rescuing Mistress Judith from the lions that daunts me."

"You'll have no need to do that," said Raquel. "Papa always says that she is a lion herself. She fears nothing and no one. You watch. The lions will scatter like mice before her.''

''That must be where you get your courage, then,'' said Daniel.

''Raquel, Daniel, come along,'' said Judith. ''We must hurry.'' And the three of them, escorted by two foot soldiers, headed for San Feliu.

A furious hammering on Marieta's door heralded the arrival of troops. ''Open, or we shall break the door in,'' said a loud, calmly confident voice.

''This shutter is unfastened, sir,'' said another voice.

''Then go in. Take Johan with you, and be on your guard.''

In no time at all, two men, booted and spurred, wearing light armor and with swords in their hands, emerged from Marieta's parlor and unbarred the front door. Their sergeant entered, and made a rapid assessment of the scene. ''More light,'' he roared.

Two men entered with torches.

''There is a dead woman in the room on your left, Sergeant,'' said the man who had entered first.

''Who is she?''

''It may be Marieta, sir,'' he said cautiously, knowing well who it was, but reluctant to claim too much acquaintance with the woman.

''Ah. Bring in the prisoner,'' said the sergeant to those outside, and another officer arrived, pushing a miserable-looking Guillem de Montpellier in front of him.

''Who is in the house, man?'' snapped the sergeant.

''Lup,'' he said. ''It was Lup who arranged everything. It was his idea—''

''You will have time for that later. Who else?''

''Just Pons Manet, the wool merchant,'' he said. ''And her—in there.'' He shuddered violently, and began to weep.

''And the two of us, Sergeant,'' called Isaac from the

end of the hall. "We are in need of assistance, here. My young apprentice is injured."

Before the guard had walked the length of the corridor, hoofbeats signaled the next arrivals. The captain of the Bishop's guard strode in, followed by the Bishop. "What have we here?" asked Berenguer. "Master Isaac, is that you?"

"It is, Your Excellency, and what we have here is your witch," said Isaac wryly. "One witch and one sorcerer's apprentice. In front of you, you find the entire plague of witches and sorcerers that attacked the city."

Berenguer snatched the heavy torch from the guard who was carrying it and held it up over the trembling Guillem and Ferran, who was slumped on a bench up against the wall, apparently unconscious. "Who is he?"

"Guillem de Montpellier, Your Excellency," said the captain. "I questioned him a few days ago at your request. You have his deposition."

"Indeed. And I suspect I will have another one soon. And that?" he said, thrusting the torch at Ferran.

"That person, Your Excellency, seems to be my brother," said Pons Manet doubtfully. He stepped closer to the helpless man, and looked down at him. "He speaks to me with my brother's voice, and claims me as kin, but how he can be my brother I do not know. We have believed for these last ten years that he was dead."

"Does he look like your brother?" asked Berenguer.

"The eyes have something of him, but look at him, Your Excellency. Crippled and disfigured as he is, it is difficult to tell."

"He was a handsome man, as I remember," said Isaac. "Tall and strong, if somewhat crude in his manner."

"If it is Ferran," said Pons, "he has fallen greatly— into servitude to this Guillem. Even so, to assist in the witchcraft that caused my son's death—his own nephew's death—how could he fall that far? He has been deceived and worked upon by his master. He is a pitiable creature now.''

''Pitiable!'' screamed Ferran, raising his head and looking his brother in the face. ''I take your pity and fling it in the dung heap along with your stinking corpse. No one works upon me. I work upon others. I am in control, Pons. I am, you weak, shivering little bastard son of a whoring mother. You're no brother of mine. How could you be my brother? You?''

The sergeant moved forward to stop the flow of words, but the Bishop held him back with a gesture. ''Let him speak,'' murmured Berenguer. ''He condemns himself out of his mouth.''

''Surely he raves,'' said Pons. ''My brother would never speak thus.''

''Don't call me brother!'' he shrieked. And in one sharp movement, he rose to his feet, and his right hand, which had been clutching his breast, flashed with a gleam of metal in the torchlight. He lunged at Pons Manet. ''Seize him!'' said the captain, pushing Pons out of the way. The sergeant thrust with his sword; as two men leaped toward him, Ferran took one more step forward and fell to the ground with the sword in his side. His thin-bladed dagger hit the tiles with a clatter as his hand fell open.

The sergeant snatched up the dagger and bent over the injured man. Isaac knelt down, felt Ferran's head and neck, and placed his hand on the man's back. ''I do not think anything can be done for him now,'' he said at last. Berenguer crossed himself, and murmured a prayer.

''He's dead,'' said Pons in a voice drained of emotion. ''How can I mourn for the man who killed my son? Ten years ago, despite his faults, I could mourn. If only he had died then. God help me, my head aches, and I am weary.''

''Sit quietly, Master Pons. I must attend to Yusuf,'' said Isaac. ''Then I will examine your head. Let someone be sent to inform Master Pons's household,'' he added, and the sergeant beckoned to one of his men.

Hushed voices at the door drew their attention away

from the scene in front of them. "Who is there?" asked Berenguer.

"It is Master Nicholau Mallol," said the guard. "And also—"

"Is my father-in-law here?" asked Nicholau, walking down the hall.

"I am here, Nicholau," said Isaac as he probed Yusuf's shoulder.

"Papa Isaac," he said with relief. "Are you unhurt?"

"I am untouched. Yusuf has a sore shoulder, and a cracked bone, but he will live."

"Bring him to our house. It is close by, and Rebecca will tend him."

"An excellent idea," said the Bishop. "Then we can wait till the morrow for explanations."

"Yes," said Judith, who had moved quietly in the door in the wake of the others. "It is the best idea. We will come with you."

"Judith?" said her husband in astonishment. "Is it you?"

"And who else would it be?" she asked with her usual sharpness. "That poor girl came to our gate. Someone had to help."

"Where are all the other inhabitants of the house?" asked the Bishop hastily.

The men all looked at each other. "I do not know," said the captain. "I sent a man to look around. Has he returned?"

"Yes, Captain," said the sergeant. "He found no one. They have all disappeared. The servants, the girls—all of them."

"Wise creatures," said Isaac. "Judith," he added, reaching for her hand, "this is Nicholau—your son-in-law."

"Good evening," said Judith, looking narrowly at him, and making a slight curtsy in his direction. "These are strange circumstances in which to meet."

"Indeed they are, Mistress Judith," said her son-in-law, and bowed.

When Pons Manet had been given over to the care of his attendants, two of Berenguer's guards placed Yusuf on an improvised litter and carried him the short distance to Nicholau Mallol's house. Nicholau opened the door to the little procession and called his wife.

"Oh, Papa," said Rebecca as she hurried to the hall, where everyone was crowding in, starting with the litter bearers. "I was worried about you. What has happened to poor Yusuf?"

"He has injured his shoulder," said her father. "Have you room for him? I do not want him moved any farther this night."

"Certainly, Papa," she said. "Please—put him in the room at the top of the stairs. The maid will show you," she said to the men carrying the litter. "Did you find—"

"Zeynab?" said Nicholau. "We did. And she is free again, and unhurt."

"That is wonderful," said Rebecca in preoccupied tones. "I was so worried. My dear, where are we going to put her?" she asked. "Never mind. We can make up a bed—"

"We will keep her until she is well enough to leave. Naomi is looking after her."

The voice from the shadowy figure in the doorway struck Rebecca dumb.

"Mama?" said Rebecca, and took a step tentatively toward her. She hesitated a moment, and then threw herself into her mother's arms, burying her head in her bosom. "Oh, Mama, have you forgiven me?"

Judith stroked her hair and then held her away from her to look at her. "Forgiven you?" she asked. "Certainly not. I won't say that I've forgiven you," she said. "But I am very happy to see you."

"Oh, Mama," said Rebecca. "You never change."

"Nor do you, Rebecca. They say," she added, "that I have a grandson. May I see him?"

"Yes," she said, "come and see him. He's so beautiful, Mama. He's asleep, but—"

"We won't wake him," said her mother. "Not to-night." And the two women disappeared quietly in the direction of Carles's chamber.

NINETEEN

One of the inmates of Marieta's house was found easily enough the following morning. She was at the fair, watching the musicians and jugglers with glowing eyes, and looking longingly at the stalls that sold sweetmeats and savory grilled tidbits. The member of the Bishop's guard who had recognized her walked up and touched her gently on the shoulder. "Hola, little girl," he said.

She jumped and turned, pale with fright.

"You used to work for Marieta, didn't you?" he said. "I remember you. You opened the door."

"Only sometimes," she said, looking pale and frightened. "Mostly I worked in the kitchen." Her lips trembled. "Are you going to arrest me?"

"For coming to the fair?" he said, laughing. "It's no crime."

"I've never been to the fair before. She never let us come to fairs." She stopped and looked nervously around. "I heard she was dead," she said. "That's what they say."

"But you knew she was, didn't you?" he said. "Isn't that why you all ran away?"

She burst into tears, and stood there, speechless and

helpless. At last she wiped her eyes with her sleeve and sniffed. "He killed her, that Lup did," she said in a low voice. "He killed her with his hands and threw her into her own parlor. We thought he'd kill us, too, so we ran as fast as we could without even taking our things."

"Are you hungry?" he asked.

She nodded.

Holding her by the arm, he took her over to the food stalls, and bought her a grilled sausage, and bread, and a little cake. He waited until she had wolfed it down before he spoke again. "Will you come with me and tell the Bishop what you saw? Then I will share my dinner with you in the canteen, and they might let you go back and get your things."

"Will they arrest me?" she asked dully.

"You have done nothing to be arrested for," he said. "And who knows? Perhaps someone can find you a place in a more respectable house than Marieta's."

She looked warily at him, believing nothing, balancing the possibility of an immediate dinner against the long-term probability of arrest. She shivered with the cold that fatigue and hunger bring. It was no contest. "All right," she said. "I'll come."

"Where are the others?"

"Here, most of 'em. Some of the girls are working," she said. "One of the slaves is trying to get back to the south. One went home. She's lucky."

"Perhaps your luck will change now," said the guard cheerfully. "Come along. No one is going to hurt you."

"Your Excellency," said Isaac. "I received your message."

"And you have arrived with commendable promptness. After last night's bungling and errors, I begin to think that no one in this city can deliver a message correctly. How is His Majesty's protégé?"

"Yusuf? He does well. Young bones do not shatter easily. The collarbone is cracked, and painful, but it will knit quickly enough, and cleanly. I shall leave him at Rebecca's for another day or two, until he is able to walk home without too much pain. It will give him an excellent excuse to rest from his lessons for a while."

"And the Moorish girl?"

"Like Yusuf, she is young. A few days of rest and good food and she will be better than she ever was. I will bring her over this afternoon so that she may give her deposition, if you like."

"Certainly. It is a mere formality, though."

"Why is that?"

"We have found one of Marieta's kitchen maids. She, and two or three others, saw Ferran Manet strangle her mistress and stuff her in the parlor. They all ran. They were terrified of him."

"One can understand why," said Isaac.

"And so, with Ferran Manet dead, and Guillem de Montpellier talking without a pause ever since he was taken, we need no more evidence of the scheme."

"It was a scheme, then."

"Oh, yes. A scheme to strip Pons Manet of all his money. They tell me that Ferran always was a clever fellow."

"He was. Too clever to prosper," said Isaac. "Did you know him?"

"No. He had left the city before my arrival here."

"All those things that happened to Pons—those unfounded accusations—keeping a Moorish mistress, and the rape charge against his son—were instigated by his brother?"

"So Guillem says. What he claims not to know is what happened to the boys. He said that the boys were never supposed to die. He thought they were just to be cozened, or threatened, and were to get the money from their families."

"He believed that Pons Manet would turn over an entire fortune—impoverishing himself, his wife, and his elder son—because Lorens asked for it?"

"I do not know if he believed it," said Berenguer. "But he wants us to believe that that was what he thought."

"What were they given, according to Guillem?"

"At the ceremonies? Two things. The juice of Byzantine poppy, burned under their noses, or mixed into wine. And an Egyptian herb which causes enchanting visions. But never enough to do them harm. He swears that by every saint whose name he can remember, and by a few other things as well."

"Nothing else?"

"Nothing."

"I know these substances. They can kill," said Isaac, "if given in sufficient quantities. But not in the way that those young men died."

"What do you think he used?"

"Sometimes our preconceptions confuse us, my lord Bishop. I was sent for to a young man who walked in his sleep and had nightmares and visions and no appetite, and who then died in quite another manner. In some ways the symptoms were those of the poison that men call belladonna."

"And which is that?"

"The juice of the nightshade. Not uncommon. I had thought they were being slowly poisoned, until the substance built up in their bodies so they could resist it no longer. That is, until I was present at Lorens Manet's death and could examine the cup and the urine. Belladonna can cause those terrifying visions, but I think someone concocted a special mixture for Ferran Manet, containing other agents—including spasmodics."

"An apothecary here in Girona?"

"Possibly. But more likely elsewhere. I believe that Ferran always intended to kill all three boys in order to terrify Pons. He may not have realized how secret they kept their friendship, even from their families."

"An evil man with a wanton disregard for life," said the Bishop. "And I suppose the woman who delivered the poison was Marieta. She was under the common height, and that fool Ramon did keep saying it was a small woman.''

Isaac did not reply for a moment. ''I do not suppose it matters much now what subtle mixture was created for the destruction of those lads. It was only important while the victims were still alive, and there was hope of rescue for them.''

''Indeed. And as painful as it was, I am relieved that it is over. Now,'' said Berenguer, shuffling through the documents on his table, ''do you know one Maymó Momet?''

''Certainly, Your Excellency.''

''What can you tell me about the dispute over the courtyard behind his house?''

A few days later, when the fairgoers had dispersed, and the traders and merchants and performers had packed up their belongings, and unsold goods, and profits from the fair, and left, the band of players was still in town. They had petitioned for permission to perform a work imbued with piety and learning, and had set up their stage in the cathedral plaza.

Most of the town was there, it seemed. Children raced up and down the cathedral steps, bumping into workmen who had come from the tavern, and were using the steps as convenient seating. Groups of women stood together circumspectly and gossiped about their not-so-circumspect neighbors.

The Bishop remained in his study, dealing with a rash of problems that had built up over the past few weeks, signing travel permits, granting permission for disputes to be heard over everything from the property lines of a jointly held courtyard to accusations that a certain debtor had been harassing the two men who had lent him money. He looked at the stack of petitions and sighed.

Isaac was at home. After a few days of biting cold, warmth had returned to the city, and he sat with the sun on his back and Judith beside him, in the courtyard.

''I cannot tell you, Judith,'' he said, ''how much pleasure you gave me by coming to Rebecca's house that evening.''

"I went to see the Bishop," she said, "because that Moorish girl said you were in danger."

"And is the Bishop not a gracious man, my dear?"

"He can afford to be," she said. "But he did send men right away," she admitted grudgingly.

"And is our grandchild as beautiful as his mother says?"

"Oh, Isaac, you are unfair. Of course he is. But he would be, wouldn't he? And why has Rebecca only one child?"

"She is young," said her father. "She will have more."

"What will happen to that Marieta's house, now that they have hanged Guillem?"

"There will be long wrangles, no doubt, my dear, but I am sure it will carry on as it was. These places usually do."

"Zeynab will not have to go back?"

"Oh no. She has her freedom."

"What will happen if they discover that she delivered the messages and gave the boys the poison that they drank?"

"Judith, my dear! Be careful what you say. That is a very serious accusation. What makes you think she did those things?"

"She told me," said Judith. "It was much on her mind. She couldn't read the messages, and she didn't know what was in the vials. She thought it was juice of the Eastern poppy."

"And it may well have been. As far as the law is concerned, Judith, there are witnesses, honest citizens, who have sworn in good faith that Marieta delivered the poison. They recognized her. That was the conclusion of the good judges, and therefore that is what happened. Zeynab was never anywhere near those three boys before each one died."

"But, Isaac—"

"Would you have her hanged for delivering a packet? And start up the outcry over witches once more?"

"I see," said his wife. "She is an innocent creature in her heart."

"I agree with you. Where is Raquel?"

"She has gone to visit Dolsa, to take her more of the herbal mixture you had given her. You were away, and we thought it no harm for her to take some over."

"I cannot imagine that there was any hurry for it, but I do not object," said Isaac. "It was kind of Raquel. Ibrahim could have been sent."

"I had other work for him to do."

"Since we have been left in peace for the moment, Judith, I must speak to you again about Raquel. You are making her life a misery by pushing this match with a cousin she has never seen. She is not like Mordecai's daughter, who can go cheerfully and boldly off with a stranger, and hope for the best."

"If you wish, husband," said Judith mildly, picking up her needlework. "There are many other matches. If she prefers one here, or there, as long as it is a good, respectable match, I have no objection."

"You don't? You have overcome your fear that she will never marry?"

"I think there is little danger of that," said Judith sweetly. "But you must work Yusuf a little harder. There is much he is to learn if he is to replace her."

And in the cathedral plaza, Dolsa, wife to Master Ephraim, the glover, stood with a group of neighbors to watch the presentation of "Daniel in the Lions' Den."

A handsome young man bounded onto the temporary stage, and bowed extravagantly to the audience. The jests and laughter and conversation ceased almost at once. In the silence that ensued, he recited in rolling tones a summary of the biblical history of Daniel, bowed again, and retreated.

A haunting melody on the flute floated out from behind

a painted tree, and then a slender young woman, hardly more than a child, stepped forward from her hiding place behind the tree. She was dressed in loose and modest garb of brilliant colors, after the Moorish fashion, and playing on a wooden flute. Still playing, she began a delicate, stately dance.

The woman who was standing beside Dolsa pushed back her veil and spoke. "That's Zeynab," she said. "Daniel, look! It's Zeynab. Yusuf, come and see. Oh, Mistress Dolsa, it's the Moorish girl we rescued. She told Papa she could earn her own living."

They watched fascinated, until the moment when the king, splendid in bright robes and paper crown, rolled aside the stone to the lions' den, and the handsome young man came out in triumph, surrounded by two prancing lions with masks, tails, and manes. Following them from the den was Zeynab, playing her flute. The lions bowed and came down into the audience with hats to collect what coins they might.

"Have you noticed, Mistress Raquel," said Daniel, "that whenever you are around, I am surrounded by lions? You are a dangerous acquaintance."

"Am I, indeed?" said Raquel demurely, with a sharp look at Mistress Dolsa, who was deep in merry conversation with one of the stage lions.

"It is fortunate that danger can be an amusing occupation," he said and threw a penny in the hat.

Then up on the improvised stage, Zeynab finished her melody. Daniel took her by the hand and bowed deeply to the crowd, turned, and winked at Zeynab. She grinned in pure joy, raised her flute in the air, and waved at Yusuf and Raquel.

Everyone cheered.